Also]

The Aurora Trology:
Chasing the Wind
A Time to Dance
Under the Sun

Then, Not Now

Gill Wyatt

Heartsease Publishing

ISBN: 9780957423732

CHAPTER 1

A heavy mist hung in the air. Darkness had consumed him.

Ken Stanton stood beside the grave – if you could call it a grave, for as yet it had no headstone. His grey floppy hair was unkempt and he hadn't shaved in days. The funeral flowers lay dead on top of the grassy earth, but he hadn't the heart or the strength to move them.

He had placed a small wooden cross over the place where Edith was buried and attached a laminated photograph to it. He remembered the day he'd taken that photo. Edith had been sitting on the harbour wall at Ryde in the Isle of Wight – she loved the boats and enjoyed watching them coming and going. She wasn't one for travel, but she loved the Isle of Wight.

He'd been standing a long time. He walked up and down a little to warm his feet before returning to gaze once more at the photograph.

It was the most natural photograph he had of her because he had caught her unawares. It was also the last photograph he had taken of her, just four months ago. Yes, she was old, but to him she was beautiful right up to the day she died. It wasn't that he was blind – if he studied the photo he could see the wrinkles and the age spots – but all he saw now was the person inside.

He had been attempting to film the seagulls, but while she was engrossed in the boats he flipped the camera to photo mode and quickly snapped the picture. Her expression was one of deep reflection, one that he had seen more often beside the sea than anywhere else. Her striking white hair fell in waves to just above her collar and her blue-grey eyes blended with the sea and the sky.

That had only been in June, and within a month she had gone. She had left him alone in this weary world.

He read the words on the nearby graves, wondering what he would write on hers when the time came. *In loving memory... Gone but not forgotten... At peace.* It was all just words. He rubbed his hands together briskly. This damp was getting inside his bones.

Initially all he had felt was numb, but now he was lost; he could barely think straight enough to speak. He was filled with... nothing, absolutely nothing. There was no point to life and no reason to go on. He was trapped in a living death.

'At least she didn't suffer long,' a neighbour had said one day, which hadn't brought him any comfort then and didn't now. '*I'm* suffering,' he had wanted to reply, but that just sounded selfish. Yes, the neighbour had only been trying to make conversation, was just being kind, but it had made him angry for a while. He didn't know whether he was angry with Edith for dying, with God for letting her die, or with himself for not having been a perfect husband to her.

He stood briefly beside a freshly dug grave gazing at... nothing... but soon returned to Edith's. He didn't want to leave yet.

In the end, his anger gave way to deep sorrow. He had known that it would – that was the way with bereavement.

He had experienced it many times before but never as deeply as this. Of course, he would not have wished his wife's suffering to continue, but suffering comes throughout life; it doesn't wait until death comes knocking. Nobody ever sees the tears of those who do not complain or moan, and his Edith never had.

Edith had only been a teenager when her mother died; much later, Ken had watched as she patiently bore her father's dementia – caring for him even when he no longer recognised her and confused her with her mother. She never mentioned his incontinence, or the number of times he woke in the night.

Ken had envied her patience and energy. She loved others so much that she made it look easy, which hadn't always made her popular; people often envied what they saw as her strength.

But he had also seen a different side to her – she had cried at her father's confusion, shed tears when people said hurtful things. Yet even then she maintained that the tears of others mattered more than her own.

Just because she didn't make a public show of her sorrow didn't mean that she didn't suffer. She had suffered more than anyone would ever know. But she wasn't suffering now, he was. She was with the angels in heaven, he was certain of that.

He picked up the cross and held it close for a while, unaware of the mud it smeared on his chest.

'Edith, my Edith!' he cried. His cry hung in the mist. Nobody heard. Nobody felt this loss like he did.

The pain gripped his chest and wouldn't let go; his breathing was laboured. If something didn't give way soon he would implode.

There was no point to living any more. She was his life, his love. 'Why? Why my Edith?' he asked, but still he got no reply.

Slowly, he turned and wandered back through the garden of remembrance.

He sat down on a bench and stared blankly at the dead leaves floating in the pond; in times past he had walked through here and noticed every detail. There was barely discernible rain in the air now as the mist began to clear.

Ken put up the hood of his anorak and rose to leave. Not that he had anywhere else to go, really. Home was an empty, lonely place.

His joints were painful and his six-foot form stooped as he walked home. He knew he was wallowing in sorrow – feeding it, even – but he couldn't stop. His mind was full of memories, good and bad.

Back at home, he hung up his wet anorak on the peg over the radiator, turned on the gas fire in the lounge and briefly warmed his hands.

He put on her Elvis album and played 'Always on My Mind'. It was how he felt today. He knew there were little things in his life with Edith that he could have done better. They were small details in the bigger scheme of things, and he was only torturing himself with this song, but the words were mostly true; she *had* been always on his mind, no matter where he went, and even now she was still here at the centre of his life.

His failures plagued his mind, but he wanted to remember the good times too. He played another of her favourites, 'Can't Help Falling in Love'. She chose this song for their golden wedding celebration and they danced to it as the band played. It was their song; for him it always would be. His life would never be the same, but he wanted to cling to what he had now.

In an odd way, the grief tied him to her forever. He was scared to let it go – scared that he would lose her altogether, afraid that her face, her touch, her voice would disappear as if into the mists, and that she would fade from his view. He felt as if she might already be drifting from him.

He'd had no time to say goodbye, no chance to speak of all the times he'd hurt her and to ask her forgiveness, and yet he was glad that his Edith had not gone on to live the half-life of one who survived a stroke but couldn't speak or move – that would be no life at all for his darling wife. It was far better that he should be the one to suffer, even though it didn't feel that way.

He switched off the CD player.

In a way, it made it a little easier to think of her escaping a living death and not about how deserted he felt – as he had so often felt since her death. Somehow, he needed to learn to live again, but he had no idea how to start again at seventy-eight. He had known how to live and love once, but that was then, not now.

CHAPTER 2

The next morning, Ken woke when it got light, got up and sat on the bed for a moment to catch his breath. Some days he would wake up and reach out a hand, expecting his wife to be at his side, or look up when he heard a noise, thinking she would walk into the room. Each time it happened disappointment overwhelmed him.

These days he found he was talking to himself, answering the television, or sometimes sitting and staring at the street, where busy feet would pass by, carrying people who didn't even know he existed. He had to resist the urge to knock on the window and wave to people he'd never met. Just a smile or a little wave would make a difference.

When Edith was here he would wake to the joy of the dawn, pull back the curtains and bring her a cup of tea. Often he would hum a song – but these days even getting up to make a cup of tea was an effort. Since her death he had taken the cup of tea back to bed and later struggled to get up all over again.

For the last couple of years they'd relied on each other so much, taken living for granted, until the day when the clock of his inner life slowly ticked and tocked and ground to a halt: the day when the heart that he'd loved had stopped.

He dropped his feet out of the bed and onto the floor, shaking his head gently to wake up to this death of a life he now lived. He pulled himself up to a sitting position and waited for the stiffness and pain in his knees to subside before stretching out his legs a few times and rising cautiously to his feet.

Somehow he must drag himself through the immeasurable hours that would make up the day again, until it was time to sleep once more. Sleep numbed the pain of meaningless action, but at times even that eluded him.

He put on his black-and-blue-striped dressing gown and stopped for a second to stroke the soft silk of hers, which hung next to his on the back of the door. He had missed the scent of her since the day he packed up her clothes in the boxes his elder son, Peter, had brought round so they could dispose of her life. Ken wished that he had found enough strength to stop Peter from taking it all away; it had given him no time to get used to the idea that Edith was no longer here.

His son had always been practical. 'You won't be needing any of this, so the sooner we get rid of it the better.'

It had felt to Ken as if Peter was getting rid of every memory of his darling Edith. *Or maybe he just couldn't cope with the memories that all her belongings triggered,* he thought. It was hard to know with Peter.

But Ken was glad that the dressing gown had been left behind. He lifted it down, held it close to his face, grateful that he could still smell the sweet scent that was hers, and with the back of his hand he wiped away the gentle tears that fell. He returned the dressing gown to its place, wondering how long the scent would linger.

Once he'd put the kettle on, he went into the lounge and opened the curtains. It was a dull autumn day with a light mist suspended in the air. He noticed the neighbour's cat jump from the fence in fear as it saw him appear at the patio door. Even the cat had turned away from him – just a touch, a stroke, any contact with something alive would awaken the senses so numb from loss.

Back in the dining area, but unable to bear the intensity of the emotions evoked by sitting at the table that he and Edith had shared for so many years, he sat in the chair by the window, enduring a snatched piece of toast spread with marmalade that he had found in the fridge. The kitchen used to be tidy and have a kind of order about it, but now the cupboards contained packets and jars all rammed in together, with the things he used most at the front. There was no real order.

He gazed out of the window at the garden. 'You were beautiful once,' he said to the tree in the midst of the lawn, the one with the falling leaves, whose colours faded now in the throes of death. He knew that quite soon it would be stripped back to the bare bones of a skeleton.

As the days got darker and colder, joints that were already painful would get stiffer and his movement would become slower. But for now he must stop his mind rambling into fields of depression and darkness and think of the things that needed doing.

The promise of help that Peter gave him on the day Edith died had given him comfort, but now, as he stared at the garden, which needed preparing for winter, Ken knew that it was all up to him. *Can I do it myself?* he wondered, and yet he knew it would be foolish to try. The house wasn't exactly in bad condition, but if he looked carefully he could see all the work that needed doing. *Just keeping it clean and uncluttered is too much to manage,* he thought.

Perhaps he had jumped to conclusions when Peter had said that he would help. In fairness, Peter had never liked gardening... and maybe Peter hadn't been offering as much help as he had thought; after all, he had a job to do and a family to spend time with, and Ken couldn't expect too much.

However had Edith coped all those years? He felt right now that he had no hope of keeping things in order. He let out a slow sigh. At least there were memories of Edith hidden among the mess.

I'll feel better later on when Peter comes to take me shopping, he thought. He was looking forward to getting out and seeing people, and if his son took him to the local shop he would see people he recognised and maybe even have a chance to stop and chat.

Ken washed his plate and cup and left them on the side to dry. Drying them up and putting them away was a pointless exercise.

Onward and upward, he thought, inhaling deeply. *I won't let fearful thoughts get the better of me.* He found a cloth, gave the kitchen a wipe and a tidy, and then got out the vacuum cleaner.

He'd hardly started the vacuuming when the vacuum cleaner stopped picking up the fluff and dirt. The bag clearly needed emptying, but he hadn't a clue how to do it.

He was still trying to empty the bag when the telephone rang. It was Peter.

'I know you need food and your stock's getting low but I'm busy at work, and shopping takes time, so I can't get you there today. Don't worry though,' he continued, without giving Ken a chance to speak, 'I've done you an order online. It should give you everything you need. The van will arrive between four and five – just make sure that you're in when he calls.' Peter said a brief goodbye and hung up.

'Make sure that I'm in! Where the hell does he think I'll be?' Ken said out loud when he put the phone down.

It's okay for him, he thought, continuing his rant inwardly, *he goes out to his work, home to his family, and then to the pub once a week to meet his friends.*

Anger was a relatively new feeling for Ken; he'd never been an angry person, but these days he got angry with himself, with Peter, and even at times with Edith for leaving him alone. Sometimes the anger extended to God. It frightened him a bit, as if an alien was taking over his mind. *I guess I'm just disappointed,* he thought, breathing deeply to try to calm himself.

Ken was scared that his frustration would drive his son further away, so all he'd been able to say on the phone was 'Okay.' But inside, his heart sank a little deeper, and he couldn't keep himself from thinking that his life was over now.

After putting down the phone, he sat by the patio door in the lounge again, wishing that he could wake up and discover that it was all a dream. He began to wonder whether it was time to go into a home; he didn't want to live alone. He would cry if he could, but his heart felt heavy and grey. Occasionally a few gentle tears would fall but the deep sobbing that he felt could bring healing eluded him. Today he would sit, as he had so many days, and pray that someone would call.

After a while, he got up and looked again at the vacuum

cleaner. He'd seen Edith do this often, and he was normally the one who could find out the way that things worked. After examining it for a while, he succeeded in opening the appliance up more by some little fluke than by logic. With a shrug he took out the old bag but had no idea where she kept the spares. He hunted in the drawers and under the stairs, and eventually emptied the old one and reused it. He put it back together not knowing whether he'd done it right or not, and then hoovered the lounge without moving a thing out of place – he didn't care about dirt that he couldn't see.

Free at last of the housework, he walked up and down the lounge and then stood by the patio door once again. He'd hoped to walk down to the end of the garden path to the greenhouse, but it had started to rain.

The greenhouse had been his favourite pastime since he retired. There was something satisfying about watching seeds grow into plants, especially when the produce started to ripen. In the past he'd often felt the urge to sing or hum as he worked, but nothing in him wanted to sing now. The song of his heart had been lost.

He would need to put the greenhouse to bed before the winter frost.

Who cares, he thought, *what does it matter if I step out into the rain and get wet?* So he put on his shoes and set off down the path.

As he stood in the greenhouse and watched the rain drip down the panes of glass, he thought of the tears that he wished he could shed. *Just think,* his heart told him, *of all of the times in the past when you shared your sorrows and joys with your wife.* Loneliness washed over him.

He remembered the time when she had come to the greenhouse alone to pick tomatoes for salad, for their tea. A toad had jumped out from behind the pots. Edith had shot out of the door, down the path and back into the house, then closed the door and leant against it as if she had an enemy in pursuit, and just at that moment she'd caught his eye.

'What's the matter?' he'd asked, but she started to cry with laughter.

'I feel stupid. I just ran from a toad – I had no idea that your greenhouse was home to a toad!'

'Ha!' he'd replied. 'You should see the old hedgehog that lives in the shed. He got in through a hole and he's made his bed in a cosy little corner.'

It had been such a funny sight because she'd been wearing pink fluffy slip-on slippers, which fell off her feet as she tried to run, so the run turned into more of a fast shuffle. A sad smile crossed his face at the memory.

He struggled to manage the greenhouse a little more each year. Edith had helped with the watering last year so he feared that his gardening days were now over. He couldn't really see how he could manage alone.

If the tables were turned, he thought, *what would Edith have done?*

He smiled to himself because nothing would stop her from doing the things that she wanted to do.

He picked up a measuring jug from the shelf and carried it down the path in the rain, filled it up at the tap by the shed, and leant precariously on the fence and the walls as he struggled back to his plants in the greenhouse.

He sighed; though bedraggled and wet, he was content

with his small success.

Perhaps it wouldn't be too much of an ordeal this year because it was too late in the season for most things. There were a few houseplants that he had kept in the greenhouse, but it crossed his mind that the best thing to do with those anyway was to bring them into the house – it would soon be getting too cold to keep anything in the greenhouse.

While he was out there, he tidied up the pots under the greenhouse shelving. He would do more another day.

He'd depended on Edith for so many things and he knew he was set for an uphill struggle, but by the time he sat down for lunch he felt a little more upbeat, satisfied with the morning's work.

After the Tesco van had pulled up in front of the house, the doorbell woke him from his sleep in the chair by the patio door. He got up, a bit drowsy but still conscious that the man would be busy, not wanting to talk for an hour or more, which was always his temptation when someone called. He found it hard to suppress the longing for company when anyone came to visit because it happened so seldom. When he had constant company he had craved solitude, but to have solitude as his only companion was miserable.

The delivery driver was jolly and kind. 'Shall I empty these crates onto the worktop?' he asked, but he had started already; he lifted the crates with ease.

Ken was still drowsy, and a little unsteady on his legs, but the driver finished the task in the blink of an eye and was soon taking his crates and saying goodbye as he left the house. He closed the door behind him.

Ken was alone once more. He piled some things into the

fridge without much of a system, set the microwave timer and put in one of the dinners-for-one that had just arrived. After that he put the frozen food in the freezer and left the dry goods in a box in a corner of the kitchen.

He thought about how much fun it had been when Edith had taken him with her when she went shopping. She dropped him off before she parked the car, and he would go and fetch the trolley. He always pushed the trolley because Edith had a list. She not only knew exactly what she wanted; she also knew in which aisle she would find things. He often tried to put little treats into the trolley while she wasn't looking, but she would always notice and take them out again.

When they were first married, and he was just a junior civil servant and she was an infant schoolteacher, they had had little money and she had got into the habit of trying to save every penny. She still did it even when money was no longer a problem.

He couldn't be bothered to lay out the cutlery on the table just for himself, so he put his dinner on a tray and took it into the lounge. Evening was falling; the darkness was eerily silent. He pulled the curtains shut and put a CD on, but the music he played to drown out the noiselessness brought back bittersweet memories of lighter times.

A blanket of gloom fell over the room. He picked at his dinner. *They were wonderful times,* he said to himself. But his reminiscence was over now; those days were dead and gone. Greyness was his lot now.

CHAPTER 3

The next day dawned as grey as the one before it, but, against all his expectations, something had changed for Ken. This state of affairs had gone on too long; this wasn't the way to play the game of life.

He pondered his lot wearily. Could he have done more to avoid this loneliness? ... He even accused himself of having lived a life entirely about himself and his wife, with no room for anyone else, of protecting their cosy little twosome no matter what.

But he rejected that thought almost immediately. *Don't be silly – we always had time for the children, the extended family, our friends and neighbours.*

He'd forgotten, until he sat and thought about it now, how often they had shared their life with others. He was being hard on himself, he knew, but somehow couldn't stop. Still, he wished that he had done more for Edith while she was alive.

He had to stop his mind from dwelling on negative thoughts and allow himself to remember the many times he had helped out – such as looking after the children while Edith went out with her friends or visited family. He enjoyed it for a while, but was always grateful when she came home. *I have no idea how she managed to look after them when they were small and I was at work,* he thought. *Life was different back then. In the last couple of years our world shrank, but not out of choice.*

He recalled the times they had shared with neighbours and friends, and he knew in his heart that on many occasions he had sacrificed what he wanted in order to give others pleasure. His self-reproach was just a misguided way of trying to make sense of his loss.

He thought about the many times he'd played chess with his neighbour, George, right up until he died, even though the poor man suffered from dementia for the last few months. He also recalled the times that he'd babysat Peter's three children, despite not knowing what they'd get up to. They tended to play him up a bit, but he never minded how long it took to read stories to them and put them to bed. He laughed to himself at the thought of those days – he was sure they chose the longest stories just so that they could stay up longer.

In the first two weeks after Edith collapsed and died, his elder son, Peter, and the three grandchildren had been kind – they'd arrive one by one and made sure he had all that he needed. Ten weeks later, they seemed to have forgotten about him. Or maybe they thought he was alright and should have got over her death by now? In the last week all he'd had was a phone call from his granddaughter, Meg, a quick call from Peter, and a Tesco delivery because his son was too busy to take him shopping. He had never envisaged them dropping their visits so quickly.

He'd mistakenly thought that they'd carry on caring for ever. Maybe he was foolish to have taken their help for granted? He had to admit to himself that he'd started to sit back and expect them to do all the things that Edith would have done... But he realised now how impossible that would be. They had lives too; he had to remember that.

His heart became heavy. His life and his hope were extinguished the day that she died. He tried to stop himself mulling it over and over – he knew that his mood was deteriorating – but she had filled so much of his life. When he looked around, he was shocked at the state of the house. In the kitchen the shopping was mostly still piled in boxes.

The pride that his wife took in dusting and cleaning was missing. He couldn't care less; there was nobody to impress. Most of the time, as long as the things that he needed each day were accessible, he dismissed the idea of doing other tasks – they were totally unnecessary. In fact, even keeping the house up to this standard was enough of a challenge while his energy levels felt low.

No matter how hard he tried, he could not find the strength to keep up with all the tasks that Edith had undertaken, and he held out little hope that his strength would ever return. As far as he knew, he might never recover from losing her. He knew the theory, he knew that time was meant to heal the pain, but he couldn't really believe it.

He barely had the stamina left at the end of each day to take himself up to bed. In fact, he had sometimes slept in the chair by the patio door; and even when he did sleep in bed, his sleeping was fitful and he felt still more depressed in the morning.

When he lay down at night, he found it hard to shut off a mind that tortured him with images of Edith, with things that they had done together. Even though he knew better, he reproached himself again. *If I had looked after her better, maybe she would have lived longer... Surely there was more I could have done to keep her alive, to keep her here with me.*

He couldn't escape her, and in a way he didn't want to. She was there, everywhere he looked. Peter had removed her clothes but Ken could see her personality in the design of the rooms, in the soft furnishings, even in the shrubs and plants in the garden.

He and Edith had done everything together, and they'd been married for fifty-two years. In his mind, when they married, it would last forever. *The young,* he thought, *have always felt immortal.* Now, the empty space beside him was like a vast gorge – nothing could ever fill it.

***

When Ken woke up the next morning, he was determined not to let yesterday's miseries continue into today.

Later on, he would go down to the local shop and buy a newspaper. Since the advent of round-the-clock news on television, he had stopped getting a paper so often – in recent years he had aimed to buy one just once a week. But lately he hadn't even managed that. Today was Wednesday, which made it nearer to two weeks since the last one. Time to put that right, to look outwards.

In order to shut out the silence while he had breakfast, he put on a CD. He enjoyed watching the birds in the garden. This morning there was a veritable fiesta of sparrows; they were his favourite birds, so full of energy and playfulness. Today felt like a good day; he'd almost forgotten what that felt like.

He decided that this morning he would tidy out the greenhouse and shut it up for the winter; that way he needn't worry about it again until the spring.

Breakfast over and done with, Ken shuffled down the garden and into the greenhouse. He picked all the small green tomatoes that had failed to ripen and put them to one side – he would transfer them to the windowsill in the kitchen, where they had a chance of catching whatever warmth was left in the sun when it shone. Then he pulled up the tomato and cucumber plants from the growbags and put them in the composter. He tried to empty the growbags a bit at a time, but bending down was painful so he gave up. He would ask Peter to do that for him on his next visit.

He took the houseplants into the house, brushed down the greenhouse shelves and cleared everything away. When he had finished, he shut the door. Once the growbags had been removed that would be the greenhouse sorted for the winter. It had been one of his major hobbies in recent years and he couldn't help wondering what he would do with his time all through the winter months. The sun had lost its warmth and he knew that winter was just around the corner.

It felt warm back inside the house. Still determined to make more of the day, Ken sat down for a while with the financial records and started to sort out some of the remaining paperwork in Edith's name. There wasn't a lot but it would be good to get it done. She had her own bank account, which he still hadn't closed. He'd put that off because it would entail going to the bank, talking about Edith's death to a stranger.

He got a mug of coffee and sat at the table, laying out the papers he needed in front of him. There weren't many, but concentrating on anything was hard right now. Edith had hated filling in forms and maintained that she was bad at maths, although Ken thought it was more that she was afraid of it.

By lunchtime he had finished the paperwork. He let out a sigh. Finally, he was beginning to get a grip on life.

CHAPTER 4

In the afternoon, Ken recalled his plan of going out to buy a paper. He changed from his slippers to his shoes, put on his jacket and set off. He wouldn't need a bag; he could tuck the paper under his arm.

On the way he met a couple he hadn't seen for a long while.

'We've just got back from four months in Australia visiting our daughter and son-in-law,' the woman said.

As he listened, Ken tried to remember their names. The man barely said a word, and the woman spoke with a slightly pretentious air. His son Ben had been in school with their daughter.

'Of course – what's your daughter's name?' Ken asked, desperately digging for clues to their identity.

'Marie,' the woman replied. 'We're Brenda and Jack. They used to all hang out in a group when they were in school.'

A light suddenly dawned in Ken's memory. 'Oh yes, I remember now. My wife, Edith, died recently... my mind is still a bit fuzzy.'

'Oh, I'm so sorry to hear that.' Brenda's cut-glass tone had softened. Jack nodded slightly, avoiding Ken's gaze.

'You must come round for coffee,' Brenda continued. 'You know where we are, don't you?'

Ken said 'yes' only because he couldn't bring himself to

say 'no'.

'Just pop round any time,' she added.

But Ken was already on his way. He hated the act of telling people, but he couldn't move on until people knew.

As he stepped down into the shop he could see at once that it was busy, and he had to wait quite a while at the till. He smiled to himself; the shop had always been a bit disorganised. It was only ever half-stocked with goods, although the staff were always kind enough to look in the stockroom for anything that wasn't on display.

If the big supermarkets were run like this they'd have gone out of business by now, he thought. *It's only their convenient position that keeps them going.*

The assistant was friendly, told him she hadn't seen him for a while, and chatted much more than she should have done considering the length of the queue behind him, but Ken was grateful and put the change in the charity tin by the carrier bags.

There was a crash behind him just as he was about to leave the shop, and he turned slightly to see what had happened – in the process, he tripped over the step at the door. He landed on his left arm and cried out in pain.

A customer left the queue and came to his aid, helping him back on his feet again. When Ken tried to move his arm he felt agonising pain.

'You may have broken it,' the customer said. 'We'd better call an ambulance.' Then she shouted out to the shop assistant, 'Can someone get a chair for him to sit on? Oh, and some ice for his arm?'

Ken heard the assistant call over the tannoy, 'Jenny to the till immediately, please.' A young girl appeared from the stockroom and the assistant on the till told her what to do. Jenny brought a chair from behind the counter and then went off to the freezer to get ice.

Ken felt faint but the customer helping him was very reassuring. 'Don't worry, the ambulance won't be long,' she said. 'Do you have someone we can call for you?'

Ken tried to reply but his voice was shaky. 'My son... but I don't know his number. Oh, he's the manager at Conlan's, the car dealers on Champion Street,' he added. His head was swaying a little.

'Take some deep breaths,' the kind customer said.

Ken did as he was told and the faintness faded. By the time the ambulance arrived he felt a lot less faint but was still in a lot of pain.

The paramedic supported his arm in a sling and escorted him to the ambulance. 'Jenny got hold of your son and he'll meet you at the hospital,' the customer said. 'Don't worry. You're in good hands now.'

He did worry. Now Peter would think of him as even more of a nuisance. He didn't want to be a burden – maybe Peter was right to worry about him. Perhaps he should go into a home – that way he wouldn't be any bother to anyone. He wasn't worried about the injury; it was just that now all the things he had planned to do would be impossible, and he'd only just started to get the house back in order.

The paramedic noticed his expression. 'Are you alright?' he asked, once they were on their way.

'My son will have had to leave work to go to the hospital,' Ken said. 'I don't want to be a nuisance to him, but I don't seem to be managing well since my wife died.'

'How long ago did she die?' asked the paramedic kindly.

'About twelve weeks.'

'Well, that's no time at all. Gosh, you've done well to be out and about. You'll manage – you'll see,' he said.

They chatted some more, but not for long as they arrived at the hospital in a matter of minutes.

'I'll be alright walking,' Ken said as the paramedic attempted to get him into a wheelchair.

'It's safer if we take you in the wheelchair,' the paramedic replied, and Ken complied.

Peter was pacing up and down outside A&E.

'What happened?' he asked the second the paramedic wheeled Ken out of the ambulance.

The paramedic replied, 'Your dad just tripped up on the step at the local store.'

The paramedic helped Ken out of the wheelchair and made sure he was registered at the desk, and then left him with his son in the waiting room. 'It looks fairly quiet,' he said to Ken as he was about to leave, 'you shouldn't have too long a wait.'

'Why did you go out? I had your shopping delivered! You shouldn't have needed anything.' Peter's tone was anxious, abrupt.

'I fancied reading a newspaper. I can't just stay in all the time. I never see anyone,' Ken said.

'But you knew I'd be round in a few days,' Peter replied.

Ken shrugged. 'I tripped over the step at the corner shop. It could have happened even if someone was with me,' he said.

Peter wasn't swayed. 'I think it's best if you don't go out without someone with you in future,' he said.

Ken muttered under his breath, 'Then you might as well book me a place in a Swiss clinic now.'

'Now you're just being silly,' Peter replied.

Ken wanted to ask Peter how he would feel if he saw nobody all week, if his only contact was the Tesco delivery man because his son was too busy, and the rest of his family too, but he decided to say nothing. Inside he was burning with anger but he couldn't afford to alienate Peter.

Not much passed between them over the next three quarters of an hour. Finally, Ken was sent for an X-ray and fortunately the queue there wasn't long either.

When the casualty officer put the X-ray up on the screen the break was clear, but the bones were not aligned.

'I'm really sorry about this,' the doctor said, 'but I'm going to have to admit you because we'll need to give you an anaesthetic and put a pin in that. We can't do it today because there's a lot of inflammation, so we'll put you on the theatre list for tomorrow morning.'

Ken looked worried. 'I haven't got anything with me.'

Peter sighed. 'Meg will have finished work now. I'll get her to go round to yours and pick up some things for you and bring them in,' he said.

'Thank you,' Ken said, and he meant it. He liked his granddaughter Meg.

'I'll wait until you're settled into a ward and then I'll go home and get in touch with her,' Peter said.

'That's very good of you,' Ken said to his son. 'I'm sorry to be a nuisance. I don't mean to be a burden to you.'

Either a twinge of conscience or the fact that the doctor was still in the room softened Peter's attitude towards his father, and he placed a hand on his good arm. 'Don't worry, they'll get you sorted,' he said.

They didn't have long to wait until a porter came to take them to the ward. He brought another wheelchair for Ken.

'That will stop you falling over,' Peter said. It was almost a joke, and Ken laughed.

The ward was bright and modern, and as the porter wheeled him towards a bed, the man in the next bed said, 'Hello.'

Maybe this isn't so bad after all, Ken thought.

A healthcare assistant helped him into the chair by the bed, got him a jug of water and a glass, and checked his blood pressure and pulse.

'You've missed the afternoon cup of tea,' she said kindly. 'I'll find someone to get you one.'

'That would be lovely, thank you,' he replied.

'If you're okay now I'll get back to work,' Peter said. 'I need to be there to lock up.' He stood up and brushed down his pinstriped suit. 'I'll try to come in later.'

***

After Peter had left, the man in the next bed hobbled over and introduced himself. 'I'm Eric, I broke a bone in my ankle when I fell off a ladder. My daughter said I shouldn't have been up a ladder.'

'I'm Ken and it's nice to meet you. I tripped over a step at my local shop. My son says I shouldn't have been at the shop!' He laughed. 'It feels a bit strange in here after being all alone at home.'

'It does at first, but you'll get used to it. Are you in much pain?' Eric asked.

‘Not too bad since they gave me an injection. They’re hoping to set it tomorrow if the swelling has gone down enough. How long have you been in here?’ Ken asked.

‘Three days. They set it and sent me home to start with, but I was in a lot of pain and when they X-rayed it, it wasn’t in quite the right place, so they reset it under anaesthetic. They kept me in to make sure it stayed in place this time! I’m going home on Friday.’

Before Edith’s death, being admitted to hospital would have made Ken feel anxious; he would have worried about her. But right now he was enjoying the activity and the company.

A hospital volunteer brought him a cup of tea and a menu for tomorrow’s meals.

‘Whatever you do, never order a small portion of anything,’ Eric called across. Eric had a loud and cheerful voice and his bright blue eyes twinkled even through the thick glasses that dominated his face.

The volunteer laughed. ‘He’s right. You’d have trouble finding it.’ Then she added, ‘Order all the meals for tomorrow because we’re not sure exactly what time your operation will be.’

Once she’d helped Ken fill in the form, Eric threw his towelling dressing gown over his flannelette pyjamas and hobbled across to Ken’s bedside on crutches.

‘I’ll show you where the television room is,’ he said.

There was nothing in the room except a television on a cheap stand, a wooden coffee table in the centre of the room, and upright, winged granny chairs around the edge. The room was painted magnolia and the carpet was a riot of clashing colours.

'Do you like football?' Eric asked.

'Yes,' Ken replied. 'I used to take my sons to every home game when I was younger.'

'Me too,' Eric said. 'I think there's a game on tonight. We could come in here after dinner. Nobody else comes in here much, so we could watch it together.'

Ken was delighted. He had a friend!

'So,' Eric asked as they walked back into the ward, 'you have other children?'

Ken nodded. 'I have another son, Ben, who lives in Cyprus.'

As they reached the ward Ken saw his granddaughter arrive. She stopped at the nurses' station to ask directions so he called out to her. 'I'm here, Meg!'

She was wearing tight jeans and an ochre-yellow top that co-ordinated well with her dyed-black hair.

'The things some people will do to get attention,' she said, laughing as she came towards him, and gave him a not-too-tight hug. 'Seriously, though, Granddad, I don't think Dad is very pleased with you going out on your own.'

Ken nodded. 'He didn't seem very pleased. But I can't stay in all day with nobody to talk to. I'd go mad!'

'I'd be the same,' she said. She handed him a box of Lindor chocolates. 'I brought you these. Your favourites, aren't they...? I'll open them for you.'

She opened the box and helped herself, which made her granddad laugh.

He was quick to follow her example, though, taking one and opening it straight away. 'Oh lovely! Your grandma never let me buy them. She said I'd get fat.'

'Well,' she said, 'they're just a little treat while you're in here.'

Meg paused and then took out a carrier bag from her rucksack. 'I went to your bungalow and got you some pyjamas and other things I thought you might need while you're in here,' she said. 'I see you've got a paper. Is there anything else I can get you?'

'Buying the newspaper started all this. I went to the local shop to buy it and tripped over the step. I'm sure I'll manage with what you've brought me. Thank you for doing that. I think your dad was a bit stressed.'

Meg pulled up a chair. 'Don't be too cross with Dad. I know he isn't being very kind at the moment. Mum thinks he hasn't really come to terms with Grandma's death. You know how fond she was of him...' She paused. 'I've noticed that he's put on weight since Grandma died. I reckon he's comfort-eating.'

Ken nodded. 'You're probably right about that, Meg. You're very wise.'

'Shall I put these things away in your bedside cupboard?' she asked, although she was already doing it. 'I bought you this squash on the way here too.' She put the bottle down on the bedside locker next to the jug of water.

He laughed. 'You're nearly as organised as your grandma was.'

'Ha ha, not really,' she replied. She was looking around the ward, taking it all in, when Eric smiled and said, 'Hello!'

'I'm Eric,' he continued, 'and I'm keeping an eye on your granddad. He's a bit of a handful.'

'He always has been,' replied Meg, getting up and offering him one of Ken's chocolates.

'Don't worry about him,' Eric whispered as she

approached his bed.

'I'm less worried about him in here,' she said. 'I was worried about him on his own.'

'It *is* very lonely in that situation,' Eric replied. 'I'm hoping your granddad and I can meet up when we leave here.'

'He hates to put anyone out. He thinks he's a burden on everyone. He probably won't invite you, but then he'll wish he had.'

'Then I'll invite him,' said Eric. 'I think we'll get on really well. I hope he thinks so too.'

She winked. 'That would be brilliant.'

Meg went back and sat down beside her granddad. 'I'll go in to the bungalow tomorrow and tidy up a bit,' she said.

'Thank you,' Ken said. 'I hadn't even done the washing-up. I was going to wash up the lunch and dinner things at the same time.'

'I already washed those up when I went to fetch your things,' she said. 'But I can't promise a lot because I'm not the tidiest person in the world.'

They chatted for a little while longer and then the dinner trolley arrived.

'It looks as if you'll be having a meal soon, so I'll leave you now,' said Meg. 'I think Dad is going to try and get back here for visiting time this evening, but don't worry if he doesn't make it. We'll ring up in the morning and find out what time you're scheduled to have your operation.'

'Thank you, Meg,' said Ken. 'It was lovely of you to fetch my things for me.'

'No worries,' she said cheerfully, then she kissed him on the cheek and left, turning to wave to Eric on her way out of the ward door.

The healthcare assistant arrived to find out what Ken wanted for dinner. Eric called across once again. 'Fish and chips is the best choice. You don't get a lot of chips, but the fish is quite nice.'

'I'll bow to my neighbour's superior knowledge,' Ken said.

Eating fish and chips wasn't easy with one arm in a sling. Ken tried to cut the fish with the fork but it was a slow process and the plate kept moving across the tray. When he attempted to hold the plate still with the broken arm he winced with pain. Eric noticed.

'Oh sorry,' he said. 'I should have thought. Let me cut it up for you.'

Apart from the pain, Ken reflected, he was enjoying it here. *I'm enjoying it more than I should,* he thought. *This is more fun than being at home on my own.*

***

'How is the pain?' the nurse asked after dinner.

'It's getting worse again,' said Ken, so she offered him an injection.

Soon after that, the doctor came to see him. 'I'm Doctor Coral. I just need to check a few things to make sure you're okay for the operation tomorrow.'

Ken nodded and the doctor sat down beside him. He asked Ken the questions on his form, took blood, and then got up to go.

'That's fine. The anaesthetist will come to see you early tomorrow morning but I'm sure it will be fine. I'll write up some sleeping tablets for you tonight, as you might find it difficult with the pain in your arm and it would be good to get a night's sleep before the operation. Your operation is scheduled for ten in the morning, so that means you won't be able to have breakfast ... The operation won't take long, though, so you should be fine for dinner in the evening – if the operation is on time.'

No sooner had the doctor left than Peter arrived with his wife, Sarah.

'I've had a word with the nurse and your operation should be tomorrow morning,' Peter announced as soon as he reached his father's bed.

Ken nodded. 'Yes, the doctor has just been, he says I should be okay for it, hopefully about ten. I have to see the anaesthetist first but the doctor says it should be fine.'

'We need to discuss how you're going to manage when you get out of here,' Peter said.

Sarah put a hand on his arm. 'Let's just get your dad better first and worry about that later,' she suggested. Ken had always thought that Sarah was good for Peter. She was less intense, and generally a lot more relaxed. Peter liked things organised, which was probably why he always got on so well with his mother.

'Well, I'm a bit concerned that you haven't been managing on your own at home,' Peter said. 'I called in at the house just now to see what state it's in, and it's quite untidy.'

'Meg said she'll go round and tidy up a bit,' Ken replied.

'I'm not sure what good that will do!' Peter exclaimed, before adding, 'Anyway, that's not the point, Dad. You just don't seem to be coping.'

Ken sighed and paused a moment, staring at the floor. 'I haven't found it easy without your mother. I miss her terribly.'

It was the first time he'd been able to talk honestly to Peter, helped along by Meg's insightful comments earlier, and Sarah's presence now. His eyes shifted from one to the other. 'I can't just pretend it hasn't happened.'

He smoothed the bed cover, considering whether to continue. 'Some days,' he said eventually, 'I can barely be bothered to get out of bed – there just seems no point. I know it will improve, but it *is* only three months since your mother died.'

Peter looked taken aback, but Sarah answered him. 'Have you thought about meeting with someone from Cruse? They do bereavement counselling and also arrange meet-ups for people in this sort of situation.'

'I'm not in any real rush,' Ken said. 'I do feel lonely without Edith, but even with my limited knowledge of bereavement I don't think three months is very long. Given time, there are interests I've considered taking up, and I've just met Eric in the bed next to me, here...' He pointed to Eric's bed. 'He's widowed too.'

Sarah laughed. 'That's a good idea, as long as the interests you're thinking of don't include abseiling and rock climbing! Perhaps we've neglected you a bit,' she added. 'We should have talked through some of these things with you.'

Ken shrugged, and then winced with pain. 'Ouch, I shouldn't have done that... It's not your fault,' he continued. 'I don't think I was ready to think about making a life for myself until the last few days, and even now I have times when I think I should just give up and go into a home.'

Sarah smiled. 'I can see why you would say that, Dad, but I don't think you're really ready for that yet. You might just need a bit of help and support. I'm sure that can be arranged.'

'I think so,' Ken replied.

'Maybe we could ask for you to see a social worker while you're in here. They would know what services are available.'

'Oh, I don't think we need all that,' Peter interjected.

'Actually, Peter,' Ken said softly, 'I think Sarah's right. I have spent all my life getting by, never asking for help, and now might be a good time to acknowledge that I *do* need some help. I can't tell you just how fed up I've been at home on my own all the time. I need to see people, and I know that realistically you and the rest of the family can't be visiting me all the time.'

Later, as Sarah left the ward with Peter, Ken saw her speak to the nurse in charge. He saw the nurse turn around and pick up a set of notes and write in them. Ken liked Sarah – she listened better than Peter, and if she wanted something doing, she was never afraid to just get on and do it.

He felt hopeful now. He had never liked asking for anything for himself; he had always seen it as selfish. He was beginning to see things differently and it had taken this accident to make him change his mind.

Every cloud has a silver lining, he thought, laughing to himself. That was one of Edith's favourite sayings.

***

That evening, he watched the football with Eric. It was a rather uneventful game, with no goals for either team, but he didn't care. It was just good to have company.

When the game was over, he got help from the nurse to get ready for bed.

'I might as well go to bed now,' he said. 'The arm is a bit painful anyway.'

She adjusted his pillows and got an extra one to put under his arm for support. Once he was comfortable, she offered him painkillers and sleeping tablets. He took both.

As Ken lay in bed, he tried not to think about the operation the next day. *Sufficient unto the day is the evil thereof, as my Edith used to say,* he recalled with a sorrowful smile. *Her words follow me everywhere.*

CHAPTER 5

Ken woke only once in the night; the night nurse gave him an injection for the pain.

He felt a lump in his throat as he thought about what it must have been like for Edith when she had her knee replacement all those years ago. His mind wandered back to those days. *I bet she was worried about me managing at home, looking after her,* he thought. Eventually he fell back to sleep again.

In the morning he was woken up by the healthcare assistant at eight o'clock. They'd let him sleep a bit longer than everyone else, seeing as they couldn't bring him a cup of tea because of his morning operation. For a brief moment he couldn't remember where he was, and he looked around to get his bearings.

'You look confused,' the nurse said. 'You're in hospital – do you remember?'

'Yes, of course,' he said. 'Just for a second, I'd forgotten.'

Taking his temperature, she told him, 'I can't give you anything to eat or drink because as things stand you'll be having the operation this morning.' Then she took his pulse and blood pressure. 'We can't give you tablets, so do you want me to get someone to give you an injection for pain?' she asked.

'I'll be fine,' he said. 'I'll ring the bell if it gets too bad. I'll just be glad to get the operation over with now.'

‘It won’t be long now,’ she replied with a sympathetic smile. ‘We’ll get you ready for theatre a little later.’

When the ward manager came around to say good morning to the patients, she introduced herself to Ken. She was tall and held herself very erect, but she wasn’t as stern as she looked.

‘Ah,’ she said, ‘you’re Ken Stanton, aren’t you?’

‘Yes, Sister,’ he said.

‘You can call me Lynne.’

‘That seems a bit informal,’ said Ken.

‘That’s the way it is these days,’ she said. ‘You can call me Sister Lynne if that makes it easier.’

He agreed to try. As she turned to walk away, she added, ‘Oh, I almost forgot. Your granddaughter has just rung to wish you good luck. She said her dad sends his love.’

By the time Ken could smell the breakfast trolley, one of the nurses, Marie, was getting him ready for theatre. It didn’t take long.

‘I’ll leave the curtains round because the anaesthetist is on the ward and will come to you next,’ she said. ‘Once we have confirmation of what time you’re going to theatre, I’ll come and give you your pre-medication.’

Ken nodded. ‘Thank you.’ He’d had an operation before, a long time ago, and he remembered that the injection had made him a little bit drowsy.

The anaesthetist came and introduced himself. ‘I’m the one who will be making sure you stay asleep during your operation,’ he said.

Ken laughed. ‘I’d better be nice to you then.’

‘Indeed you had,’ he replied. ‘I know the doctor has already done this, but I just need to listen to your heart and lungs. He's already filled in the form for me, so if they're okay you're good to go.'

He did the usual breathe-in, breathe-out, tap-tap stuff, listened in a few places with the stethoscope, and declared that Ken was fit for anaesthetic. He pulled the curtains back and left, and Ken read yesterday's paper for a while to pass the time.

At nine o'clock the nurse came to give him the injection. 'We're all set for ten o'clock,' she said, 'which is good news because orthopaedic surgery can sometimes get delayed because of emergencies.' She gave him the injection and left the curtain pulled around the bed.

It wasn't long before Ken started to feel a bit drowsy. He tried to continue reading the newspaper but eventually his eyes wouldn't focus any more. The next thing he knew was the nurse returning to take him to theatre.

'Hello, Ken,' she said. 'You're about to be the star of the show.'

He smiled, but he was barely aware of what was going on around him. The nurse helped him onto the trolley with the assistance of the porter.

'Good luck,' Eric called after him as the nurse accompanied him to the lift that would take him down to the theatre.

Ken still felt drowsy. Nothing was quite in focus and it was all a little bit like a dream. Faces appeared above him, and then he went to sleep.

***

The next thing Ken knew was when he woke up on the ward. As he looked around, his eyes tried to focus; they were still heavy and he struggled to open them. He closed them again.

At midday the healthcare assistant came round to take his blood pressure and pulse, and when she moved his arm he opened his eyes again. This time his focus was stronger.

'Hello, glad to see you're awake,' she said cheerfully.

'Did the operation go alright?' he asked as he leant forward to look more carefully at his arm.

'Absolutely fine!'

He could feel the weight of the plaster on his arm and lifted it slightly to inspect it further. He attempted to move his other arm too, but it was a bit awkward with the drip in the back of his good hand.

'Don't worry,' the healthcare assistant said. 'We'll take that down as soon as you're drinking. You can have a tiny sip now if you like. You have to take it slowly, though.'

She poured a tiny amount of water into a medicine cup and he drank it. It felt good on his dry lips. She saw him rubbing a drop into his lip so she offered him Vaseline from the tray beside him.

Ken hadn't noticed Eric standing behind her, leaning on his crutches.

'She's probably got lipstick in her pocket if you want a little of that,' Eric said.

Ken smiled. He liked his new friend and really hoped they would meet up after they left the hospital.

Sister Lynne came down the ward and stopped by his bed. 'I've just had a call from your son, Peter. He wanted to make sure you were okay and says he'll come to see you at about two o'clock.'

'Thank you, Sister Lynne,' said Ken.

The student nurse pulled the curtains around the bed. 'I'll wash your face and hands and clean the rest of the blood off your arm. They're not very good at that in theatre. Then I'll get you back into your pyjamas. Eric will tease you mercilessly if you get up wearing that gown.'

The first time she tried to get the drip through his sleeve she got it the wrong way round and ended up with the drip bag coming out through the neck. They both laughed.

'I always have trouble with these,' she said.

The arm with the plaster on wouldn't go through the sleeve at all, so she did up the top button over his arm.

Once she'd finished, she gave him a bit more water than last time but still only a little in a medicine cup. After that she helped him to sit up, propped him up with pillows, and then pulled back the curtains and placed the bell by his right hand.

'I'll pour you half a glass of water. Wait a few minutes and then drink it and see how you feel,' she said.

Eric came over to him. 'You look as if you should have a parrot on your shoulder,' he said.

Ken laughed. 'Well, at least I don't walk as if I have a wooden leg,' he said.

Eric was never far away that day; he was quite content to pour water for Ken when he needed it and get things out of the locker for him.

'I bought you a paper,' he said. 'I thought it would give you something to read while you're stuck in bed.'

'Thank you,' Ken replied.

On the dot of two o'clock, Peter arrived, and kissed his

father on the head. Ken smiled to himself; Peter had always been punctual.

'Sarah sent you these biscuits. She made them for you last night. I think she's worried you'll starve to death in here.'

'Oh, what a lovely thought. Say thank you to her for me.' Ken held up the biscuits for Eric to see. 'Hey, Eric, we're alright for a midnight feast now.'

Eric gave him a thumbs up and smiled.

'I hear from the sister that the operation went well,' Peter said. 'I'm still quite concerned about how you'll manage at home, though. We've been talking about it at ours. Meg thinks you could do with some help.'

The conversation was turning a bit negative for Ken's liking, and he began to feel a little downhearted. But just when he was about to change the subject for fear of sinking deeper into depression, Meg arrived.

She had a teddy under one arm, which she handed to Ken. 'I thought you might be feeling lonely so I brought you some company.'

Peter looked horrified. 'What the hell is he going to do with that?'

'Cuddle it when we're not here,' she said as she gave her granddad a hug. 'Unless Eric is going to do that too, which I doubt.' She looked over at Eric, who burst out laughing.

'Ha,' he said, 'when he's not using it I might have a cuddle.'

Meg sat the teddy on the top of the locker and it stared down at Peter, which amused Ken.

'He's watching your dad,' Ken said to Meg, and she laughed too.

Her father's frown and stern voice interrupted Meg's laughter. 'Can we be serious for a moment? We need to talk about how Granddad is going to manage at home.'

She adopted a sober expression but caught Eric's eye. He sported an expression of mock reprimand and wagged his finger at her behind Peter's back. She tried not to laugh and just winked at him.

'The social worker is coming in this afternoon and will talk with you about what help you need at home,' Peter said. 'Sarah has spoken to her on the phone.'

Meg shrugged. 'Why don't I just go and stay there for a couple of weeks? Granddad might need someone to come in and help him get washed and dressed at first. But I'd be there in the evenings and at weekends to do anything else. Would that work for you, Granddad?'

'I'd like that,' he replied. 'After a couple of weeks I'd be more used to managing the house with my arm in plaster.'

'And you could always ring if you needed me to come over after that,' she added.

'We need to see what the social worker says,' Peter said. 'And I expect she will have some suggestions about how you manage in the longer term. It would be good if you could get some long-term help with the cleaning.'

***

Meg had left by the time the social worker arrived. She introduced herself as Anna, and Ken instantly liked her.

She offered respite care for a couple of weeks in a nursing home, but when Peter put Meg's suggestion to her she was happy to try to accommodate them.

'He'll need someone to come in and help him with personal care,' she replied. 'You can take it week by week and see how you manage. Most people don't take as long to adapt as they expect. We can arrange that, or help you to arrange it yourselves if you prefer.'

She turned to Ken. 'How were you managing before you had the accident?'

Peter opened his mouth as if to answer, but the social worker put up her hand to stop him. 'I'm interested in how *you* think you were managing,' she said, directing her comment to Ken.

'I've found it very difficult without Edith,' he began. He felt tears welling up as he spoke of her again. He fought them. 'We did everything together. She was the one who could still drive so she took me everywhere. We did a lot less in the last few months because she got very tired, so I stopped doing the things that I'd once done. When I was still driving I used to go to the library. I went to an art group too, but the little things in life began to take so long that I never got around to doing any painting at home, so I stopped a couple of years ago. I don't know what to do with my life now.'

He paused as if deciding whether to confide in her further. 'I've also found it lonely, which makes me feel a bit depressed at times. It's only three months since Edith died.'

As he spoke he choked up a little, and he saw that Peter wiped away a tear himself. He realised in that moment that he hadn't fully recognised the loss the rest of the family had felt when Edith died.

He turned back to Anna. 'I couldn't see any point in tidying the house or clearing the garden. There was nobody to do it for any more... without her, day after day just dragged on. Some days I see nobody all day... that's why I decided to go out alone, and I'm not sad I did because at least I see people in here.'

'Three months isn't very long,' Anna said. 'Maybe you need help to re-establish your life. There are people who can help you do that.'

Peter looked from his father to Anna, and back again. 'I'm sorry,' he said to Ken. 'I didn't realise you were lonely.'

'I felt... stupid,' Ken said. 'Why should I need company at my age? And I know your job is demanding, Peter, and Sarah is busy at school.'

'I found it hard to talk about Mum,' Peter said, looking away. 'Staying late at work was better than having to live with what I was feeling.'

'And I didn't realise that. It felt as if everyone else just carried on with their lives as if nothing had happened. I would have been happy to talk about your mum.'

The social worker had sat back in the chair. She let them discuss how they felt for a while and then brought their focus back to the current situation. 'I think it's an important step that you've all taken in sharing how you feel. We do need to set up some help, though.'

'Will you help us to find someone to help Dad with washing and dressing and maybe to make sure he has some lunch? I'm sure Meg will do most of the other things while she's there.'

'I think we should set up someone to do personal care every day until you feel you're managing okay,' she said to Ken. 'They can help until the plaster cast is removed if you need it. And when you're on your own, maybe someone twice a week to do some cleaning. We can ask Age UK to send someone to see what help you need when you get home from hospital, and they'll help you get back to your hobbies too if you like.'

Ken cheered up again at this. 'That would be good. I really think I'd like to get back to my art group.'

'I'll see what I can organise and give Peter a call,' she said.

***

Once Peter and the social worker left, a nurse came to help him sit in the chair.

'You've managed plenty of water now. I think you can have a cup of tea. I'll take down the nil-by-mouth notice so they don't miss you out. When you've managed that okay, I'll remove the drip. But I'll leave the cannula in just in case we need it to give you any medicine.'

She put a table in front of him and placed his arm on a pillow on the table.

When the tea trolley came round, Eric was sitting with him again as they exchanged phone numbers.

'Do you have a mobile phone?' Eric asked him.

'Only this old thing,' Ken said, leaning over and taking it out of the locker at his side.

'You should get a new one,' Eric replied, reaching into his dressing-gown pocket. 'I talk to family and friends on Facebook on mine. They haven't always got time to talk on the phone, but at least I have some communication with them – especially my nephews and nieces.'

Ken looked a little downcast. 'I'm not very good with

technology.'

'Ah, we'll change that,' Eric said, his voice exuding confidence. 'Does that mean that you don't use a computer much, either?'

'No, I don't have a computer,' Ken replied.

'But you said that you have another son in Cyprus,' Eric said with a quizzical expression on his face. 'How do you keep in touch with him?'

'I send him letters now and again. I don't hear from him much. If I go to Peter's house they use Skype so I can talk to him for a while then.'

'Wouldn't you like to be able to do that any time you wanted to?' Eric asked.

'I would... I've tried using Peter's computer. He helped me to set up an email account, but I don't use it because I never bought a computer.'

'Well,' Eric said, 'if you can afford one I can help you to set it up and then maybe get a taxi over from time to time to show you how things work.'

'I'd like that,' Ken said. 'I'm likely to be a bit slow, though. Peter got fed up trying to show me the same things again and again with email. I didn't use it often enough to remember how.'

'The young ones take it all for granted. They don't understand that it's all completely new to us. Don't worry – I took ages to learn to Skype, but my daughter in Australia keeps in touch regularly that way.'

A nurse interrupted them. 'I've been in touch with the doctor,' she said, addressing Ken, 'and he's spoken with the social worker. We'll keep you here tomorrow and Peter will fetch you on Saturday. That way your granddaughter says she can be at home when you get there.'

'That's brilliant. Thank you,' Ken replied.

By the time the early evening meal arrived Ken was hungry. He sat beside his bed at his table, feeling for the first time that he could live again. He knew that sometimes friendships like these didn't continue, but he had a good feeling about Eric. For some reason they connected.

That evening, after the visitors had left, Eric's wife came up in conversation.

'For three years I was her carer. She had dementia and what terrified her the most was the idea of being "sent away". I told her that she was fine with me and that I would look after her, but I did have times when I was so exhausted I thought I would have a breakdown. The family begged me to let them put her in a nursing home, but I wouldn't do it. She was still my Annabel, even though towards the end she knew nobody but me, and even then she sometimes thought I was her dad. For months after she died I was totally lost and lonely... not only that, but I constantly remembered times when I was impatient with her. If I lost my patience with her, she would cry like a child and I felt so mean.'

Ken was pensive. 'Do you still think about her?'

Eric smiled. 'Oh yes, but I don't torture myself anymore. I had counselling for a while. Now I realise that by keeping her at home, even if I did get impatient from time to time, I kept her where she wanted to be. The doctor once told me that it was likely she'd be more confused if she went into a home. That was my thinking too – that she'd be better off surrounded by familiar things. Maybe I was wrong to keep her with me as long as I did, but now I just think, well, I made that decision and we did our best.'

As Ken lay in bed that night, he knew that he and Eric would talk about it all again. He also knew now that he would take all the help he could get. He was anxious about going home; just remembering the weight of the greyness in that empty house made him recoil.

Meg would be there, at least for a little while. Now, though, that wasn't enough. He needed to take things slowly, but he wanted a plan to make his life meaningful again.

Eric and Peter had talked about counselling. He had heard about Cruse before – yes, bereavement counselling might be a good idea – after all, he had been with Edith for over fifty years, and they had known each other since their schooldays.

Painting was something else he wanted to do again. Even if he couldn't get to places by bus, he wasn't short of a penny or two; there was nothing to stop him getting a taxi.

As soon as he got home he would write down his life plan. Meg would help him. No doubt she'd add ideas of her own too. Sitting at home alone over the last few weeks, he had thought that his life was over; he had given up hope of ever dragging himself out of the pit of despair. Now, although he still carried the burden of grief, he sensed possibility too – it was as if a switch had been flicked in his head.

CHAPTER 6

Ken woke to an awful commotion. He picked up his watch, which he'd been keeping in his locker as he was unable to strap it to his arm. It was only half past six.

The curtains had been pulled shut around the old man three beds away, and trolleys were being dragged behind them to his bed. *I'm sure that was the defibrillator that they just took away,* Ken thought to himself, propped up in bed.

Watching the scene unfold, he couldn't help but think about how fragile life is. *It's important to make each day count,* he thought.

Hannah, the healthcare assistant, came across to him. 'Are you alright, Ken?' she asked.

'Yes,' he replied, though in truth he was a little shaken.

'It's a bit unsettling, isn't it,' she said kindly. Ken nodded.

***

After breakfast, an occupational therapist arrived.

'I'm Tanya,' she said in a very soft voice. 'I've come to show you ways to wash and dress with one hand. It's likely to take you a little while to start with, but you'll soon get the hang of it.'

Ken was wearing a T-shirt with short wide sleeves, and she showed him how to take hold of it at the back of the neck and pull it over his head. He didn't find that bit hard, and they talked for a while about clothes that are easy to get on and off. He managed almost everything she showed him but was stumped by his shoes.

'You could get a pair of trainers with Velcro,' she suggested. 'That's what a lot of my patients do.'

'That's a good idea! I've been struggling to tie my laces for a long while,' he said. 'I can't get them tight enough. I'll give Peter a ring and see if he'll get some for me.'

Tanya declared his first attempt a success. 'If your granddaughter is going to stay with you for the first fortnight you probably won't need help,' she said. 'Now, I'll book you in to our little kitchen this afternoon and see how you manage there. You may just need someone to help you with lunch.'

After the kitchen assessment, Ken was pleased with himself. 'I nailed it,' he said to Eric. 'I passed my washing and dressing assessment and the kitchen stuff too.'

'So you'll be going home tomorrow then, I guess,' Eric said. 'I'm going this afternoon. My daughter is coming to collect me. They had to arrange someone to help with the cleaning. I said I'd manage but they didn't agree.'

This time, it was Ken who walked across to Eric's bed. 'Shall we decide when to meet up for coffee now? We can always ring to change it if one of us has an appointment or something. I'm happy to take a taxi to somewhere near you.'

Eric put his newspaper down on the bed. 'Brilliant idea,' he said. 'Tuesdays and Thursdays are usually good for me. There's a café on Townsend Street, just at the end of my road, if you're sure you don't mind getting a taxi. That way

I can hobble down there on my crutches.'

'That's great if you're okay with it,' Ken replied. 'What's it called?'

'Cara's Café. They do the most wonderful cappuccino.'

'Sounds ideal,' Ken said.

After lunch, Eric's daughter came to pick him up. The ward felt quiet without him but Ken decided to enjoy it; tomorrow would be busy and a little strange.

He thought he'd feel lonely again when Eric left, but there was constant activity on the ward and he'd chatted to one or two of the other men, so at least he wasn't alone.

He knew Meg wouldn't be in to visit him this evening – she'd already said she'd be at his bungalow sorting things out so that she could stay there. He imagined that Peter would come in for a short while. But Ken didn't mind being alone tonight.

***

Ken spent the next morning relaxing. He knew Peter had to work today; he'd assumed that his son would pick him up at lunchtime and drop him home, and had been a little concerned that it meant Peter wouldn't get a lunch break, but Peter had reminded him that he only worked a half day on Saturday.

Meg would be at his bungalow to meet him. Following his successful washing and dressing session, and the help that Tanya had given him yesterday in the occupational therapy kitchen, he was feeling more confident about managing at home.

He bought a newspaper and settled in his chair. He had

packed everything into the case that Peter had brought in last night, and the bed beside him was now stripped of bed linen. Sister Lynne was on duty this morning and she brought him details of an outpatient appointment and medication to take home with him.

Peter arrived at quarter past one. 'Are you ready to go?' he asked. Ken nodded. 'Yes.'

Peter picked up the case and Ken followed him. On the way out of the ward, Ken stopped to say goodbye to the staff. It was strange to be leaving. So much had happened in such a short time.

Peter put a box of chocolates down on the desk. 'You've not only sorted his arm, but you've been a great help to us all,' he said to the senior nurse at the desk. She looked up from the notes she was writing and smiled. 'Thank you,' she said.

'Thank *you*,' replied Ken. 'If it weren't for this,' he said, lifting up the arm in a cast, I'd have thoroughly enjoyed it.'

The ward manager laughed. 'If it weren't for that you wouldn't be here.'

***

When they arrived at his bungalow, Meg was on the doorstep. 'Welcome home,' she said with a cheerful bounce in her voice. 'You must be glad to be back.'

He smiled. She was dressed in purple jogging trousers and a red sweatshirt.

'Well, in a way,' he replied. 'I'll miss the activity in the hospital, though.'

Peter left to get home as there was paperwork he wanted

to get done. Meg made them coffee and sat with her granddad near the patio door.

'I've been thinking,' he said as he gazed out of the window.

'Mmm?' she replied.

'Life seems to rush by at such a pace, and there are so many things that I'd like to do that I've never got round to.' He stopped, uncertain whether to continue. 'I think I should make a list of all the things I'd like to do before I die.'

She laughed. 'They call that a bucket list,' she replied. 'Everything you want to do before you kick the bucket. We'll sit down this evening and write it out.'

Once they'd drunk the coffee, she unpacked his case and put everything away. Then she took him into the kitchen. 'We can start by finding places for all the tins of food that you've shoved in this box in the corner. Grandma would have had a fit if she'd seen this.'

Ken laughed. 'I can see you'll have this place back to normal in no time.'

Meg looked apologetic. 'We were so busy doing all the things we do every day that none of us realised how unhappy you were. Sorry, Granddad.'

He put his hand on hers. 'I didn't know what to do to get out of that pit. It seems strange that I had to break my arm to find out.'

'Grandma used to say that every cloud has a silver lining,' Meg said, laughing.

That evening, after they'd had dinner, they sat down in the lounge and discussed his plans. Meg got out a sheet of paper and wrote *Bucket List* at the top. 'So,' she said, 'what do you want on this list? What unfulfilled dreams do you have?'

'Much of what I want to do is go back to doing things I once did,' Ken said. 'I want to go back to an art group. That was always my favourite pastime.'

She wrote it down at the top of the list. 'And what else?'

'I want to make some new friends.'

'Well, you just did that. You are going to meet up with Eric, aren't you?'

He nodded. 'Yes, next Thursday.'

'Brilliant.'

'Before your grandma died, we did talk about going to Cyprus to visit your Uncle Ben, but I don't suppose I could manage that now – not on my own,' said Ken with a sad expression.

'Dad said that Uncle Ben and Auntie Jane are coming over for Christmas next year...? But I still think you should go and visit them there,' Meg said. 'We can all help you this end, and I'm sure Uncle Ben would pick you up at the other end. Or...' she paused for a moment and raised her eyebrows. 'If you went at the right time of year... I could come with you!' She was suddenly animated.

From that moment the bucket list went out of the window as Ken and his granddaughter embarked on a virtual journey. They continued to work out all the details of their trip until Meg realised that they'd got side-tracked and brought them back to earth.

'Okay,' she said, picking up her phone. 'Before we go any further, let's see what it would cost.'

After a few minutes on the internet and a few scribbles on paper she concluded, 'It depends a bit on what time of day you want to go.'

She entered a random date and scrolled through pages on a comparison website. 'I thought British Airways would be a lot more expensive but they're not as bad as I expected. It looks as if some of the companies have deals if you go into the travel agent's. It's worth considering what time of day you'd prefer to go.'

He nodded lightly. 'You're right. I hadn't thought of that.' He considered it for a moment. 'I'm not sure these days that I'd cope with an overnight flight, or arriving in the middle of the night.'

'The flight times look good with British Airways but I'll see what deals they can do us. I'll go into the travel agent's when I'm in town in the week... but you need to get that arm sorted first. We'll plan it for next year. Now,' she said, changing the subject, 'what else needs to go on this list?'

Ken had got so excited about the possibility of a trip to Cyprus that he couldn't think about anything else for a short while. 'Well,' he said eventually, 'I'm not sure I need the list after all.'

He relaxed back into the chair. 'I thought I needed a lot of new, exciting things, but if I get back to my art, make new friends and spend time with family, that will probably be enough.'

Meg put down the pen. 'So, nothing else?'

'Oh! I would like to start going back to the library.'

She wrote that down too. 'I'm going to leave this list on the coffee table,' she said, putting it down with the pen beside it, 'and whenever you think of anything, you can just add it to the list. And,' she added, 'I might write a few things on it too, like learn how to tidy the food cupboard.'

Ken laughed. He could see that he was going to enjoy having Meg here for a couple of weeks.

She went into her temporary bedroom and brought out the jumper she was knitting for Amber, her sister Stella's young daughter. Then they sat and chatted until Ken was too tired to stay awake any longer.

It took a lot of effort to change into his pyjamas. As he lay down to sleep, he contemplated how much better life was now. There were new and exciting things on the horizon.

CHAPTER 7

On Sunday morning the carer arrived as arranged by the social worker. She introduced herself as Angie. Nothing seemed too much trouble for her, and the ease of conversation made Ken feel as if he had known her for years.

'You're actually managing fairly well,' she said. 'It's quite difficult anchoring the toothbrush while you squeeze the toothpaste onto it, and putting the lid back on is pretty hard too. With a bit of help on these new ways of doing things, you'll be able to do most things on your own soon enough.'

By the time Angie left, Ken was clean and presentable and readier to face his first full day back at home than he'd expected.

He rested for most of the day, with Meg always ready to fetch whatever he needed, but as the daylight faded he decided to walk down to the local church for the evening service. Since Edith had died he had occasionally attended evensong at half past six.

'It's not my scene, but I'll come with you,' Meg said.

'You might like it tonight,' he replied. 'It's a special service called "Advancing". I heard about it a couple of weeks ago and had been trying to pluck up the courage to go because the church was a connection to Edith. When I broke my arm I didn't think I'd make it, and I was surprised to find I was disappointed! It's a service to remember our loved ones who have died. It's about moving on. We'll light a candle for them.'

'Sounds good,' she said. 'I'll come with you and light a candle for Grandma.'

They sat quite near the back; the church was almost full, which didn't happen all that often. Ken could see that Meg was a little uncomfortable to start with. But he saw her wipe away tears too, as he and many others did. When the time came to light a candle for the loved ones they had lost, Meg took her granddad's hand.

'Can we go together?' she asked.

He nodded, and when the vicar handed him the taper to light his candle, Ken moved aside to share it with Meg and they lit the candle together. They returned to their seats in tears, and neither of them could sing the final hymn.

'It's strange,' Meg said to him on the way home. 'I feel terribly, terribly sad at losing Grandma, but oddly comforted.'

'I feel the same,' Ken said, 'but I feel as if I have just given myself permission to move on. Not leaving your grandma behind, but taking something of her with me into the rest of my life.'

She took his hand again as they walked back around the corner to the bungalow. 'Me too,' she said. 'I didn't realise until just now that I was scared that I would totally lose her. I feel now that she has influenced how I live, even in her death.'

Ken had always felt close to his granddaughter, but never as much as today. At the hospital he had realised how much loss his son had felt at the death of his mother, and today he recognised those feelings of loss in his granddaughter.

When they got back to the bungalow Meg put on the kettle and brought out a chocolate cake that she'd been saving for tea. 'We can celebrate a new beginning with a cake,' she said.

'How lovely!' he exclaimed. 'I didn't know you could bake cakes.' Then he turned towards her. 'I'm sorry,' he said. 'I was so numb from my own pain that I couldn't see anybody else's.'

'I'm just glad I came with you,' she said. 'I only came because I was worried about whether it would upset you, but I found it helped me to express my own sadness.'

She put the tea down on the coffee table in front of him and then he produced an old biscuit tin. 'I found these when I was going through your grandma's things. They're mostly photos. I was afraid to look at them on my own and I wondered...'

He didn't finish the sentence, but she replied, 'Of course I'll go through them with you – as long as you tell me the stories that go with them.'

Most of the photos were old black-and-white ones, but some were recent enough that Meg recognised the people in them.

'I was thinking about this the other day,' said Ken as he fingered a photo of him dancing with Edith at their golden wedding celebration. 'We danced to Elvis's "Can't Help Falling in Love".'

'I remember that,' Meg said. The softness in her tone told him that she was deep in thought.

He got up, put on the song, and shared the memory

with her. They talked for the rest of the evening about her grandmother.

'I remember her driving me to a school hockey match. For some reason Mum and Dad were busy and she volunteered. She was the most vocal supporter.'

He laughed. 'She could be very loud.'

'Especially when she was singing,' Meg added, 'which was quite often.'

'Her family... was everything to her.' He paused, a little choked, then changed the subject. '...and do you remember how she always took an umbrella with her? It didn't matter if it was a sunny day. She packed it when we went to Cyprus in the summer!'

'"Well, you never know",' Meg said, quoting her grandmother. They both laughed.

When Ken went to bed that night, he fell asleep instantly.

***

On Monday morning Ken could feel the tension in the air. Meg was rushing and dropping things in the process. She made sandwiches for herself, and while she was at it she made some for her granddad so that he didn't have to worry about lunch.

'I've left your sandwiches wrapped in cling film in the fridge,' she called as she rushed out of the front door. 'Try not to get into any trouble!' she added, shutting the door behind her. Ken let out a sigh as he heard it shut.

Meg hadn't had time to wash up before she left, so he set about doing it one-handed. He found it more difficult than he expected and eventually decided to leave it until his carer, Angie, arrived. She could probably show him a better way to approach it.

He was just about to go to the garden and fill up the bird feeder when the phone rang. He picked it up and it was someone from Age UK.

'Hello,' she said, 'my name is Kate. I've had a call from the social worker who visited you in hospital. She thought you might appreciate a visit from someone to see how you are getting on. My job is to visit people who've been in hospital. Sometimes it's hard to get back on with your life again. I wondered if you'd like me to visit.'

Ken knew that this was one of those opportunities he had promised himself he would take. If he was going to go forward then he needed help.

'That would be lovely,' he replied. 'When would you be able to come?'

'I can do either tomorrow or Friday,' she replied.

'That's great because Thursday is the only day I am out,' he said.

'What about tomorrow morning? I could come at, say... eleven o'clock?'

'That's fine,' Ken replied. 'I'll be up and dressed because the carer will have been by then. I'll see you tomorrow then.'

He put the phone down, and as he passed Edith's photo he couldn't help picking it up and speaking to her. 'I hope I've got this right, but I don't think you'd want me to sit around getting miserable. In fact, I think you'd tell me off if I did.' He put the photo down and then remembered that he had been going to feed the birds.

He went down the garden and topped up the bird feeder in the apple tree. Then, as he put the bag of seed back on the shelf in the shed, he spotted the resident hedgehog. It was curled up in the corner, so he didn't disturb it. *That could have been me hibernating if I hadn't broken this arm,* he thought.

***

When Meg got in that evening she was exhausted. 'I had two important meetings today and I was almost late this morning,' she said. 'Pull up a stool beside me so we can talk while I cook.'

'That's my fault for slowing you down,' Ken said as he moved a stool closer to her. 'I'm sorry.'

'No, no, Granddad,' she replied, turning to face him. 'I'm often late. I leave home late and then drive like an idiot to get to work on time, and then if the traffic is bad I'm late anyway.'

'Does that get you in trouble?' he asked.

'No, not really, because I always get the work done and I often stay late. But I don't feel good about it.'

'You don't need to make my sandwiches – I'll manage. It will just be slow but I have plenty of time...'

Ken suddenly remembered the phone call. 'Oh! I forgot to tell you – I've got a lady – Kate, she said her name is – coming tomorrow from Age UK. She visits people for a few weeks after they come out of hospital and helps them get their independence back. I thought I'd ask her to help me get back into an art group.'

'Good idea,' said Meg as she picked up an onion and

began to slice it. 'Do you know if the group you used to go to is still running?'

'I don't know, but I have the number in my address book of the lady who used to run it. Peggy Day, I think her name was. I could have a look now.'

'Yeah, do it while you think of it,' she said.

He found the notebook on the shelf under the telephone table in the hall. 'Here it is,' he said in a triumphant tone, 'I have her number.'

'That's great,' Meg said, 'and if she isn't running it any more she may well know of another group. Anyway, I'm sure this lady from Age UK would track one down for you.'

'I feel as if I've lost confidence,' he replied. 'I used to be able to do all those things for myself, and for your grandma.'

'Ah well, that's why Kate is coming, isn't it? She'll help you with that and I'm sure you'll get your confidence back soon.'

She smiled at him – a slightly embarrassed smile. 'I mean, I wouldn't have thought that the church could help me, but it did. We've been a very independent family, but we all need a little help sometimes.'

CHAPTER 8

On Tuesday morning Ken nagged Meg out of the house with plenty of time to get to work.

'I can do it myself,' he said to her as she fussed about how he was going to get breakfast. 'I'll just be a bit slow, but I've got all day.'

'I'm going, I'm going, Granddad,' she said as she picked up her laptop and work bag and left.

When she'd gone he decided he'd try frying an egg and some bacon. He could just about grip the frying pan with his left hand once he'd got it onto the hob, despite the plaster cast, and managed even better than he had hoped. *Everything just takes longer,* he told himself.

After he'd finished breakfast, and very slowly washed up, he sat down to read a book and wait for the carer.

After Angie had left, he continued reading a little longer until Kate arrived, almost on the dot of eleven o'clock, and he took an instant liking to her. She had an open, friendly face and was dressed in bright colours.

'Hello, I'm Kate. We spoke on the phone yesterday.'

'Come in, it's nice to meet you,' Ken said as he stood back from the door to let her pass. 'Would you like a cup of tea or coffee?'

'I'd love a coffee if you're having one,' she replied. 'Do you find that difficult to do with your arm in plaster?'

'I'm getting used to it,' he answered. 'My granddaughter

does most of the work in the evening when she gets back from work. She'll be here for my first two weeks. By then I expect I'll be managing most things.'

'Well, I'm available for up to four weeks, so if you do find you aren't managing everything I can help you to make other arrangements,' she said.

'That's good to know.'

'What things do you think would help you regain your independence?' Kate asked as they waited for the kettle to boil.

'Well, I've been thinking about re-joining an art group. I went to one up until about two years ago, but my wife and I found that doing everyday things was taking longer and I gave up. Since she died I've missed having company, but I've given up all my hobbies.'

'What group did you go to?'

'I went to a group run by Peggy Day in the community centre on the Dalton estate. I have a number for Peggy but I'm not as confident these days. I'm a bit afraid of ringing her.'

'I can do that for you,' she said, 'or I can get through to her and then if she still runs the art group I can put you on to her.'

'That's a good idea,' Ken agreed. 'I've got her number here.' He handed Kate the address book, open at the right page.

Kate rang the number, and to Ken's surprise it turned out the group was still running. Kate handed him the phone. He made it clear that it would be a few weeks before he could return, as one-handed art wouldn't be easy, but he found out the day, time and price, and agreed that he would attend as soon as he could. Organising it all was much easier than he expected.

Ken made the coffee as Kate continued chatting. 'Are there any other groups you'd like to join, or people that you'd like to get back in touch with?'

Ken told her about Eric. 'I'm meeting him this Thursday. I'm quite hopeful that we'll be good friends because we got on so well in hospital. Oh,' he added, suddenly remembering, 'there is one other thing, although it is possible that Eric would teach me.'

'What is it?'

'I was chatting with Eric about the possibility of getting a laptop so I could Skype my son in Cyprus,' Ken continued, 'because at the moment I only get to talk to him if I'm at Peter's house, which isn't very often. Only trouble is, I don't know how to use a computer.'

They moved into the dining area and made themselves comfortable. Kate sipped her coffee, then put it down on a coaster. 'Well, if you're interested, we do have volunteers at our centre who can help you to learn how to use a computer. They would help you set up an email address, go online, order online, set up Skype – anything like that.'

'That would be brilliant. I'll talk to Eric and to Peter and try to find out which computer would be best for me,' he said. 'I might be a bit of a slow learner.'

'That's no problem. You can learn at your own pace.'

She left him after an hour, having made an appointment for the next week and promised she would find out about computer classes. He had agreed to look out his old art equipment and also find out which computer would suit his needs.

***

Ken hardly waited for Meg to get through the door that evening before he began telling her his news. She was delighted. 'By the time I leave here you'll have your social life sorted,' she said.

'I have to wait for the plaster to come off before I can start painting again, though.'

She shrugged. 'I don't see why. You should get out your easel and give it a go tomorrow. You paint with your right hand. You'd just have to rest your palette on a surface beside you.'

It got him thinking. *Maybe she's right.*

'I'll get everything out and have a try tomorrow,' he promised.

'Find your things tonight and I'll help you set it up. Some of the paints might have gone solid,' she pointed out. 'If so, you could take a taxi to that craft shop on the business park. I can't remember its name.'

He got up to look for his art equipment while Meg cooked the dinner.

Eventually he located a box in the spare room but couldn't lift it.

'I've found the box,' he said, 'and my canvases are behind it, along with the easel.'

'Okay,' she said, 'we'll get them out after dinner.'

As they ate, they discussed his art. 'I remember you

painting,' Meg said. 'Mostly birds.'

'I've always liked the birds, ever since I was a young lad living in the country. I guess that's why I still encourage them into the garden every winter.'

'At least here you're still on the edge of the countryside, so they do come into the gardens,' Meg said. 'It's a beautiful place to live. I wouldn't want to live in a city.'

'I guess a small town is a good compromise, although I do miss living further out in the country sometimes,' he said.

After dinner, Meg moved the box into the dining area so that he could investigate while she washed up. The used brushes and palette had been left perfectly clean, and there was even a pack of new brushes.

'Some of these oil paints do look a bit of a state, though,' said Ken. 'I think I *will* go to the craft shop. I just need to decide what colours I want.'

Meg went back into the spare room to set up the easel and found a pile of canvases behind it; some were used and some were blank. She took hold of two blank ones and moved them into reach, then she caught sight of an oil painting of her grandma. 'When did you do this?' she asked.

'I'd forgotten I'd done that,' he said, taking it from her. 'That was for her seventy-fifth birthday. So, three years ago.'

'It captures her personality. Did you always paint in oils?' she asked.

'I did,' he replied. 'I got quite good at oil painting, at one time. But I've been wondering about trying something new, with watercolours. I think I'll have a look at them too when I'm at the shop tomorrow. I want to begin all over again.'

He sat quietly for a while. *Long ago,* he thought, *before the children, before the weekly grind of the office, this was a big part of my life. Even two years ago I was still painting now and then.*

He felt as if something was stirring, rising in him. As if a part of him was beginning to come alive again.

CHAPTER 9

On Wednesday morning Ken stayed out of Meg's way while she got ready for work.

After she'd left, he rang a local taxi firm. He was determined to get his artwork started again. He arranged to be collected at eleven o'clock, and then had to make sure he'd had breakfast before Angie arrived.

He ended up short of time for the washing-up once again. *Not to worry,* he thought, *I can do it after lunch.* But when Angie heard he was going out, she quickly washed up for him before she left.

With all that taken care of, and with nothing more to do but wait for the taxi, Ken began to feel really excited about his plans.

The taxi arrived on time, and the driver agreed to wait outside the shop for him.

Ken bought more oil paints, a set of watercolour paints and a large sketch pad, and then headed back outside to the waiting taxi.

He was pleased with his purchases, and even more pleased with himself. When he arrived home, he paid the taxi driver and went back into the house, stopping to pass the time of day with a neighbour, but only briefly; he couldn't wait to try out his new paints.

After changing into clothes that had only been worn in the garden in recent years, Ken picked up a blank canvas and put it on the easel. It felt strange, almost as if he didn't know what to do. First, he chose a pencil and outlined the harbour that he held so close to his heart; this was where he would begin with watercolour painting.

He changed his mind after a few minutes and took out his new sketch pad.

The harbour was pretty well engraved in his mind, but he felt that a photograph in front of him would help to fill in the details. As he searched for a photo, he came across one of Meg as a little girl in the arms of her grandmother.

'I can't believe that was twenty-four years ago,' he mused.

Studying the image, he resolved to paint it secretly as a present for Meg's kindness. *She mustn't know,* he thought, *and I need to get it finished for when she leaves so I can give it to her as a leaving present.*

He had to be clever about this because Meg was no fool. She would get suspicious unless he got going on the painting of the harbour at the same time.

He continued looking through the photographs until he came across one of the harbour, and then he took both photographs into the spare room.

Today he would start the harbour painting but also sketch an outline of Meg and her grandmother on another canvas and then put the photograph and the canvas in the wardrobe where Meg wouldn't find them.

He picked up the sketch pad and began to draft a layout for the harbour. First, he drew a faint line for the horizon and the line of the harbour wall, then he drew the outlines of boats and put little marks where he would paint seagulls.

He recalled the harbour on a warm spring day. It hadn't

been a very bright day but the slate-grey sky almost blended with the sea, except for the fact that the sea had subtle green tones. The tide was high and the waves slapped against the harbour wall. Seagulls floated just inside the harbour, drifting slowly inwards. All of a sudden they would take flight and fly high in the sky to catch the thermals, then soar back down to the water and begin the process again. He envied the seagulls.

Sudden awareness awoke him from the memories that were distracting him. Beautiful as they were, he needed to concentrate. He put the photograph out of sight and began to sketch out the initial impression of the harbour and the waves. He could only mark the canvas faintly; he didn't want the lines to show through the watercolours.

Next he mixed the paints to the exact colours he wanted. He would begin with the sky, the way he always had. The sky he pictured had many tones, so he filled the palette with a number of different colour mixes and began his first wash with just water, in order to create the soft edges for the clouds, before working in the strongest blue-grey mix.

He used loose brushstrokes to give it texture. While it was all still wet, he developed the clouds. He darkened the base of each cloud and then took a while to soften the edges with a wet brush, gently bleeding the colour away to blend it in. Then he added more paint to sections of the sky to vary the depth of colour.

It felt strange creating with paint again, as if he was bringing back a part of himself that he had lost, or a friend that he hadn't seen in a long while. It returned easily despite the fact that most of his past paintings were in oils. He had only used watercolour paints once in a while in the past, but this scene lent itself to that style.

Time passed quickly when he was painting. Standing back to take a look at the painting, he put the brush in the jar of water and suddenly caught sight of the time on the old carriage clock. It was gone two o'clock and he hadn't even thought about lunch.

If I defrost a pot of soup from the freezer, he thought, *and have a wholemeal roll with it, then it won't take long and I might have time to do a little more painting...*

He rushed through lunch, washed up and got back to his easel as fast as he could.

***

By the time Meg came in from work he'd finished the sky and drawn in a few more details of the harbour wall. That would be what he tackled next, but for today he would put the painting away and spend time with his granddaughter.

'Let me see what you've done so far then,' she said when he told her he'd been painting.

He noted the smile on her face when she saw what he had done, and the way she looked at him with pleasure.

'I haven't seen you this alive since Grandma died,' she said. 'Nor have I seen you with paint in your hair!'

He laughed.

'It's lovely, Granddad,' she added as she looked at his work from a distance and then close up.

'Thank you,' he replied, 'although I haven't done any painting for a long while so I'm pretty sure it isn't that lovely really – but I have enjoyed it.'

'Carry on if you want to,' she said. 'I'll cook dinner in a

little while.'

He shook his head. 'I think I'll stop now. I haven't tidied the bedroom and it's a bit of a mess.'

'Oh!' Meg said as she went back into the hall to hang up her coat. 'Before I forget altogether – remind me at dinner to tell you about Cyprus. I went into the travel agent's in town.'

'Okay!' Ken said, the excitement evident in his voice as he bounced off to tidy his bedroom with more of a spring in his unsteady step.

Tidying up had never been one of his strengths. Generally he was happy to live with his muddles, but he was making at least some attempt to keep things a little tidier now that Meg was here.

'I don't know why you worry about tidying,' she called to him. 'You know I'm as messy as you are.'

'That may be,' he called from the bedroom, 'but if the place is untidy your dad doesn't think I'm coping. I don't want him booking me into a home just when I'm getting my life back together.'

Meg laughed. 'Don't say that, Granddad. He might book me into a home too if that's the standard he's using for coping.'

Her granddad laughed too, and busied himself while she cooked dinner.

When he'd finished tidying up, he sat in the dining area gazing at Meg over the book he'd got out to read. The open-plan kitchen diner had been Edith's idea when they moved into the bungalow. They had often talked when she was in the kitchen and he was in the dining area.

Meg's cooking was as creative as the rest of her life. She

rarely used a recipe and she made it look easy. He returned to his book, but he heard her singing quietly to herself and it reminded him of Edith in her younger days.

'Your grandma used to sing when she was cooking,' he said.

'I remember that. Sometimes she used to put on an Elvis CD and sing along.'

'In a deep voice like Elvis,' he laughed.

He got up and went to the kitchen to fetch the cutlery and then laid the table ready for dinner. Somehow it was worth it for two.

Meg put the dinner down on the table. 'We could never have had curry with Grandma here, could we?' she said.

Ken laughed. 'No, she was a bit of a traditionalist when it came to food.'

'But she cooked the things she liked really well,' Meg said.

'She did. She went to cookery lessons after we got married because she couldn't cook at all. She'd make cakes that never rose and bread that was as solid as a rock. But she soon picked it up.'

'She certainly did,' said Meg fondly.

Ken looked up at her. 'So,' he said, 'what did you find out about the possibility of going to Cyprus?'

'Oh yes!' she exclaimed. 'It's a good job you reminded me...' She jumped up from the table briefly and came back with a notebook.

'I wrote down what the guy in the travel agent's said because I knew I'd forget that too. Okay...' She started flicking through her notes. 'I've talked to him about two different ways because I wasn't sure whether Uncle Ben had space to put us up. If he can put us up at his house, then we really only need to arrange flights and airport transfers. If not, we need to find an apartment nearby in Limassol.'

Ken thought for a moment. 'I've only seen pictures of his house – they've moved since I was last there,' he said. 'I'm trying to remember how big the house looked in the photos. Maybe we need to ring Ben and find out what he would suggest.'

'We could do that tonight,' Meg suggested.

'I think they're two hours ahead of us. So we need to be careful what time we ring.'

'If we ring straight away then we should be okay,' Meg suggested. 'Shall I ring him now?'

Ken smiled. Meg was like her mother. 'That's a good idea. Do you have a phone number for him?'

'I think so. It should be in my phone.' She found the number and dialled it.

'Ben Stanton,' came the reply as Ben picked up the land phone.

'Hi, Uncle Ben, it's Meg.'

'Meg? Oh, Meg, I wasn't expecting to hear from you.' Ben was always a bit disarmed by surprises. 'Is everything alright?'

'Everything's fine,' she replied. 'I'm staying with Granddad to keep an eye on him for a couple of weeks and we've been wondering about coming over to Cyprus in the spring for a bit of a break.'

'Okay,' Ben replied slowly, as if uncertain. 'Is Granddad up to the travel?' The tone was questioning, suspicious even.

'Well, I'm sure he will be by then, if we come over in

about March. He said he'd like to come, and so would I, so we decided that he might be able to if I accompany him and keep him out of trouble.'

Ken nudged her. 'Hey,' he said, 'I'm no trouble!'

'What do you mean,' she whispered, laughing. 'Look at all the trouble you've caused *me*.'

'So are you thinking of staying with me? Or in a nearby apartment – or somewhere else?' he asked.

'Well, I rang to ask what you'd suggest. Obviously, we'd like to see you and Auntie Jane and the kids, but we'd also like to see a bit of the island so I'd need to hire a car.'

'Why don't you leave it with me, and I'll speak to Jane when she gets in. We might have room, but we also have friends who have a fabulous apartment near the sea, with two bedrooms, so that might suit you better. It's about half an hour from here but much more convenient for everything else. I'll give you a call at about this time tomorrow and let you know what she says.'

Meg was over the moon. 'I've never been to Cyprus,' she said as she cleared away the dinner things, 'and I haven't seen my cousins for years. It will be fantastic if we can sort out the arrangements.'

She helped her granddad as he carried things to the kitchen. He was humming to himself. Agreeing to go in the spring would give him time to recover from the accident and feel more emotionally stable. By then, he hoped, he would have a much fuller social life.

As Ken lay down to sleep that night he remembered the last time that he and Edith had travelled to Cyprus. *That must have been fifteen years ago,* he thought, *when Ben's children were still young.*

He imagined himself reconnecting with them all, and fell asleep contented.

CHAPTER 10

When Ken stirred the next morning, he felt refreshed. He must have slept through because he didn't remember waking in the night as he usually did. He could hear Meg padding around in the room next door and assumed it was about eight o'clock.

He had been surprised when she declared at eighteen that she wasn't going to university. She was bright enough to, but he hadn't reckoned on her determination to get on at work. As a housing officer she dealt with some difficult situations at times, but she seemed to take it all in her stride.

He picked up his glasses from the bedside table, put them on and looked at his watch. He was right. It was almost eight. *Thursday,* he said to himself. *I'm meeting Eric for coffee today, as long as he's okay. I'll give him a ring at about nine.*

He laid out the clothes he would wear to meet Eric and couldn't help laughing at himself. This was his first social outing since Edith had died. He felt like a teenager going to his first party. He chose brown corduroy trousers and a sandy-brown short-sleeved shirt that he could just about get over the plaster cast. On top of that he would wear his moss-green V-necked jumper, which was the only one he possessed that would fit over it.

He put on his dressing gown and went into the kitchen to make his tea. 'Tell me if I'm getting in your way,' he said as he met Meg in the hallway. 'I'm just getting a cup of tea and then I'll be out of the way.'

'I'm running a bit late,' she said. 'If you're making tea could you make me a cup of coffee?'

He laughed. She was always running a bit late. 'Of course,' he said, shaking his head. 'I'll leave it on the side by the kettle.' He made her coffee and took his tea back into the bedroom.

It was usually about quarter past nine by the time Angie arrived to help Ken, and she'd promised to make sure she was on time today. He looked forward to her visits; not only was she very patient and encouraging throughout all his frustrations as he washed and dressed, but he also enjoyed chatting with her as he did so. He was pleased with the progress he'd made and was feeling much more confident now.

His day was planned out, which felt good. This morning he would meet up with Eric, and this afternoon he would continue with his painting. *Maybe I'll do a bit of the oil painting of Edith and Meg,* he thought. *She won't expect me to have done much of the watercolour painting because I'm going out.*

He heard Meg leave the house and emerged from the bedroom to make breakfast. He fancied a bowl of porridge and a slice of toast. *I might treat myself and Eric to a slice of cake,* he thought. All sorts of things were going through his mind. *I hope we get on as well as we did in hospital... I hope we can stay friends and meet each week. Maybe we could do other activities together as well...*

After a few moments, though, he told himself off, reining in the excitement a little. *Just take today's meeting as it comes.*

At nine o'clock he rang Eric to make sure he was still okay to meet up, then rang to book a taxi.

True to her promise, Angie was on time, and he was dressed and ready long before the taxi was due, so he went out into the garden and replenished the bird feeder.

After that he sat and read for a little while, getting up every now and again to pace the floor and look at the clock.

The taxi arrived on time. Ken put on his scarf and waterproof jacket, picked up his wallet, locked up the bungalow and got into the taxi. The journey was only about ten minutes, and he arrived outside Cara's Café just before eleven, as they had arranged. Two minutes later, as he stood outside, he saw Eric in the distance using crutches to hobble down the road.

'Go in and get a table,' Eric called to him. So Ken went inside and chose a table by the window. It would be so good to see Eric.

'Blimey, that was hard work,' Eric said as he plonked himself down on the seat opposite Ken.

'I never thought,' Ken said. 'As I was getting a taxi anyway, I could have got it to come past your house and picked you up.'

'Oh yes, I never thought of that either,' Eric said. 'Not to worry, I imagine the exercise was good for me. How's your arm coming on?'

'It just makes everything take so long, not to mention that it limits what clothes I can wear. I've learnt how to get clothes on and off by myself now, so that's not too bad, and I'm pretty good at washing one-handed, but it is a bit frustrating. Then every now and again I forget about it and only remember when I get a twinge of pain. How are you managing with your leg?' he asked.

'Well, I get down to the shop at the end of my road with the help of the crutches, but it's such an effort that if I go anywhere else I get a taxi,' Eric replied. 'I'm still not allowed to weight-bear for six weeks so I might as well get used to the crutches.'

'Does it hurt your arms using crutches?' Ken asked.

'I've got used to it – it just takes so long to get anywhere,' Eric replied.

The waitress appeared with her notepad. 'What would you like, gentlemen?' she asked.

They ordered two cappuccinos and two slices of the delicious-looking carrot cake on the display stand.

'Must be one of our five-a-day,' Eric said.

'I would think so,' Ken replied. 'If Edith was here I wouldn't be allowed cake. She'd warn me I'd put on weight.'

They chatted for an hour and a half and then decided that they would also order lunch, and then chatted for another hour before Ken called for a taxi to take him home. While they waited, they made an arrangement to meet up again the following Thursday at the same time.

The taxi dropped Eric home first, and when Ken got home he realised that he had a bit of time to work on the painting of Edith and Meg before Meg got home.

He got out the canvas, photograph and paints, and began to paint, starting with the background. The background of the photograph was light honeydew, the colour of their lounge at the time. Ken mixed up the colour on the palette as close to the original as he could and used a palette knife to apply it to the canvas in a thin layer. He would need to leave it to dry overnight, so he took it down from the easel and put it back into the wardrobe.

Next he cleaned the palette and knife, dried them and put them away, and got out the watercolour painting of the harbour. He had promised himself yesterday that he would tackle the harbour wall today, so he mixed up different tones close to the colour of the stone that made up the wall. The wall was a kind of dirty yellow-grey. He used a brush and roughly washed the area of the harbour wall, mixing in some of the other colours on his palette from time to time to vary the colour slightly across the wall. After that he built up the colour by gradually adding other washes in places, over the top of the underwash, with an old, rough brush.

He put the brushes in a jar of water, wiped his hands on the old cloth that he kept on the easel, and went off to make a cup of tea while the painting dried.

As he gazed out of the patio door at the birds around the bird feeder, he considered his day and smiled to himself. Breaking his arm had been a blessing in disguise. Not that he wanted the pain and inconvenience, but it had somehow awoken him to a life that he would not have imagined was possible at his age. He had thought that his life was over, had longed for death, even, after Edith had died, but now he was beginning again.

He sat for quite a while before returning to the painting. He was short of time today because of the hours he had spent with Eric, but he didn't regret it. Eric and he would become good friends, he was certain of it now.

He returned to the painting, and added the defining lines around the stones with pen and ink before putting a few thicker lines in places with a fine brush. The art of painting had come back to him once he'd started. He'd forgotten just how invigorating it was.

***

That evening, Ben rang as he said he would. Jane had spoken to the friend who owned the apartment near the sea and said that they could have the use of it for a negligible amount, just so that electricity was covered.

'The best thing to do,' Ben said to Meg, 'is to get estimates for flights to Larnaca, but don't book anything yet. Make sure your granddad is okay first. If you do come out for a visit I'm sure we can give you lifts from the airport.'

When Meg came off the phone she was very excited. 'The apartment is a short walk from the shops in one direction and very close to the sea in the other. Uncle Ben's house is about half an hour away. I think we should go.'

'I quite agree,' Ken said. 'We'll need to make sure we hire a car for when we arrive. Maybe we could even collect it from the airport – that would save Ben or Jane coming to collect us.'

'And they drive on the left so it wouldn't be too difficult,' Meg added. 'We won't need too many extra clothes because it won't be exceptionally hot or cold.'

They decided that they definitely wanted to visit Cyprus, and Meg agreed to sort out a week that suited her work schedule and book it off. Then she would contact Jane and get her to book them into her friend's apartment.

'I don't know why I've never thought of visiting them

before. I somehow always expect them to come here,' she said.

'So do I,' Ken replied, 'but this is a great idea and it will give me something to aim at.'

They sat for almost another hour discussing all the things they would like to do in Cyprus, and then Meg headed off to her room, yawning.

'I'm out tomorrow evening,' she said, 'so I think I'll get an early night.'

CHAPTER 11

The next morning, Ken was surprised to hear Meg leave the house early.

He chose to sit by the patio door with his breakfast on a tray. From there he could watch the birds playing in the apple tree. He couldn't help noticing the fallen leaves rotting on the lawn. As soon as he'd finished breakfast he would get out the rake and clear them. He couldn't expect Meg to do that. Or at least, he could make a start on it. It wouldn't matter if he got dirty as Angie had promised him a bath today.

After breakfast, he cleared up and then went into the garden, got out the rake and cleared the leaves. He could only sweep them into a pile, but that was progress. The apple tree needed cutting back, but he knew he'd be in trouble with Peter if he tried using the stepladder, so he left the tree and determined to remember to ask Peter about it.

With that done, he sat by the patio door to admire his work and watch the birds playing in the tree while he waited for Angie to arrive.

At this time of year, Edith used to go out and buy extra birdseed for the bird feeders. At one point they'd had one in the small strip of garden at the front as well as one in the back garden. She used coconut shells to make fat balls too, but that was a lot of work when the shop sold them ready-made. He would go to the garden centre this afternoon and settle for just the birdseed.

He picked up the phone and rang for a taxi for two o'clock, arranging that the driver would call back for him at the garden centre after about an hour and bring him home.

He read his book until lunchtime and then got out the sandwiches Meg had made for him. Having left the lunch things on the side to wash up when he got back, he put on the trainers with Velcro that Peter had bought for him, retrieved his waterproof jacket from the hall, picked up his wallet, keys and shopping bag, and left as soon as the taxi driver rang the doorbell.

It was a beautiful day. The pavements were carpeted with richly coloured autumn leaves and the low sun was shining, although there was a lot less warmth in it now. Ken chatted with the taxi driver all the way to the garden centre.

'I'll be waiting right here in an hour,' the driver promised. Ken thanked him and walked slowly to the entrance. An hour would be plenty of time.

He wandered through the outdoor section of the garden centre, stopping to look at the plants on his way. It wasn't even November yet, but the shop assistants were stocking the shelves with Christmas decorations and gifts ready for the early shoppers. He browsed the Christmas area for a little while but eventually decided that he had better buy the birdseed before he completely forgot what he'd come for.

On his way to the till he came across a pretty floral notebook that he thought Meg would like, so he put it in his basket along with a packet of locally made fudge and a book called *Greenhouse Gardening*, and headed for the till. *I'd better get a move on,* he said to himself. *That taxi will be waiting.*

Once he'd paid for the goods and packed them into his bag, he went to find his taxi.

Back at home, Ken made a cup of tea and took the birdseed into the garden to top up the feeder. He considered painting the sea in his watercolour, but he was tired and decided to sit down with his new book instead.

Meg got in late from work as she'd been in a lengthy meeting, but she cooked a quick stir-fry for dinner so that she was ready when her friend from work collected her for an evening in the pub. It was strange to spend the evening without her.

Ken decided to sort through a box that he'd found in the spare room. He set it down on the dining table and started to sift through its contents.

Most of it was just odds and ends that the children had brought back from school trips and then, later, from holidays abroad, but right at the bottom of the box, wrapped up in burgundy material, was a small, hand-carved wooden box. The box was lined with red velvet and inside was a cotton bag of coins. It must have belonged to Edith because Ken had never seen it before.

He picked up the coins and fingered them. They were definitely foreign but he had no idea which country they were from. But no matter how intrigued he was, he would have to wait to find out. Meg would look up the coins on the internet. Right now he regretted not having a computer.

It occurred to him that having a computer was something that he hadn't put on his bucket list. He picked up the list and added it before returning to the box.

Most of the contents were only worth putting in the bin, Edith's old payslips, receipts, gift bags that Edith must have thought were pretty and she might use one day. He smiled to himself – 'You never know,' he could hear her saying.

There was a plastic bag full of felt-tip pens. He tested each one – most of them had dried out. He really didn't want a house full of rubbish. He fetched a black bag and disposed of the majority of the contents of the box. But despite the fact that the items the children had brought back from trips were mostly useless, he couldn't bring himself to get rid of them. They were a part of his past.

He placed the things he wanted to keep on the table. There was an old guiding book that must have belonged to Edith because he could remember her in the Guides when she was younger. It was a scrapbook with newspaper cuttings, programmes and old photos; he wouldn't get rid of that. He scrutinised a photo of Edith as a young teenager. Even in a photo from her youth he could still pick her out.

For the rest of the evening he sat down with a glass of red wine and watched television. It wasn't something he did all the time but he did like the occasional crime drama; he enjoyed trying to work out who the criminal was before it was revealed.

When the episode finished, he decided to go to bed. Much as he would have liked to paint for some of the evening, he'd done enough for one day; he would paint the sea tomorrow. Meg would probably stay in bed all morning and he would get on with some painting. He rarely had a lie-in.

***

Apart from the fact that he stirred slightly when Meg came in, he slept through the night. Since he had begun to rebuild his life, Ken had slept much better. Sleep had been elusive while he was trying to work out what his life meant without Edith. *I think she would be proud of me,* he said to himself when he woke up on Saturday morning.

Just as he expected, there was no sound from Meg in the morning. He didn't blame her for staying in bed; she worked hard. He got up and had breakfast on a tray. He decided to sit, as he often did, in the chair by the patio door. It was a clear morning, which Ken suspected meant it would be quite cold outside.

The sparrows were already fluttering and playing around the bird feeder. The apple tree was almost bare now, so he could watch them more easily. He enjoyed his breakfast. Saturday was usually the only day that he bothered to cook breakfast. It was one habit that he'd continued after Edith died. In the past she would have cooked it for him, but he was perfectly capable of doing it himself.

After breakfast, Angie arrived and Ken got washed and dressed with minimal help. He knew he wouldn't need her for much longer, and it occurred to him that he would miss her when she no longer came.

Once she had left, he set up his easel in the spare room and placed the canvas and photograph ready for him to continue the oil painting. Edith's dark hair would be the next thing he would paint because it would take a few layers to get the texture and depth of colour he wanted; when Meg was born Edith had still had a lot of dark tones in her hair. He would need to swirl the paint slightly to capture her curls, too.

It was strange how he needed the photograph in order to remember the details. Somehow it made him feel that her memory was slipping away from him. He felt sorrow wash over him. He had managed to keep depression at bay over the past couple of weeks by staying busy, but as he looked at the photo now it triggered memories that overwhelmed him.

He went and sat down in the lounge, and for the first time he wept without restraint. Before long the sound of his sobs woke Meg up, and she came into the lounge.

'Are you okay, Granddad,' she asked softly, although it was blatantly clear that he wasn't.

'I will be, my love,' he said between sobs.

She sat beside him and rested her hand on his arm. 'You're doing great, Granddad,' she said, tenderness in her tone. 'You and Grandma were together so long, it's bound to take a long while to come to terms with her death.'

'I feel as if I'm forgetting her. I don't want to lose the memory,' he said. 'I can't picture her like I used to.'

'Maybe you never really did,' she said. 'Perhaps the way we see someone is dependent on other things, like the smell of her perfume, the sound of her voice, the touch of her hand.'

He nodded as he wiped away tears with his handkerchief. 'I was just looking at a photograph of Edith and I realised that I couldn't picture her without it.'

'I think we should make up a photo board of all your favourite photographs of Grandma,' Meg said. 'I'll go out later on and buy one and we can do it tonight and hang it in the lounge.'

Meg made a cup of tea and went back to bed for a while. Ken regretted having woken her; he knew how much she loved her Saturday morning lie-in, especially when she had been out the night before. He crept quietly back to his painting, but feeling in his heart that it had been good to cry.

As he began to mix the paints he felt the same emotions rise again. There was nothing he could do – one day, Ken believed, he and Edith would be reunited for eternity, but for now they were separated. And he would not have wished her to stay; not if she was suffering. So, somehow, he had to let her go.

With renewed enthusiasm he set about capturing the colour and texture of Edith's hair as it was at the time of Meg's birth. There were white streaks – he remembered that when he thought hard. Some shades of grey or white hair appear dull or harsh as people age, but even when Edith's hair went completely white he saw it as distinguished. Indeed, he had talked her out of dyeing it. Her hair, like her personality, was beautiful just as it was. She had called him a flatterer when he said it and they had laughed.

Maybe he didn't remember every detail of what she looked like, but he had so many memories of their conversations and the funny little things that she said and did. *I'm lucky,* he thought. *So many of our friends are divorced or live almost separate lives, but we were the best of friends. When everything else became difficult, we were still friends.*

He smiled now. That was the truth. During his depression he had thought that he had not been good enough for her – that he should somehow have been more than he was – but now he felt only gratitude for the times they had shared. He hadn't been perfect, but he could accept that.

The base colour that he chose for Edith's hair was a mixture of dark brown and black, but when the sun caught her hair, as it did in the photograph, there were rich seams of red too; he would add those in the next layer, along with the white streaks. The lighting would be all important in this painting; he needed to get it right.

Somehow, by allowing the tears to come he had sharpened the memory. *I think I was so afraid of losing the memory,* it dawned on him, *that I clung to her and couldn't clear my mind.*

He picked up the photograph. *I will let you go, my love. I will set you free.*

He could imagine her now – imagine her returning the favour, imagine her replying: *And I set you free too, my love.*

After half an hour's work, he put away the oil painting and took out the watercolour of the harbour. Today he would attempt to paint the sea. That was much more difficult. He wanted to capture the variety of colours, the movement, and the way that the light played on the surface.

He wanted to express how the swirling waves hit the harbour wall, how the light shimmered on the water, how the blends of blue, green, grey and brown ebbed and flowed, reflecting the light and shade of the sky; all these intrigued him.

There was something captivating about the sea, something that drew him. He had always had a hankering to live by the sea but it had never fitted in with work or family commitments, especially as his career advanced; there had always been something to hold him back. Maybe, just maybe, now was the time. He pondered the possibility as he blended the colours on his palette. He didn't want to blend them completely; he wanted them to contain veins and lines of other colours, just as the sea would.

When he had finished the first layer of the sea, he stood back from the easel and looked at it for a few minutes, picturing what he would do next. Then, leaving it on the easel to dry, he took the brushes to the kitchen and was surprised to find that Meg had got up.

'I was just lying in bed reading and I thought I might as well go to town and get that photo board this morning,' she said. She was still in pyjamas; it took her a little while to get organised on a Saturday. She poured a bowl of muesli and milk and added a little fruit.

'That's not much of a breakfast,' her granddad said.

Meg shrugged. 'Ha ha, you haven't seen me out shopping,' she said. 'I'll probably end up buying a doughnut.'

'I might walk down to get a newspaper,' he said, 'but probably not a doughnut.'

'Don't you go tripping over the step again or I'll be in trouble as well as you,' she said. 'I can always get the paper for you while I'm in town. Unless you *want* to go out, of course.'

‘Yes, I need to get out,’ he said. ‘It looks a reasonable day.’

Meg changed into jeans and a cobalt-blue jumper and put on her black Gore-Tex jacket. ‘I’ll take the car,’ she said. ‘Do you want me to drop you off at the shop?’

Ken winked as he declined the offer. ‘I need the exercise,’ he said. ‘Don’t worry, I’ll be careful.’

After Meg left, Ken tidied his bedroom, put on his coat and scarf and walked down to the local shop. All he bought was the paper, and none of the conversations he had were particularly thrilling, but he’d got out of the house and he felt better for it. He navigated the step at the shop without any problem and wandered slowly home, made a cup of coffee and sat in the lounge.

When Meg returned she showed him the photo board. ‘They had silver-coloured ones as well,’ she said, ‘but I liked the rugged wooden one better.’

‘I agree. That will definitely look good on the lounge wall,’ Ken replied. ‘I’ll get out the box of photos later on and put them on the table. If you’re not going out we could sort them out this evening.’

‘I’m not out this evening,’ she said. ‘I can’t keep up the pace two nights in a row.’

He laughed. ‘Are you getting old?’

‘Maybe,’ she replied with a giggle.

Meg put the kettle on and spooned coffee into a mug, made her drink, and sat down beside her granddad on the settee. ‘I expect I’ve got some more up-to-date photos on the laptop,’ she said. ‘I’ll have a look this evening while you look through the box. I can print them off at work on Monday.’

'That's a good idea,' Ken said. 'Most of my photos go back a few years.'

That afternoon Meg went round to a friend's house, so he set to work on the oil painting again. He found more and more often that he was comfortable on his own. When Meg went out he didn't feel alone now. He was slowly coming to terms with Edith's death. Making a life for himself had been the key to it. But nobody could ever take her place, and he felt certain now that he would never totally forget her as he had once feared. Making a photo board would help him to picture her every day too.

In the evening they sat down after dinner and Meg searched her laptop photo files while Ken rummaged through the photograph box. He handed her a photo of Edith with a golden retriever.

'Oh, I'd forgotten you had the dog,' she said. 'I loved that dog. I used to sit on the floor and lean on him. He never complained.'

'I remember that,' Ken said with a reflective smile. 'He was a lovely, patient dog.'

'Conan, wasn't it, his name?' she asked.

'Yes, although that was only a part of his pedigree name,' her granddad replied.

'I think you should put that one on the board,' she said, and he nodded and put the photo aside.

She came across a file of photographs on the laptop from the Christmas before last, when most of the family were gathered at Peter's house as usual. 'These are nice,' she said. 'Grandma is holding Stella's baby in this one... And this is one of my favourites – both of you with Stella and the baby. Amber seems so grown up now. It doesn't seem possible that photo was taken only two years ago.'

'I keep thinking that about all these photos,' said Ken as he pondered the past. 'It seems like yesterday that you were born – or your dad, come to that.' He picked up a photograph of his wedding. 'I remember that day so clearly.'

'So your fears about forgetting Grandma are unfounded then,' she said. 'If you can remember your wedding day, and you can still picture Grandma like that, then you're not going to forget what she looks like in a hurry, are you?'

Ken laughed. 'Sometimes,' he said, 'you are too wise for a twenty-four-year-old.'

They carried on selecting photos from the box and the laptop, until eventually Meg got up. 'What about a beer?' she suggested. 'I think we've earned it.'

Ken agreed. 'That's a really good idea... You do realise,' he added, 'that we have far too many photos for that board?'

She nodded calmly as he spoke. 'I do, but that's a better position to be in than not having enough.'

'Very true,' he said. 'But I think I've had enough of hunting through photos for today.'

'Me too. I'll print off the ones we've chosen on Monday at work if I have time. They'll only be on paper but I think it will look okay if I mount them on card.'

'Thank you,' said Ken, turning towards her. 'Not just for doing the photos, but for being here.'

'The time has gone fast,' she said. 'I can't believe a week has gone already. You've managed really well.'

'I like to think so,' he replied. 'By the time you leave I'll be fine.'

‘I’m certain you will. I was worried about you when you first left hospital, but I think you’re much better in yourself now.’

When Ken lay down to sleep that night, he felt a measure of satisfaction. He felt he’d made progress, and it was good to hear that Meg agreed.

CHAPTER 12

Ken slept well and woke late on Sunday morning. He suddenly realised that the carer would be here soon – Angie was having a day off, and her colleague Marie would be helping him for the first time – so he forced himself out of bed quickly.

Marie was almost as lovely as Angie, and she seemed very impressed with the progress Ken was making. 'You'll be putting us all out of a job,' she teased him.

Once she was gone, Ken took up his book and wondered when Meg might stir.

In the end, Meg didn't wake up until almost eleven. She emerged from the bedroom still looking drowsy.

'I forgot to tell you,' she began in a slurred voice, 'we're going to my parents for dinner. We need to leave here at about half past twelve.'

'Oh right. That's nice of them,' Ken said. 'Do I need to dress up?'

'Well, I'm not!' she exclaimed.

'Casual it is, then.'

'I reckon you'd find it quite difficult to wear a suit with that arm in a plaster cast anyway,' she said with a grin.

'I hadn't thought of that,' he replied, wondering what he should wear instead.

'Anyway, I don't think you need to worry about your outfit too much, Granddad.'

'But I was thinking,' he said, 'maybe we should take a family photo. I'd like a photo for the new beginning.'

'Oh, that's a good idea. If I take it on my camera then we can upload it onto the computer and I can print it off with the others at work tomorrow.'

'That's great. Then we can do the photo board tomorrow night and get it finished. Otherwise it will sit around here like all my other unfinished projects.'

Meg laughed. 'I'll go and get ready.'

'That's another good idea,' he laughed. 'I'll make you a coffee while you do.'

'Thanks, Granddad. Just leave it in the kitchen and I'll come and fetch it.'

She picked up the coffee on her way back from the bathroom, but by half past twelve she still hadn't reappeared from her room.

'Meg, we're going to be late,' Ken called. 'You know what your dad is like for punctuality.'

She almost ran out of the bedroom. 'Okay, I'm ready,' she said.

They arrived at Peter's by one o'clock, as they were meant to, and dinner was served soon afterwards.

It was good to sit up at a table with the family. With the exception of Meg, Ken had little opportunity to see Peter's children. Meg's elder brother, Stuart, and his wife, Karen, arrived with their two young boys just after Meg and her granddad. Their younger sister, Stella, arrived with two-year-old Amber about half an hour later. Peter had started dinner without her. Ken saw Meg smile to herself; at least she was never quite as late as Stella.

Peter soon began to quiz Ken. 'I hope you're not going

out by yourself anymore?' he said.

'He's fine, aren't you, Granddad?' Meg said. 'Of course he goes out. You can't expect him to stay in all day.'

Her granddad nodded. 'I know you worry about me, Peter, but I'm fine. It was just an accident. It could happen to anyone.'

'But you *are* a bit unsteady on your feet, so that makes you more likely to fall than most people,' he said.

The conversation continued and somehow came around to the subject of Meg and her granddad's trip to Cyprus. The alarming thing for Ken was that it was Peter who brought the subject up.

'It appears,' Peter said, addressing his father, 'if Ben is telling me the truth, and I have no reason to doubt him, that you and Meg are planning a trip out to Cyprus.' He paused in disbelief. 'How on earth do you think you're going to manage?'

Ken took a deep breath. Discussions of this nature were never easy with Peter. He took life too seriously and he always liked everything to be neat and organised.

'I know that you worry about me, son, but I'm managing much better than you realise. The only thing I *really* need a carer for now is when I want a bath – Angie won't be helping me with washing and dressing much longer... She does think I might need support with a few other things when Meg leaves, though.' He paused.

'So how will you manage that when you're away?' Peter asked.

'We're not planning on going until the spring, so I'll be better by then. The arm will be out of plaster and I'll be a lot stronger.'

Peter tightened his lips and flared his nostrils.

'We'll only be half an hour away from Uncle Ben anyway,' Meg said. 'Was he concerned about Granddad, then?'

'No... Well, he didn't say so, but that's not the point.' He turned to Ken. 'He was just checking up on how you were.'

'Don't worry,' Ken said. 'I honestly will be a lot better by then. I wasn't managing before because I wasn't coping with your mother's death. I can't say I'm over it now, but I'm gradually improving and I have plans for my life.'

'Such as?' Peter asked.

'Well, I was wondering about joining a gym.' He glanced up to gauge the reaction and then continued. 'I was talking about it to my friend Eric, the one I met in hospital. Because of the arthritis, Eric thinks I can get vouchers from the GP.'

Meg looked enthusiastic. 'Exercise is meant to be good for arthritis – it keeps the joints moving. You'd have to take it easy at first but then I imagine you'd have a personal programme that would take your starting point into consideration,' she said.

Peter looked sceptical. 'Would you go on your own?'

'Well, Eric and I have been talking about going together. It's just an idea at the moment.'

'Do all gyms do it?' Meg asked.

'To be honest I don't know anything about the scheme at the moment. I only know what Eric told me and he hasn't looked into it yet,' he said.

'Well, I guess that's the first step then,' Peter said.

Noticing the anxious look on his son's face, Ken began

to think that maybe Peter had just been concerned for him all along. *Maybe,* he thought, *he isn't trying to control me after all.* Ken resolved to give him the benefit of the doubt.

They continued with dinner, and later all sat chatting in the conservatory for a little while.

'I didn't know you'd talked to Eric about the possibility of going to a gym,' Meg said to her granddad.

'No, I never got round to mentioning what we discussed, did I?' he replied. 'It was just something he suggested in passing.'

'I think it's a great idea – especially if you do it together,' Meg said. 'I've often thought about joining a gym – quite a lot of my friends go, so I could go with them.'

As dusk began to draw in, Meg suggested that they go home. But first she took the family photo her granddad had requested, which took far longer than necessary because Amber refused to co-operate until she was bribed with chocolate.

When everyone was in place, Meg set up the timer on the camera, but she took too long getting into position and had to do it all again. The final result, however, was fine, apart from the fact that the chocolate bribe ended up around Amber's mouth. Ken didn't mind.

Finally, Meg and her granddad got back to the bungalow and passed a quiet evening. Ken went to bed early to read. Despite the exhaustion of the week, he was content. Life was looking better.

CHAPTER 13

When his appointment at the hospital came around, Ken could hardly believe that nearly two weeks had passed since the accident. So much had changed in so little time.

The appointment was for ten o'clock, but he knew by experience that appointment times were never precise. He'd arranged with Angie that he would wash and dress on his own so that he could be ready early. It had taken quite a while but he had succeeded.

He wanted to take something with him to keep him occupied while he waited. A book was an option, but experience also told him that it was quite difficult to concentrate with all the noise in a hospital. Maybe he could take a sketch pad. The problem with that was that people always wanted to know what you were doing. *Perhaps that doesn't matter,* he thought. *I could just tell them.* So that was what he decided to do.

He had breakfast, changed into suitable clothing, and put his sketch pad and favourite sketching pencil into a bag. He had already arranged for hospital transport to take him to the appointment and he knew that they were sometimes quite early, so by nine o'clock he had his coat on ready. It turned out to be a good decision as the transport arrived at ten past nine.

The transport picked up two other people on the way to the hospital and arrived at ten to ten.

Dora, one of the two people in the transport with him, was also going to the orthopaedic outpatients department, and as they could both walk they went together while the driver fetched a wheelchair for the other woman. Ken and Dora registered at the reception desk and they were both sent to the X-ray department.

'I guess they just want to check on the progress we've made and make sure everything is alright,' Dora said.

'I imagine so.' Ken nodded. They walked together to the X-ray department and took seats in the waiting area. While they waited, Ken listened to the story of how Dora had fractured her wrist when she fell over a pothole crossing the road, and they bemoaned the state of the roads until Dora's name was called.

Left alone in the waiting room, Ken reflected on how isolated he had felt at first after Edith had died, when there were obviously plenty of interesting people out in the big wide world – he just needed to find ways to meet them.

Well, breaking my arm seems to have had that effect, he thought wryly, *but there must be better ways of meeting people!*

He passed the time making rapid sketches of the people around him. Fortunately none of his subjects asked him to explain himself. Eventually his name was called, and he passed Dora in the corridor.

The radiographer positioned Ken's arm and took two X-rays. After that Ken was sent back to the waiting room in the orthopaedic outpatients department, where he found Dora waiting for the doctor. They sat and chatted for a while and then Dora was called in to see the doctor. Ken was called next, almost as soon as Dora came out.

'Did it go okay?' he asked her as he got up.

'Yes, it's healing and in absolutely the right position,' she replied with relief.

Ken followed the nurse into the doctor's room and sat on the chair beside the desk. He could see his X-ray on the computer screen in front of the doctor.

'How does it feel?' the doctor asked.

'I only get occasional twinges now. It itches a bit, though,' Ken replied.

'I'm not surprised,' the doctor said. 'But it's healing very well. We'll see you in another two weeks and make a decision then.' He called to the nurse to request that an appointment be made for two weeks' time.

While he was at the reception desk Ken made sure that they knew he and Dora were waiting for transport, and then he went back to the waiting area.

Ken found Dora and sat down. 'I guess we just have to wait for the transport now,' he said, then added, 'The WRVS shop is just along the corridor – would you like a drink while we wait?'

'That would be lovely,' she said. 'I'll come with you. We got seen so quickly that there's no way the hospital transport will be back just yet.'

'Ah, well,' Ken said, standing up. 'I'm not in a rush.'

They wandered down to the shop and Ken treated them to a bar of chocolate each as well as coffee. 'I shouldn't have the chocolate,' he said, 'but life's too short for counting calories.'

Dora laughed. 'I quite agree,' she replied.

Ken smiled to himself as he looked at Dora. She wasn't the sort of woman he was attracted to – she had no fashion sense, for one thing – but he was enjoying her company and found her laugh infectious. Since fracturing his arm he had met quite a few people that he got on well with, people who might help to widen his circle of friends.

'How long ago did you fracture your wrist?' he asked as they wandered back to the waiting room.

'Three weeks ago. The doctor wants to see me in another three weeks and they hope to be able to take the plaster off then. They think I'll need physiotherapy because the fracture is at the joint and it may well have seized up a bit after six weeks in plaster. And what did the doctor say to you?' she asked.

'They want to see me again in two weeks,' Ken said, 'although they expect that the plaster will stay on for another two after that. It's healing well, though. They don't think I'll need physio because it will need to gradually gain strength. They'll give me exercises, though.'

'It will feel weak,' she said.

'I'm sure it will.'

They talked about family next. Dora couldn't contain her excitement about her younger son getting married. 'He found it very difficult after he got divorced. It cost him financially as well as emotionally,' she said.

Ken sympathised. 'It's very hard for young people to afford property these days.'

They chatted for a little while longer and then the hospital transport driver arrived. They'd only had to wait about half an hour.

'Are you both ready?' the driver asked.

Dora nodded and Ken said, 'Yes,' as they both got up to leave.

'Don't forget your scarf,' Ken said, handing it to her.

In the back of the hospital transport they exchanged telephone numbers and agreed to stay in touch.

***

It was a cold day, so as soon as Ken got home he put the kettle on and made a cup of tea. He didn't feel like lunch just yet, although it was nearly time for it – probably the effect of that chocolate bar at the hospital.

He took it with him into the spare room and got out the oil painting, frustrated with himself that he hadn't made more progress. At this rate it wouldn't be finished by Saturday when – and he couldn't believe it had come around so quickly – Meg was due to return home and leave him to fend for himself. He talked sternly to himself. *You have plenty of time this afternoon and you need to virtually finish this painting today.*

Once he had got out the paints and the palette he quickly mixed the colours he needed for the faces and began work. He needed to get things in the right order so that he created the right textures.

He set the painting on the easel and looked at it, standing back to get a better view. He took the photograph in his hand and looked carefully at the detail. There was pure love for that baby in Edith's eyes, for their dear granddaughter Meg. He wanted to capture that look in the eye, that love.

Very carefully, he transferred that expression on Edith's face to his canvas. The smile lines, the wrinkles – every little detail was important to express that love. He needed to show the way that she held Meg so close and the way that Meg's eyes tried to focus in that special way that tiny babies' do. Each held the gaze of the other – this was what he wanted to show.

He worked for less than an hour before he decided to have lunch, but there were only tiny touches to add now anyway.

His late lunch took longer than he had planned because he picked up some of the photos that he and Meg had chosen for his photo board and he got a bit carried away with the memories. As he returned from memory lane, he remembered the painting and almost jumped to his feet.

By mid-afternoon he had done all he could to the painting, so he put it back into the cupboard to dry and settled down with a book for a while. He was reading *The Book Thief*, which Meg had brought with her. She had finished it and declared it an interesting read, so Ken had picked it up and started it. She was right. He struggled to put it down.

At about quarter to four he sighed as he pushed the book aside and convinced himself to do a little watercolour painting. He wanted something to show Meg so that she wouldn't get suspicious about how he was spending his time – he wanted to make sure that he kept the oil painting hidden.

As he began the painting, he found he wasn't very enthusiastic because he was eager to get back to the book, but once he'd got under way he soon became absorbed in it. The major background of the painting was now complete, so he began the intricate work of painting the boats. Some of the boats were tied up in the harbour and others were moving. He needed to make the movement evident in those that were sailing, and the motion of the sea had to be realistic around the stationary boats.

He loved that part – bringing a picture to life. *I can't wait to get back to the art group,* he thought.

After about an hour he needed a break and decided to cook the dinner. Meg had got diced beef out of the freezer before she left for work, and he'd noticed that she had bought a can of red wine sauce. He knew he had frozen veg in the freezer, so with some difficulty he started to make a casserole of beef in red wine.

More than once, he got frustrated with himself, so once the casserole dish was finally in the oven he took himself off to the lounge to recover.

Meg breezed through the door at around six and threw her laptop bag down onto the settee. 'It's cold out there this evening.'

'Put the gas fire on if you like,' Ken said. 'The central heating has come on but it might take a while to heat up the room.'

'Thanks,' she said. 'I think I will – just until it warms up a bit. Don't you feel cold?' she asked.

'I've been in the kitchen with the oven heating up ready for dinner. I'll carry on in a minute,' he said.

She nodded. 'What are you cooking?'

'I found the red wine sauce so I've added some frozen veg and it's all in the oven. I thought I'd save you the bother of cooking tonight,' he replied.

She turned on the fire and sat for a few moments with her coat on. 'Well, let me know if you need my help.'

Eventually she warmed up enough to take the coat off

but she kept her scarf on.

'It doesn't help that your old Fiesta's heating system isn't so good these days,' Ken said.

'It is very old.'

He determined at that moment that one day he would get her a new car. Maybe that wouldn't be fair to his other grandchildren, but Meg was the one who had given up her time to help him, and her encouragement had changed him. She had been a part of the process of his recovery and he was more grateful than words would express; but he wouldn't tell her now.

'Never mind, have that seat, close to the fire,' he said. 'You'll soon warm up.' Then he headed back to the kitchen to check on the casserole and put the kettle on.

'Thank you,' said Meg as he returned with a coffee for her. 'I printed off those photographs from my laptop for you, by the way. So we could finish that photo board tonight.'

Ken began to set the table. 'I'm sorry dinner's a bit late,' he said.

Meg looked delighted. 'Not at all!' she replied. 'There's no rush.'

Before long, Ken served the dinner and poured them a each a glass of red wine from a bottle he'd found in the back of a cupboard.

'This is extremely civilised,' she said.

After dinner they watched last week's episode of *Have I Got News for You* – Meg had recorded it, declaring that it was her favourite version of the news, which made Ken laugh.

After that, Meg suggested that they make the photo

board. It didn't take long. With her eye for design, she had soon arranged the photos on the board in a way that was aesthetically pleasing, and with her granddad's favourite photograph of himself with Edith at the centre.

'Okay,' she said, 'before I stick them all down, are you happy with the design?'

'It looks perfect,' he said.

She stuck everything in place, and by the time he had made coffee she had finished attaching the photos to the board and was positioning it on the wall. 'Whereabouts do you want it?' she asked.

'I think I'd like it in the dining area, actually,' he said. 'Then whenever I have a meal at the table I can see all the pictures.'

'Do you have a drill? I'll put it up now, then we've finished that project,' she said.

He went outside, turned on the little battery-operated lamp and rummaged in the shed. He knew he had a drill somewhere under all this clutter. He had to take out a fair number of things to find it, but eventually he located it, locked the shed up and appeared triumphantly at the patio door.

'Found it!'

It didn't take her long to drill the hole and put the photo board up.

Ken laughed. 'You didn't learn that from your father.'

'Certainly not,' she grinned. 'He's great at managing the business but I imagine the mechanics wouldn't let him near a car – he's never been a hands-on sort of person.' She put the drill down on the table. 'Takes all sorts!' she exclaimed. 'And he earns enough money to pay someone else to do all the things he can't.'

She pointed to a photograph of her grandparents dancing together. 'I think this is my favourite. You used to dance a lot when you were younger, didn't you?'

Ken reflected for a moment before replying, remembering the ballroom dancing lessons they'd had. For a short while they entered competitions, and often came third but never first. 'We weren't brilliant, but we were quite good for a while,' he mused. 'Your grandma looked lovely in those ballroom dresses. She enjoyed dressing up, said it made her feel like a princess.'

'Could you teach me?' Meg asked.

Ken sighed. 'I don't know. It was your grandma who had the real skill – she just dragged me around the dance floor.'

'But you could teach me a waltz,' she said.

He looked shocked. 'Didn't you learn that when you were younger?'

She shook her head. 'Things weren't quite what they were in your day, Granddad. I did ballet and tap for a while.'

He nodded slowly. 'I guess you're right. Things have changed. Okay,' he said, and he stood up and put a hand out to her, inviting her to dance.

She stood too, and he went through the basic steps with her. He showed her how to hold his hand, placed her left hand on his shoulder and his right hand on her shoulder blade and then described the steps.

'First, put your right foot back, then your left foot over to the side, and then bring your right foot to your left foot,' he said. He repeated, 'Right, side, together,' as they practised. 'The steps are very simple,' he said.

They went through the steps a few more times until he felt she could manage it with the music. He moved across to the CD player and put on 'Moon River'. Once or twice she moved in the wrong direction, but eventually she managed the moves more smoothly.

They practised it a few more times. 'And all the while I'm counting to three in my head,' she said.

He laughed. 'Actually, you've been counting out loud.'

When the track came to the end, he put it on again. 'We'll go through it all once more,' he said.

This time she found it much easier, and with Ken leading they got to the end of the track okay.

'You should go to lessons. You have natural rhythm,' he said.

'I'm exhausted from trying to remember where to put my feet,' she replied.

'It wouldn't take you very much practice to remember the steps without thinking.'

She plonked herself down in the easy chair, raising dust. 'Now I need a drink.'

Ken hadn't sat down yet so he went to the kitchen and put the kettle on. 'You might meet a nice young man if you go to ballroom dancing lessons,' he said with a wink as he looked over from the counter.

'Granddad!' she exclaimed. 'I'm quite happy on my own... and anyway I expect I'd have to take a partner with me if I went to lessons.'

'Mmm. Maybe,' he said as he put a mug of coffee in front of her.

'How is your painting coming on?' Meg asked him.

'You can see it if you like,' he replied, and he went to the spare room to fetch it.

'It's coming on well,' she said. 'I'm amazed at how fast you can paint a picture.'

'The final details will take a long time, though, because I have to wait for one part to dry before I can do anything else, otherwise the watercolours run.'

When he went to bed that night, Ken reflected on how long it was now since Edith had died. Every day had dragged by at the beginning, but now that he had started to rebuild his life, he had good days as well as bad ones, and the bad ones were becoming less frequent.

CHAPTER 14

Ken felt quite emotional the day before Meg was due to leave.

As he sat in the dining area, having breakfast, he caught sight of the photo board. Now, the photos no longer seemed like treasured memories – it felt as if they were taunting him. He wept a little. When Meg went, the joy would leave him again.

It was hard to lift himself out of his self-pity. He needed to make the final touches to the oil painting but nothing in him wanted to make the effort.

The only thing that forced him to carry on was the thought of Meg. He might dread the prospect of her leaving, but she deserved something special to take with her.

At last, he roused himself to return to the painting, and as he worked he found his mind began to clear. He began to feel certain that he would see plenty of Meg from now on, because they had connected on a deeper level. The thought of it made him smile for the first time all morning.

He had no place to go today – no coffee with Eric, no appointments, nothing. So he decided that after lunch he would take a walk in the park. *As long as it doesn't rain,* he thought. *But you can only go if you've finished the oil painting.* His inner voice was stern.

After a while, he stood back to look at the painting from a distance. At first he held the photograph beside it, but then he changed his mind, put the photo out of sight and followed his instinct. The expression would be captured in the tiny details – if he exaggerated those, it would put the picture out of balance. He took his time, and allowed himself to completely enter into the feelings the picture evoked.

By the time he sat down for lunch he felt emotionally exhausted, but utterly satisfied with what he had painted. The success with the painting had given him the boost he needed and he was now excited about the idea of a walk in the park.

He found his scarf and a woollen hat and put on his overcoat. It was sunny, but he felt the chill of the autumn wind as he stepped outside. The cold air burnt his lungs after the warmth of the house. He had kept the heating on today because Meg had told him that the forecast was for a cold day.

It felt good to be out. He pulled his scarf up higher around his neck to keep out the chill, and headed for the park.

As he stepped inside the park gates he saw a grey squirrel dart up the tree in front of him. He'd forgotten how much he loved this park.

He watched the swans and ducks on the pond for a short while but the cold air urged him forward. His pace quickened, and after about twenty minutes he set off for home, renewed and refreshed.

As he continued homeward he reflected on how lucky he was to have Meg as his granddaughter. *So often,* he thought, *we go through life without ever telling those we love how we feel.* When he handed over the painting and card, he resolved to tell Meg what a wonderful granddaughter she was.

In the afternoon he worked on the watercolour. That harbour was amazing, an artist's dream, and he wanted to capture it... How he longed to get back to his art club. The group had never been big, but he had enjoyed the input of others and the company, and there had never been a time in his life when he needed company more than he had since Edith died.

As he lay in bed that night, unable to sleep, he mused on the difference that this last fortnight had made. There were still a lot of changes he had to go through, he knew that, but as a result of his accident, he had met people who had helped him on his journey.

***

Saturday had come around much faster than Ken had wished, but he'd managed to finish the all-important oil painting. He just hoped that it was now dry enough to wrap.

On his way back from coffee with Eric on Thursday he'd got the taxi driver to stop so that he could get some wrapping paper and a card. It was quite possible that Edith already had some somewhere in the bungalow but he hadn't been able to locate it.

He planned to wrap the painting before Meg was even awake. There was little chance that she would be up early on a Saturday, especially as she'd been out with her friends the night before.

He crawled out from under the covers, sat for a while on

the edge of the bed to get his balance, and then put on his slippers and dressing gown. There was no rush to get dressed; he could do that later.

As it was Saturday, he would make the effort to cook himself breakfast. Cooking entailed a lot more care with a plaster cast on than Ken had previously taken, he had found, and he usually used the bigger, heavy-based frying pan because it was more stable. He cooked sausage, bacon, egg, mushroom and tomato and carried it into the dining area. The curtains were not yet opened so he pulled them back and sat down at the table.

It was strange how it happened, really – any one day could be good from the time he woke up, and another could be bad. After yesterday's low mood, today he felt alive again. Today the pictures on the photo board evoked happy memories. He was glad he was having a good day because it would be hard enough with Meg's time with him coming to an end. She was lively and full of energy; even two weeks of her influence had been enough to kick-start him back into life.

If it really happens, he thought, *it would be wonderful for us to visit Ben in Cyprus.* But if he was honest with himself, he knew that Meg had a busy life and would possibly forget all about the plan when she went home, to say nothing of the fact that she wouldn't get a lot of encouragement from Peter.

He put it out of his mind, finished his breakfast and washed up. Once he'd tidied up he decided he would wrap the painting before he got dressed, and after that he would put out seed for the birds. Meg would take quite a while to pack everything up once she woke because although she had arrived with just a suitcase, she had been home a few times and collected more things. They were liberally scattered around the bungalow.

Meg leaving was another milestone, really, because now Ken would be alone again. In one way he was sad, but in another way he knew it was a step that he had to take some time, and he had a certain sense of – well, not exactly excitement, but... progress. Success, maybe. He couldn't describe the feeling well but he was hoping that this time he could cope emotionally.

It was almost half past eleven before Meg woke up and trudged into the dining area, still in her fleecy pyjamas. She said good morning but it was barely audible.

'Did you have a good evening with your friends?' Ken asked.

'Oh yes, the band were brilliant, but we went on to a club afterwards so it was a bit late when I got in.' She went to the kitchen and poured a bowl of muesli.

'Do you want a coffee with that?' her granddad asked.

'Yes, please,' she replied. 'Quite strong – I need the caffeine.'

He made her a coffee and passed it over to her.

'I'm going to miss you, Granddad,' she said. 'And this bungalow has such a pretty garden. Dad was never much of a gardener and Mum doesn't have the time.'

'Well, you could do it. You have a good eye for design,' he replied.

She laughed. 'Do you know, I've never thought of doing any gardening at Mum and Dad's. I guess I use it like a guest house. I suppose it just doesn't seem like my own. Most of my friends have moved out of their parents' houses. Maybe

I'll try to move out too... I'd probably even enjoy it. But I feel as if I'm still quite young for all that responsibility....'

'But you're responsible enough in your job. I've always been surprised that you haven't bought your own place. Especially as you're a housing officer – you deal with accommodation issues all day! Are you content to stay at home? I'd have thought you could afford to buy your own place.'

'I've just never been good at saving.' She shrugged.

'But unless your dad is over-charging you – which I doubt – I can't see why you shouldn't be able to put some aside and buy your own house.'

'I suppose you're right. I've always thought it would be too difficult on my own,' she said. 'Perhaps I should think more seriously about it.'

Over the last fortnight Ken had thought that he was a bit of a burden to Meg; but listening to her now he realised that it was just possible that their time together had changed them both.

'There is certainly space for a bird feeder like mine at your dad's,' he said. 'That attracts the birds and they're beautiful to watch.'

'And in the summer I could get some bedding plants like you do every year and that makes the garden attractive.'

'True, and there are winter flowering shrubs – they're not always cheap but they make a lot of difference.'

'What's the plant in the corner with the pretty white flowers?' she asked.

'Winter jasmine. It will flower throughout the year,' he said. 'Just keep it in a relatively sheltered spot.'

Ken thought she looked a little forlorn. 'Are you

alright?' he asked.

'I'm fine, Granddad,' she replied. 'It's just...' She paused.

He raised his eyebrows, encouraging her to continue.

'I wish my dad would teach me things like you do.' She spoke without lifting her gaze from the table.

It must have been hard for her to say that, knowing her dad is my son, thought Ken.

'Have you ever asked him?' he said. 'The thing is, Meg, I was only thinking the other day that we don't say the things we want to often enough to the ones we love. In fact, I was thinking that because I wanted to tell you that you are the most amazing, wonderful granddaughter that anyone could have.'

Meg started to cry. Ken was surprised – he had always thought of her as confident. *We never know what people are hiding behind their masks,* he thought.

He sat beside his granddaughter and put a comforting hand on her shoulder. 'Your dad loves you very much. He *is* very protective, but then he's like that with us all. If you think about that, it's a beautiful thing that he cares so much, even if it means that he's afraid of us taking risks.'

Meg smiled, with a gentle nod. 'He knows so much about business that would be helpful in my work, but I never seem to get a chance to ask him.'

Ken didn't answer immediately, and when he did he looked her right in the eye. 'You have to *make* a chance. Ask him if he'd have time to explain a few things to you sometime.'

He paused, and neither of them said a word for a few moments. Finally, he spoke again. 'I imagine he'll be pleased to be asked – glad that you recognise his wisdom.'

She looked sad again and sounded choked as she replied, 'I feel as if I lost him long ago.'

'But he's still here,' her granddad replied. 'You can reconnect. I'm sure if he thought about it that way your dad would be sad too.'

'His life just seems to be all about his work. I feel as if I'm of secondary importance – at best,' she replied.

He rested his hand on her shoulder again. 'I think most of us expend too much of our energy on work and then realise too late that we have lost touch with those things in life that matter most.'

'So you think I should try?' she said.

Her granddad merely nodded. 'Now, are we going to gather all your things together for you to pack?' he asked.

She laughed. 'I have spread out a bit, haven't I?'

'You made yourself at home,' he replied.

She looked sheepish. 'Sorry,' she said.

He shook his head. 'Not at all, I'm glad you did.' He handed her the book of hers that he had been reading.

'Keep it if you haven't finished it,' she said.

'No, I've finished it.'

'What did you think of it?'

'It was really good,' he replied. 'Unusual, and interesting. It's not a book I'd have naturally picked up. Let me know if you come across any other books you think I'll like.'

'I will,' she promised.

When they'd gathered everything together on the dining table it was obvious that it wouldn't all fit into her case. 'I can lend you a case,' her granddad said.

'Or,' she said, picking up one of the boxes he'd emptied

when sorting Edith's papers, 'I could use this.'

'Good idea,' he said. 'But before you go I have a present for you.' With that, he headed off into the spare room.

'Oh Granddad, I don't need a present,' said Meg, almost offended.

'I never said you did,' he replied with a wicked smile, 'but I wanted to show you how much I appreciate you doing this. If I'd gone into a home for rehabilitation I might have decided that I'd be less trouble there and stayed permanently.'

'I'm sure you're not ready for that yet, Granddad,' she said.

He came out with the wrapped canvas and presented it to her with the card. 'It's just a little gift for being the best granddaughter a granddad could want.'

She looked at him, a little taken aback. 'Have you done me a painting?'

'Unwrap it. Take a look,' he said

Meg unwrapped it eagerly, then stood open-mouthed.

'Oh my goodness!' she said, holding it at arm's length. 'That's beautiful. That is just how I remember Grandma... there was a photo like this,' she added, looking across at him and catching the pleasure in his eye.

He nodded. 'I copied it.'

She balanced it on the mantelpiece and stood back. 'It's amazing!' After marvelling at it for a few moments more, she gave her granddad a warm hug.

'You shouldn't have done this,' she said. 'I've learnt a lot being here.'

Then she frowned. 'I've just realised,' she said, pausing as if confused, 'you must have been painting this all the while I thought you were just doing that watercolour painting.'

He laughed. 'I did have to be a bit sneaky.'

'Well, it is the most wonderful present,' she said. 'When I get my own place it will have pride of place in the lounge.' She picked it up and wrapped it loosely in the paper again. 'I'll put it on the passenger seat of the car right away so I don't damage it.'

Their parting was a bit sad, but there was joy in it too for Ken because he knew now that it had been good for Meg as well as for him.

We miss so much when we are too busy for each other, he thought, *but staying connected is up to each one of us.*

He determined to do his part to stay in touch with all of his family.

CHAPTER 15

On Monday evening, Meg felt alone. Her mother had gone out with friends and her dad still wasn't home from work. She desperately wanted that opportunity to reconnect and with her mother out this had seemed the ideal chance. But no, here she was, trying to make the first move, and work was still taking first place. By the time her dad came in, she was angry.

He walked through the door, said hello, heated up his dinner in the microwave and went and sat down in the lounge, flicking the remote from side to side until he landed on something passable to watch. *That is a picture of our lives,* Meg thought. She got up and went to her room.

Feeling more alone than ever now, she threw her book across the room. *Well, I tried,* she told herself – but she knew that she hadn't really made much effort. *How can I, when I'm so angry?* She needed to stop thinking like this. The most important thing was that it was in her control.

She wanted to talk to her dad about budgeting. Since talking with her granddad, she had decided that what she really wanted to do was save for a deposit on a flat of her own, but she knew that she wasn't very good with money. She tried to remember her granddad's advice. *I need to make the first move,* she told herself sternly. She put aside her anxiety about being rejected and determined to overcome her reticence.

She didn't want to intrude, but there was no other way to talk to her father. She walked quietly into the lounge and sat down beside him. 'Are you watching this, Dad,' she asked.

'Not really.'

'Can I ask you a question then?'

'Yep,' he replied, without switching off the television.

She resisted the urge to give up. 'When you've got time, can you help me with budgeting, please? I want to save up and buy a flat, but you know how poor I am with finances.'

'Yes, okay,' he said, still mindlessly gazing at the television.

Undeterred, she carried on. 'When would be a good time?'

He looked up for a brief second. 'Well,' he said, thinking for a moment, 'I'm not busy this Saturday afternoon.'

'That would be great,' she said, and got up to go to her room to ring her granddad.

'I know it's not much,' she said to him, 'but I think it's a start.'

'That's wonderful,' said Ken. 'That's not a small start, either. Given you had disconnected, that is massive. Well done! Now you have to make sure it happens. Have all your bank statements ready and anything else that seems appropriate. I knew you could do it.'

When she came off the phone, she was tearful and elated. Life was a little brighter, a little more hopeful. She picked up the painting that her granddad had given her. *Love,* she thought, *just a little love is all it takes. I love you, Granddad.* He was part of her life now in a way he had never been before. She had given her time to reconnect with him and it had been a blessing to her as well as to him. Now she needed to do the same for her father.

On Friday night she reminded her dad of their Saturday afternoon appointment and he smiled. 'I hadn't forgotten,' he said. 'I've always thought your finances were a bit chaotic.'

She smiled. In the past she would have taken offence at that comment, but since her time with her granddad she was more inclined to believe that love overlooks these things and pursues its goal. The goal was twofold. She genuinely did want a flat of her own, and she *was* bad at managing finances, but her second goal, to reconnect with her father, required her to take note of what he said, to sacrifice her pride for the sake of the relationship. She loved her dad; she just needed to know him better, to understand him.

When Saturday came around, Meg got up late in the morning as usual and was just a little afraid that her father would end up working into the afternoon as he often did. The car dealers closed at midday but he often stayed on doing paperwork until three or four o'clock. Today she smiled as he came through the door at twenty-five past twelve.

'Have I got time for lunch before we start?' he asked her as he put his laptop bag down in the lounge.

'Yes,' she replied, 'and if you're interested I've made some butternut squash soup and bought some rolls to go with it.'

'How could I resist?' he replied with a shrug.

They sat at the table together and discussed his morning's work while they had lunch. After they finished, she handed him her paperwork and washed up while he looked at it. Then she brought in two mugs of coffee and sat down beside him.

'Firstly,' he said, 'it's much better to keep all your papers and documents in one file.' He handed her one.

She smiled. 'How did you know I hadn't got one?'

'A lucky guess,' he replied. 'If you keep everything together and get in the habit of putting everything financial into a file then you can always find papers when you need them.'

'Okay,' she said. 'I'll try... I know you're right – I wouldn't dream of keeping papers in a mess like this at work.'

'I totally understand that,' he said. 'It probably feels like starting work all over again once you get home, but once you've set up the system it makes it much easier.'

She nodded.

'Then,' he continued, 'arrange them in the file so that all documents of a particular type are filed together. Like this,' he said, as he punched holes in all her credit card statements and placed them together.

He went on to point out that she had sometimes missed a payment on her credit card. 'If you miss a payment you pay a ridiculous amount in interest,' he said. 'Set it up to pay by direct debit and then that never happens – unless, of course, you don't have enough money in your account to make the payment.'

To Meg, personal finances had always been a random, casual thing, in complete contrast to her careful approach at work. She spent whenever she wanted to, but since she'd been considering buying her own place she had begun to notice where she spent money without thinking. *Being more organised is bound to help me make savings,* she thought.

This discussion led on to a friendly chat about where she might like to buy a property.

Meg shrugged. 'I don't know,' she said with a puzzled look on her face. 'I guess I can probably only afford a flat, although really I'd like a garden.'

Peter looked pensive and took a few moments to reply. 'Well,' he said, pausing slightly, 'we'll get your finances fully in order and work out how much you need for a deposit and how much the building societies will lend you.'

She still looked puzzled. 'Do you think I'm better off in a nice area in a flat, or not such a nice area in a house?'

Peter sighed. 'There are arguments for and against each. Ideally you would go for a house in an up-and-coming area, but you have to be able to predict that.'

Meg stretched out her legs in front of her. 'And,' she said, 'I guess I need to take the ease of access to work into consideration.'

Her father nodded. 'To be honest,' he said, 'over where Granddad lives is most likely a reasonable bet. How long did it take you to get to work from there?'

'About twenty minutes,' she said, 'whereas it takes about thirty-five minutes from here. Being over the other side of town does put me about forty minutes from here, though.'

'Yes, but it doesn't take anything like that time in the evening or at weekends,' her father said.

'That's true,' she said. 'I hadn't thought about that.'

Peter opened his laptop and googled the local housing market, just to get an idea of prices in the different areas. He pointed out a tiny, terraced house around the corner from her granddad.

'That's about three streets away,' he said, 'although I admit it doesn't have the same open, tree-lined effect. They're all terraced houses sitting on the pavement, but they have gardens. Some may only be patio gardens but at least it's somewhere to sit in the summer.'

'Oh my goodness!' she exclaimed, 'and they are about forty thousand pounds cheaper than the ones around here.'

He nodded. 'Yes. Mind you, there are some flats around here with small gardens, or with shared gardens. It depends on your priorities.'

They scrolled through a large number of local properties and her father gave her the pros and cons of each area and each type of property. 'Parking isn't always easy where there are old, terraced houses. Flats often have designated parking areas. Modern terraces tend to have more parking space than old ones.'

By the time he'd finished, Meg had much more of an idea about what to expect from different areas. *Granddad was right,* she thought. *Getting my dad's help is invaluable.*

'Next Saturday morning I'm not working,' he told her. 'If you get out of bed early enough we can set up all your payments as direct debits or standing orders online. That way you won't keep incurring extra charges for late payment.'

When they'd finished, she offered him coffee and they sat and talked. It was the first time for months that he had asked her about her job and she had asked about his.

Meg remembered what her granddad had said about telling other people what we feel and she put a hand on his arm. 'Thank you, Dad,' she said with sincerity. 'I really appreciate the help, you know.'

'Oh, that's alright,' he said. 'What kind of dad would I be if I couldn't help you with things like that?'

She smiled to herself. Her granddad had helped her to see a way to begin changing her relationship with her dad.

CHAPTER 16

It was six weeks after the accident before the plaster cast was finally removed. Ken felt a bit vulnerable for a couple of weeks afterwards, and cautious about answering the door at night – he was aware that he wouldn't have the strength to defend himself, should he need to.

Also, he hadn't realised how often he'd relied on Meg to open cans for him or carry heavy bags and boxes. When he remembered those sorts of things early in the day, he asked Angie to do them for him, but sometimes he forgot. Her visits were much shorter now, apart from bath days, as she just made sure his lunch was ready and helped with the few bits of housework he was unable to manage.

But it wasn't long before he began to feel stronger, and within a fortnight of having the cast removed he was able to go back to his art group.

It was strange to be back after a full two years away, but oddly familiar too. He took his painting of the harbour with him for others to critique. The response, to his relief, was positive, with just a few minor suggestions.

'I'm a bit rusty,' he said, 'and I'm much more accustomed to working in oils, but I wanted to give watercolours a go because I thought the scene lent itself more to that medium.'

John had been there almost from the start of the group. 'I can see why,' he replied. 'Have you ever used pen and ink?'

'No,' Ken replied. 'Do you think that would work for this picture?'

'Well, it could,' John replied, 'but the faint outlines you've drawn remind me of pen and ink and I just wondered whether you'd used it at all.'

Ken shook his head. 'They weren't meant to show!'

This was what he had missed. Life had become insular in the last few years and it had happened so gradually that he hadn't realised it. At the end of the session John invited Ken for lunch at the café around the corner from his house. Ken accepted.

They had years to catch up on. John had been single all his life and was devoted to his art.

'I'm holding an exhibition next year,' he told Ken. 'It's in February, but if you've got any work you've completed and you want to exhibit it, you're welcome.'

Ken was pensive. 'It's so long since I've painted anything that I have nothing to exhibit,' he said.

'Well, you have plenty of time before the exhibition. I'd be glad of excellent work like yours to put on show.'

Ken was flattered, uncertain whether John was just being kind. 'You don't have to do that,' he said. 'I'm just glad to be back.'

'I'm not just being nice to you,' John replied. 'I've always admired your work.'

John offered to drop Ken back home and they chatted on the way. As he pulled up outside Ken's house, John repeated his offer. 'I mean it, you know,' he said. 'I would love to exhibit your work.'

Back inside the bungalow, Ken considered the

morning's events. Life had taken yet another turn. He laughed to himself. *If I'm not careful I'm going to have to slow down,* he thought. *I didn't expect to be telling myself that!*

He went into the spare room and put up the easel. At the art club he had begun an oil painting of a moonlit sky over the sea, with slightly surreal colours. It was mystical and vibrant. The light exploded on the canvas in a fantasy of colour, and John had loved it.

'It has life, hope,' John had said, and Ken couldn't help thinking that somehow John was expressing his own feelings.

He missed Edith; he missed her more than words or art or anything else could ever say, but he was less devastated now. Life still offered him something. John had lived his whole life without a 'significant other' and survived – he had devoted himself to his art. *Life goes on,* Ken thought.

As he sat by the window in the fading light of dusk, Ken thought about the people he loved in his life. He wanted the next thing he painted to show deep love. *How can my art express that? What could I ever paint that would even begin to show how that feels?*

He got no answers, but it was something he would consider over the next few days. In the meantime, he would paint his picture of hope.

***

When Thursday came around, Ken woke up with lightness in his spirit. He had begun to love Thursdays. Today he was picking Eric up in the taxi and they were going to a gym in town to have an assessment.

Eric had rung up last week from the café, and they had got an appointment for this Thursday. 'We can have coffee in town afterwards,' Eric had said.

Ken was excited. For the last few years he hadn't been able to do a lot of exercise, and recently he had done nothing except walk to the park or the shops. He had noticed that some of his clothes were a bit tight and he knew that the cakes and chocolate weren't helping.

He got ready early, and packed a small bag with clothes for the gym. The taxi arrived on time.

Once the taxi had collected Eric, he did most of the talking all the way to town. He had been to a gym a couple of years earlier and knew roughly what to expect.

By contrast, Ken had never set foot inside one.

'In my younger days I played cricket,' Ken said to the trainer they were matched with, when asked about his sporting history. 'But as I got older I did nothing, and when I got arthritis it became too painful to do much. I didn't realise that exercising would help that.'

The trainer took Ken's blood pressure, weighed him and measured him. 'Well actually, all things considered, you're not in bad shape,' he said.

Ken didn't like to ask what things he'd considered.

'As you've had a fracture just recently in that left arm,' Mike, the trainer, continued. 'I'll give you very gentle exercises to strengthen the muscles. Muscle wastage is very common when you've had a limb in plaster.'

Mike was unbelievably enthusiastic, a trait that Eric later told him was common to all the personal trainers he had met.

After that Mike turned his attentions to Eric and weighed and measured him too. 'Unlike Ken,' Mike said, 'you need to be very careful how much you do on the cardiovascular machines because you don't want to strain the ankle.'

Eric looked disappointed, and Mike sat down beside him. 'One of the great things about this gym,' Mike said, once more with far more enthusiasm than it merited, 'is that we have a swimming pool. Swimming is excellent exercise.'

Mike stood up. 'Come on,' he said, 'let's go into the gym now and I'll see what you can both do. I'll do you a four-week plan, and after that I'll reassess you to see how you're getting on.'

He started Ken off on the treadmill, getting him to walk slowly at first and then gradually increase to a pace where he was still comfortable but had to work a bit harder.

With Eric it was a bit more difficult. 'We'll try you at a low level on the bikes, but not for too long until you get your strength back,' said Mike. 'I'd most like to get you swimming. Can you swim?'

'A bit,' Eric replied. 'I'm not a fantastic swimmer, and I can't see much without my glasses, but I'll give it a go.'

Mike nearly nodded his head off. 'That's wonderful,' he said. 'In fact,' he added, turning to Ken, 'our warm pool would be very good for the arthritis too.'

They both agreed to make that a part of their plan and Mike suggested that they come twice a week.

'What about a Saturday afternoon, as well as our usual Thursday?' Eric suggested.

Ken agreed. 'I'm not usually doing much on a Saturday

afternoon,' he said.

Mike showed them some floor exercises and gave each of them some strengthening exercises too, to help their recovery, before finishing off with stretches.

'That's all agreed then,' he said. 'I'll type up your personal plans and put them in this green file here.' He indicated the shelf where the files were kept.

'Great,' Eric said as they left the gym. 'Now we can nip round the corner to that café I mentioned.'

They sat down at a table by the window and chatted excitedly.

'I feel like a kid again. I think I'm going to enjoy going to the gym when I get used to it,' Ken said.

'I used to love it,' Eric replied. 'I gave up when my wife was ill. I needed to be with her all the time.'

Ken laughed as the waitress came across to them. 'Do you think we've earned a slice of cake?' he asked Eric.

'Definitely,' Eric replied, so they ordered two slices of carrot cake to go with their coffees. 'It must be good for us,' he added, 'it contains carrot.'

***

When Ken got home that lunchtime, he put on a CD of Elvis and picked up his favourite photograph of Edith as 'Love me Tender' was playing.

'If you could see me, my love,' he said, 'you'd be proud of me.'

It's a pity that she can't be here with me, he thought, *but I'm so glad that I met Eric and have found new people to spend time with.*

He felt he'd done enough for one day, and once lunch was out of the way he decided to sit quietly and read his latest book. It took him by surprise when the doorbell rang at quarter to six, and even more so when he found Meg standing on the doorstep.

'You have a key,' he said in surprise.

'It would be rude to just walk in on you now that I'm not staying here,' she replied.

He shook his head, his grey floppy hair flicking from side to side. 'No, just use it,' he said.

'Anyway,' she said, brushing lightly past him and taking off her coat and scarf, 'I just had to come by and tell you all about the time I spent with Dad last Saturday. He's helping me to sort out my finances and' – she paused for effect – 'we *chat* now.'

Ken hugged his granddaughter. 'I'm so glad,' he said. 'He's very gifted, your dad.'

'Also,' she went on, 'he reckons that I could afford to buy a terraced house on Lime Street or thereabouts once I've saved a bit. I think he'll help me with the deposit too.'

'Well,' Ken said, 'if you need any help from me let me know. I don't have as much capital as your dad but you're welcome to anything I've got spare.'

She plonked herself down on the settee. 'Oh Granddad, that's really kind of you, but I'm pretty sure now that I can afford a small place if I'm a bit more careful with money.'

'Well, you only have to ask,' he said. 'Are you staying for a coffee?'

She looked at her watch. 'Oh yes, I think I've got time. I'll text Mum and tell her I'm here, then she won't worry.'

Ken put the kettle on and told her about joining the

gym and planning to go swimming there with Eric.

'Gosh, your social life is better than mine!' she exclaimed.

'Well, you'd better buck up then,' he said. 'It's about time you found yourself a nice young man... or I'll have to go looking for one for you.'

She looked a little embarrassed. 'I'm quite happy, Granddad,' she said, 'but I was thinking about those dancing lessons. I'll go if I can find somewhere that I don't have to take a partner with me.'

Ken offered to ask Eric. 'He seems to know about almost every social event that happens in the town,' he said.

'Ha ha, you do that, Granddad,' she said. Then she changed the subject. 'Did you finish that harbour picture?'

'Oh yes, didn't I show you? Come with me.'

He took her into the spare room and she saw both the completed harbour picture and his mystical sunset over the sea.

'I love this,' she said, pointing to the new painting with a stunned expression on her face. 'You should do more like this. You could sell loads of these. It's so expressive.'

'I only really do it because I enjoy painting,' he said. 'It's not about making money... Mind you,' he added, 'John, who goes to my art club, has asked me to exhibit some of my work at his exhibition in town in February.'

'That's awesome,' she replied. 'I hope you said yes!'

Ken smiled. 'I haven't replied yet because I don't have a lot to exhibit. It all depends whether I've painted enough by then to make it worthwhile.'

'Well, I'm going home once I've finished my coffee, so you could continue with this one tonight,' she said.

He furrowed his brow. 'Are you bossing your old granddad around?' he asked with a twinkle in his eye.

'Just encouraging you,' she replied.

They sat chatting in the lounge for a little while longer and then she left. All the while he sat, he practised the arm exercises that the physiotherapist had given him when the plaster cast had been removed.

He had only seen the physio once but he felt sure that the arm was getting stronger. Sometimes he had to stop himself picking up something heavy when he felt a twinge of pain, but most of the time he followed the instructions that he'd been given.

Well, he thought, contemplating the evening ahead, *you could do a couple of hours' painting after dinner.*

He considered it and decided that he would start another watercolour painting. For one thing he liked the variety, and for another he found that painting detail in artificial light sometimes meant that he didn't like the effect in daylight. If he just painted the background for his watercolour painting he could adjust the colour later.

After dinner he began painting another favourite place. It had been many years since he had visited Ben in Cyprus, but he had been enamoured with the Church of St Lazarus in Larnaca.

The background of the sky was easy to mix because, the way he remembered it, the sky was a perfect Mediterranean blue with barely a wisp of cloud. He would draw the outline of the elongated building faintly first, with its high tower and three domes, and then begin the wash for the sky. Somewhere, he had a guide to the church, but finding it might be impossible... Then again, he knew where on the many bookshelves some of the guides were and he set about searching through them.

As he hunted, he said aloud to himself, 'This is where the internet would be handy. I guess I could easily find a picture there to give me an idea of what I wanted to paint.'

He determined to pursue the idea of getting a laptop and learning to use it.

As luck had it, he did find the guide to the church, although why he and Edith had kept so many shelves full of books and brochures for so long eluded him.

Still, right now he was glad that they had. He took the guide into the lounge and sat with it for a while, just getting an idea of what he was trying to draw.

Then he put the guide to one side and with a light pencil drew the basic outline of the building. The picture on the front of the guide was closest to what he was trying to capture. It took him a long while to get the outline just how he wanted it. The white stone against the almost harsh blue sky was what he remembered most.

There was a kind of timelessness about this church. It had survived for so many centuries and was part of a picture that went back to biblical times. There was a blinding brightness about the sky that he wanted to capture.

He couldn't make up his mind whether he wanted to paint it in watercolours or in oils, and ultimately decided that he would do one of each, starting with the watercolour. Meg was right. He should do the paintings for the exhibition and the same building painted in different media would be interesting to the viewer.

Ken smiled to himself. He was now considering his art from a different perspective.

A part of him felt disloyal to Edith now that he was filling his life with other things. It felt as if he was replacing her. He knew that such thoughts were not rational, and that he was still here and couldn't sit and feel sorry for himself for ever, and he knew that Edith wouldn't want him to, either, but he still had to fight the negative feelings.

He decided that Eric would understand and that he would chat with him about it when they next met. *That will be Saturday afternoon,* he thought with pleasure.

While he was still considering which colours to mix for the watercolour sky, the phone rang. He was surprised to find that it was Dora.

'Hello,' she said, 'is that Ken?'

He was delighted when she invited him round for the afternoon on the next day, Friday. He thought carefully. Angie would be coming in the morning, to help him with his bath for the last time, but the afternoon was free. 'I'd love that,' he said, and so it was arranged. He would walk around the corner to her house.

He got back to his painting, seriously wondering how he would fit all these new activities into his life.

I think I need a diary, he thought. *Or one of these days I'm going to forget where I'm meant to be.* Life had become busy all of a sudden.

The only day that tended to be quiet was Sunday, and by the time it came around each week he was glad of it. Sometimes he would wander to the church where Edith's funeral had taken place and attend evensong; it wasn't well attended but it was quiet and reflective.

He wanted to keep his memories of Edith alive, but he felt that he was taking better care of himself now too.

CHAPTER 17

After Angie had helped Ken with his bath on Friday morning, they sat down to talk about his future care needs.

The occupational therapist had provided him with a stool to perch on for a full wash, and he already had grab rails in place. Overall, Angie felt that he was coping well now with all his personal care and the housework, and Ken told her that he felt more confident and was happy to manage alone. She assured him that if he encountered any difficulties in future, he could contact the care company and they would arrange help.

He would miss Angie, Ken reflected as she spoke. She was so full of life and encouragement.

He was still mulling over the possibility of having some help with the cleaning, but, as Angie had said, he could contact the care company if he decided it was necessary. *The way things are going,* he thought, *I'll need someone to do the cleaning while I get on with my social life!*

Oddly enough, it was that very thought that made him decide. He didn't want to spend all his life cleaning, and if he could sell some of his art, as Meg had suggested, he would spend the money on a cleaner. He decided not to hire one, though, until he had his first payment for a painting.

All of sudden, he was setting up a business in his mind. In that case he would need a website, and therefore a laptop. Now he needed computer lessons. His mind was racing ahead... *Slow down,* he commanded it.

He went into the spare room and moved the Cyprus painting off the easel, replacing it with the mystic sunset scene. In his excitement at the thought of setting up a small business, the explosions of colour and light were easy to paint. The swirls of orange, brown and red burst from the canvas. Ken was in good form today.

By lunchtime the mystic sunset scene was in need of only a few more details, and he had painted the brilliant blue sky of the church on his watercolour painting. He was motivated now, and desperate to make even more progress with his painting, so he stopped only to butter a roll and heat up some spicy tomato soup before continuing with his work.

He finally downed tools at a quarter to two, when it was time to get ready to go to Dora's. Perhaps it was a good thing, he reflected, that he had to break up his painting frenzy with an afternoon out at a friend's!

Ken didn't make a special effort with his appearance; he didn't want to give Dora the wrong impression. It was just gone two o'clock when he rang the doorbell.

When Dora opened the door, Ken's heart sank. She had dressed up, and when he entered the lounge he saw that everything was laid out perfectly for afternoon tea; there were even flowers on the table.

He needed to ensure that she knew this was just about friendship. Not only was it not long at all since Edith's death, but Ken had no wish to replace her, no desire for another relationship. Apart from anything else, he was too busy.

He sat down where Dora indicated on the settee in the conservatory, and she sat beside him. 'How is your wrist doing now?' he asked.

'Oh, I get very frustrated with myself,' she replied. 'Everything takes so long.'

He nodded, recognising the problem. 'I miss Meg,' he said. 'I hadn't realised how much I depended on her to do the things I couldn't.'

'Do you mind being on your own again?' she asked.

'Most of the time, no,' he replied. 'I needed someone there to get me going again, but in some ways it's good to have my place back.'

'I've never got used to it,' she said.

The more she talked the more he realised that her life was very different from his. Dora looked after her grandchildren when they finished school each day and helped them with their homework. She happily did the housework, taking pleasure in keeping the house tidy. Her husband had died several years ago and she had only a few close friends. She told him that she would ideally like to meet someone and marry again, that she had never quite lost the feeling of loneliness that came from living alone.

Ken took his opportunity and suggested counselling. 'I don't think it's essential to have someone else in your life in order to feel complete,' he said, trying to be sympathetic at the same time as getting his point across.

'I miss Edith,' he continued, 'but I wouldn't want to begin that whole process again with someone else. I have other interests in my life now.' He hardly dared look up to see how she took this.

When he did, her expression was doleful. 'I don't have

any interests, apart from the garden,' she said with a shrug. 'And cooking, but it seems a bit pointless cooking just for me.'

'Well, Cruse would give you counselling if you rang them. There will be a waiting list, but I'm sure it's well worth it to re-establish and recentre your life,' he suggested.

'I enjoyed looking after someone,' she countered.

'There are a lot of voluntary organisations who would love your help,' Ken went on. 'There are so many needy people, and a lot of organisations rely on volunteers who take time to care for others. When I came out of hospital I was helped by a "home from hospital" volunteer from Age UK who reconnected me with my art club and helped with other things too.'

She looked him in the eye, pensive this time. 'Maybe I *could* volunteer,' she said tentatively. 'The grandchildren are growing up fast and I know they don't want to come here after school anymore. It's for my benefit these days. I felt a bit rejected, but maybe I should turn my attentions to people who *do* want help... I'm not sure.'

'If you do decide you'd like to do something new, there's a volunteer bureau in town. They would know who wants help and in what ways. That way, they'll match your skills to their database and give you suggestions. Or there's plenty of information online.'

'I'll have a think about it. I want my old life back, really. Change is just a little scary.'

'Change is always a little scary, but it happens whether we like it or not, so maybe it's better to choose your change,' he said.

'I wish I was as brave as you. You seem to have managed

all your change pretty well,' she said.

He shook his head. 'I was forced into change when I fractured my arm. I wasn't coping at all well before that – I was just feeling miserable and sorry for myself. Having the accident forced me to think about my future.'

He thought about the past, recalling only too well the turmoil he had felt in the first weeks after Edith died.

Then he turned back to Dora. 'Did you have a job before you had the children?'

She nodded. 'Yes, I was a receptionist at the local hospice.'

He gazed out of the conservatory window. Dora had a very large garden, mostly laid to patio but with a pond halfway down. 'Can I see the garden when we've had the tea?' he asked.

'You certainly can. I love my garden. I have a gardener who does all the work that I can't,' she said.

'Really?' he said. 'Does he have any spare time? I mean, would he do a bit for me, do you think?'

'I could ask him,' she offered.

He loved how life was coming together now that he was more honest and open. Having a gardener to do the heavy work would leave him free to do the bits he loved, like the greenhouse.

'What part of the garden do you do for yourself?' Ken asked.

'The pond, and I like to grow bedding plants from last year's seeds... like marigolds,' Dora said. 'The gardener does the shrubs and mows the lawn at the times of year that it needs it. He prunes the fruit trees, too.'

The garden was beautifully laid out. Ken thought about

Meg and her desire to design her father's garden. *Maybe she could come here and see this garden to get a few ideas,* he thought.

He gave voice to the idea and Dora was delighted. 'Oh!' she said, the pleasure obvious in her voice. 'Do you think it's good enough for that?'

He nodded as he sipped his tea and took a bite of the cream scone she had made. 'I do,' he said. 'You obviously have an eye for design.'

After they finished the tea she put on her shoes and jacket and shepherded him to the garden, unlocking the conservatory door. 'Come on, then,' she said with enthusiasm.

It was cold as he stepped outside but he didn't suppose they'd be in the garden for long.

'We'll start at the end and walk back towards the house,' Dora decided.

The garden was long and narrow. At the very end she had what she told him was a raised vegetable garden, although there was nothing there now but a few rather sorry-looking sprout plants and some purple sprouting broccoli.

'Dan – that's the gardener – raised the beds so that I could do some of the work myself.'

'That's a brilliant idea,' Ken replied. 'If my beds were raised I could do more. Bending down is a problem... I find it hurts my knees, and my back aches too if I do it for long.'

'I sympathise,' she said as she moved up the garden towards the house.

On one side of the path was a greenhouse and shed. He could see that, like his, the greenhouse had been shut up for the winter. When they came to the pond she stopped.

'There are koi in here aren't there?' he asked. 'I'm sure I saw one just then.'

'Yes,' she replied, 'but the pond is quite deep in order to help them survive the winter.'

'Does keeping them entail much work?' he asked.

'Not a lot, but I do clean out the entire pond in early autumn to make sure that the water is as oxygenated as possible before the cold weather arrives.'

He was intrigued. Indeed, a lot of things interested him now that he had more of an appetite for life. Not that he intended having a pond in his own garden – he had other things to do with his time – but he did wonder whether Meg might be interested in one.

They wandered on towards the large patio area where Dora had a built-in barbecue.

Ken didn't have enough room in his garden for a large patio, and would have no use for a barbecue, but that was another feature that he thought might interest Meg – or at any rate, it might interest Peter because he and Sarah often had barbecues for their friends in the summer.

The patio was quite sheltered and housed many plants in pretty pots. Dora certainly had a gift with garden design.

When they went back inside Ken asked Dora outright if it was alright to give her number to his granddaughter, and Dora was delighted. 'A lot of the young people that I know don't do gardening,' she lamented. 'Neither of my sons is interested.'

'I guess they're all working too hard to have time for the garden, so they design it with the least possible work in mind,' he said.

She nodded slowly – sadly, he thought. He hadn't considered it until then but she was right. Many of the gardens around him were laid to patio and had no plants or lawns. He couldn't blame their owners; life was just too busy.

They went back inside and he thanked her for the afternoon tea.

'We must do this again sometime soon,' she said. 'I've enjoyed your company.'

'Yes, and you make a lovely afternoon tea,' he replied.

'Thank you for the suggestion about the voluntary work. I would have thought I was too old, but I guess anyone can keep someone else company, or offer some support and advice. I'll have a think about it.'

'Absolutely, and hopefully you'll be able to give Meg, my granddaughter, a few pointers for redesigning my son's garden so it's more useful, and prettier all year round,' he said.

Once he'd got Dora's awkward expectations out of the way, Ken realised, it had actually been an enjoyable afternoon. He didn't think Dora really needed a partner, just some more company. Hopefully she would consider getting out a bit more now, so she could keep someone else company and give them a sense of hope and purpose in turn. *How amazing,* he thought as he wandered home, *how infectious helping can be.*

That was another subject he would like to be able to express in his paintings, but he had no idea yet how he would achieve it. He needed a small notebook to write down all the ideas he had for new subjects. He stopped off at the local shop and bought one, then increased his pace for the rest of the walk home. He wanted to get back and finish the painting he was working on right now.

As he got through the front door of his bungalow, he threw off his coat without even bothering to hang it up and went straight to the spare room. He picked up his palette and brushes with enthusiasm and set to work, rapidly adding small details.

By the time he had to start cooking the evening meal, he had finished the mystic sunset painting and set it aside to dry.

CHAPTER 18

The next day, Ken was determined to start a new painting. He had decided that he'd like to be involved in John's exhibition and had challenged himself to paint enough pictures to exhibit, but that meant a commitment to doing at least a little painting most days. He was going to the gym and for a swim with Eric this afternoon, so he needed to get everything else done this morning.

He didn't want a lot of shopping but, this being Saturday, he would buy a newspaper. He had stuck to his aim of buying one every week or so, and Saturday was the day he most often did it now.

Having picked up the paper, and a small notebook, he succumbed to a chocolate bar. He went to the checkout. Jenny, who had helped him after his fall, was serving, and after she'd asked him how he was doing and they'd chatted for a few moments, he paid and left. He still found himself being cautious of the step where he had fallen.

He was keen to get everything on his to-do list out of the way this morning, so he got out the vacuum cleaner and hoovered the lounge and dining area. Even the cleaning was less of a chore now. He would never be obsessive about it, and he would employ a cleaner once he earned a little on paintings, but he was content for now to keep it reasonably clean and tidy up himself.

When he'd finished hoovering, he painted for the rest of

the morning.

The afternoon was relaxing. Ken and Eric worked out in the gym for a short while and then went for a swim in the pool. The joy of going to a gym at a hotel was that it also had a sauna and pool, so after they had swum for a while they sat chatting in the sauna.

Here they met Helen, a young woman who could walk a very short distance on crutches but got about mostly in a wheelchair and an adapted car. Ken found her enthusiasm for life infectious.

'I come for a swim most days,' she said. 'If I'm too busy I give it a miss but I find that the exercise keeps me more mobile than I would be otherwise. When I've been ill and not been for a week or so, movement is more painful.'

'That's interesting,' Ken said, 'because even going out for a walk most days has made my joints freer.'

She nodded. 'Before I started swimming I was hardly going out. I tried to walk further and further each day but walking is too difficult for me. My GP suggested swimming.'

They continued to chat until Ken got too hot and decided that his time was up in the sauna.

'I'm going into the hotel lounge for a coffee now,' Helen said. 'Would you both like to join me?'

Eric looked delighted. 'That sounds like a great idea. We were going to a café after this anyway, so we might as well join you here – what do you think, Ken?'

'Sounds good to me!'

They got dressed and retreated to the hotel lounge. Ken admired the intricate decoration of the ceiling and the stunning plaster rose around the central chandelier. The room was lavishly furnished with a patterned thick-pile carpet and hand-carved furniture. The velvet cushions were plumped up and set in place so precisely that Ken was almost afraid to sit on the chair for fear of disturbing the layout.

Helen threw herself down into a chair. The waiter came across almost instantly. 'Hello, Helen. What can we do for you today?'

'Can we have three filter coffees, please?' she requested, and then turned towards Ken and Eric. 'Ooh, is that alright?' They both nodded agreement. 'And three of your chocolate brownies, please,' she added. 'Their chocolate brownies are to die for!' she explained to them.

Helen was a lot younger than they were but she didn't seem to mind their age. In fact, as Eric pointed out to Ken later, she didn't even seem to notice.

'So,' Ken said, turning his attention to Helen, 'what do you do?'

'Do you mean do I have a job?' she asked. Ken nodded. 'I kind of have a job. I sculpt but it doesn't make me enough money to live on, and anyway I don't like being shut away on my own all day. So I'm on Income Support because I'm not able to hold down a permanent job – I do have severe pain some days and it also takes me a while to get going in the morning.'

'That's interesting,' Ken replied. 'Where do you sell your sculptures?'

'Here and there,' she replied with a shrug. 'Believe it or not I'm a bit shy of marketing. It seems a bit wrong pushing my own work... a bit vain, somehow.'

Ken had been entertaining an idea he wasn't sharing, but

eventually he spoke up. Maybe John would exhibit sculptures for Helen or would know someone who would.

'Well,' he said tentatively, 'I paint, and I know someone who exhibits. It's just possible that he knows other sculptors. If you give me your contact details I'll talk to him about it.'

Helen's face brightened. 'I can do better than that,' she said, rummaging in her handbag. 'I've got my business card right here.' She found one and handed it to him.

'So you have a website?' Ken asked. 'Did you get someone to set that up for you?'

She shook her head. 'No, I used one of those cheap packages and did it myself. They might not be like the super-duper designs but I only need something simple. As long as it showcases my work that's all I want.'

Ken took the card. 'I'll give it to John. I imagine he'll give you a ring directly,' he said. Helen clapped her hands in delight.

Ken had taken a liking to her; she had energy and drive, even if she lacked confidence in her work. He understood that feeling – it's easy enough to create if you are that way inclined, but it's a totally different matter believing that someone else will appreciate your art. Marketing is a separate skill.

Eventually Ken said, 'I'll call a taxi – I'd better be getting back.'

'Where are you going to?' Helen asked. He told her the address. 'But we share a taxi,' he replied.

'That's no problem,' she said, in her animated fashion, 'I can drop you both home.'

'Are you sure?' Ken asked. 'We don't want to put you

out.'

'It's no bother,' she replied. 'I've enjoyed meeting you both. I hope we can do this again soon.'

After he got back to the bungalow, Ken answered a phone call from Meg.

'I've been trying to get hold of you,' she said. Dad helped me find cheaper deals for stuff like my phone and my car insurance today, so I can save up faster.

'That's brilliant,' he replied.

'He also said that if I want to do the garden, that's fine by him because he hasn't the time or the interest.'

Ken could hear the excitement in her voice and it caused a warm glow in his heart. Somehow his relationship with her had sparked a deeper relationship between Meg and her father and he was delighted.

'Before I forget,' he said, 'I met a lady recently, who happened to be going to the hospital in the same transport as me, who has a real eye for garden design. She would be happy to talk to you.' The enthusiasm rose in Ken's voice as he continued. 'I've seen her garden – it's beautiful. She has a gardener who does the heavy work and she does what she can. She seems quite knowledgeable. I mentioned you to her and she said she'd be quite happy to talk to you and show you around her garden.'

Meg sounded excited. 'I'd love that,' she replied. 'I've got a lot of ideas and I'd love to bounce them off someone knowledgeable. Anyway, we can talk about it more tomorrow if you're free because Dad has said that if I come and fetch you, you can come to dinner again.'

Apart from his art, which he was happy to do in the morning, Ken had nothing arranged and they agreed that she would pick him up at half past twelve. He was looking forward to seeing the family and sharing his week with them.

CHAPTER 19

Ken got up early on Sunday morning and intended painting, but he heard the church bells ringing and decided to go to the eight o'clock service. It was never a long service and the church brought back memories of Edith. She had attended that eight o'clock service every week until she began to find it difficult to get up and organised that early. After that she occasionally went to evensong, but she missed the quiet of the early-morning service.

He put his suit on, because that was what he had always done when he went to church, and his overcoat, because the old stone church was always cold at this time of year. Then he wrapped his scarf tightly around his neck and set off.

His heart wasn't heavy today, just reflective. Sometimes he wanted to be alone, wanted time to think of Edith. He would never forget her; he knew that now.

He knew the vicar well. In fact, after Edith died, the vicar had invited him to the church luncheon club, but Ken was afraid he'd have nothing in common with the other people there. He had declined, but as he recalled the conversation now he had to admit it was nice that the vicar had offered.

The old oak door creaked as he opened it. He was met by a cheery face. He took the booklet that was handed to him and sat alone at the side of the church. That was where he wanted to be. He watched the flickering of the altar candles on the vaulted ceiling, laid the hassock down on the floor and knelt. A flood of relief and peace poured over him. Just for this moment in time, life had slowed.

What was it about this place that spoke so deeply to your soul? he silently asked Edith. He knew she couldn't answer him, but whatever connection to Edith he could find here, he wanted it. No matter what befell her in life, she had always been serene.

He sat back in the pew as the service began. It was familiar to him; he had grown up with it, sung in the choir, even, for a while. This service had no hymns, no choir, just rich, deep words that spoke meaning even amid today's trials. There was something calming about the rhythmic intoning of the liturgy, and he entered into it. His breathing slowed as if he breathed in the rhythm of the words. He felt attuned to the God of the universe.

He kept himself to himself after the service, quietly thanking the vicar and leaving. Now he wanted to visit the grave, to talk to Edith even though he knew it made no sense.

He located the site of the grave, barren and empty though it was, and told her again how he loved her, how he thought of her every day and how proud she would be of him. She'd always gone alone to the church, and he couldn't help wondering whether there could have been another layer to their relationship if he had looked within more often, even in the midst of his busy life.

Once again he sat on a bench nearby and thought of the good times, and the hard times, and let light tears roll down his cheeks without bothering to wipe them away. He didn't leave until he began to feel cold, and he went via the garden of remembrance with its beautiful fountain and pond.

It was only as he walked home that he began to wonder about a headstone... *Or,* he thought, *perhaps Helen could sculpt an angel?* That way he would get something unique and she would get paid work.

When he got home he was cold. The central heating wasn't enough; he felt the need for the warmth of the gas fire in the lounge. Until today he had been racing headlong into his newfound future, but now he needed to stop and take stock. He made a mug of hot chocolate. It wasn't something he had often, but today it felt right, a part of this day of caring for himself.

He sat down at the table, looking out over the garden. *Today,* he said to himself, *is a day of rest.* He thought about what he would paint today but decided that his mind needed a break from his everyday activity. He would go to lunch later with the family, but he decided that he didn't want to be drawn into any activity. He would rest and relax with them, and that was all.

He smiled as he sipped his hot chocolate, surprised at how little he had known about himself until recently. He had taken life for granted – lived it without thought, hardly pausing for breath. Only when he was forced to stop, forced by his loss to face his true feelings, could he access his real self. So today he chose to rest and recharge.

***

'You're quiet, very quiet today,' Meg said in the car after she'd picked him up.

'Yes,' he replied, his voice serene. 'I've had a lot of

change and activity in my life recently and I needed a quiet day.'

Meg grimaced. 'It might not be quiet at home,' she said. 'I think Stuart and his family are coming to lunch too.'

Ken shook his head lightly. 'Don't worry,' he said, 'rest and quiet come from within. I went to Edith's favourite service at the church this morning. I think I have that quiet in me now.'

Meg laughed. 'Granddad, you do say the funniest things.'

'To be honest,' he replied. 'I spent a lifetime with your grandma and it's only now I've recognised that she knew how to find her true self by being still, not running away.'

'Interesting idea,' Meg said, although Ken wasn't sure whether she had a clue what he was talking about.

Today, as the car swept into the drive, he was ready. *Why,* he asked himself, *did it take me this long to learn to be still, to enjoy the moment – to realise what Edith had known for so long?* He had no answers. But the peace within answered for him: *It doesn't matter how long it takes; you've learnt it now.*

Meg unlocked the front door and held it open for him.

Peter was in the hall and put out his hand to greet his father. Ken took the hand and pulled his son towards him, locking him into an embrace. Peter recoiled slightly, surprised, and then returned the hug, even though he did sport a look of embarrassment.

Ken smiled to himself. *He'll get used to it,* he thought.

Peter extricated himself and led his father into the lounge. 'Dinner will be about half an hour,' he said. 'Would you like a coffee or a sherry or something?' Ken hid his amusement; it sounded formal.

'Actually,' Ken replied, 'I wouldn't have thought of it but I'd love a sherry.' *Today is a day for rest and recovery and recharging,* he reminded himself.

'Do you need any help, Mum?' Meg called to the kitchen from the lounge, where she had sat down beside her granddad.

'I'm fine at the moment,' Sarah called back. 'I'll give you a shout if I need anything doing.'

Meg knew that if her mum said that, she meant it. Sarah always enjoyed working on her own in the kitchen, usually working to a plan.

Peter came into the lounge. 'How are you managing without Meg?' he asked.

'Oh, I'm doing alright,' he said. 'I've made a few good friends since the accident. I'm just so grateful that I had Meg there for the first fortnight. It was hard to get used to doing everything with only one hand functioning properly.'

'Do you get lonely now?' Peter asked.

'Mostly I'm fine – in fact, I'm having to make sure that I take time out to be alone,' he said. 'I have bad days, but they're less frequent now.'

Ken reciprocated his son's interest. 'How are you doing – and how is the business going?'

Peter shrugged. 'Pretty good,' he replied. 'It takes a lot of hours just to keep it ticking over.'

'Do you get enough time for yourself?' Ken asked him.

'I try to but I find I'm quite exhausted a lot of the time,' Peter said.

They continued chatting until Stuart and Karen arrived with the two boys. At five years old, Ian was definitely in charge of his little brother, James. Ken laughed as three-year-old James tried, and failed, to do everything that Ian did. Not that he was always aware that he had failed. When Ian did a handstand, James tried to copy it and ended up in a heap on the floor.

A little later, Meg offered to take Ken round the garden so that they could talk about what she was planning to do with it.

She led him around the side of the house first. 'I wondered about having a shed round here, or maybe some vegetable beds. I'm not sure if it would get enough sun, though,' she said.

'You really need to talk to Dora,' Ken said.

They wandered slowly around the garden. 'It's pretty bland, isn't it?' she said.

Ken shrugged. 'Yes, but in fairness your dad doesn't have time to do the garden and it is very easy to keep as it is.'

Once they were back inside, Ken said, 'Let me give you Dora's number.'

Meg put the number in her phone.

Over dinner, Peter began a discussion about Christmas. 'Okay,' he said, as if he was calling everyone to order. 'What's everyone doing for Christmas?'

Stuart commented first. 'I think it's only fair on the children to stay in our own house, but you're welcome to come over for dinner if you like,' he said.

As the family decided on their own plans, it occurred to Ken that some of his new friends might be on their own at Christmas. And that he might just like to spend some time over Christmas with them. *After all,* he thought, *I really enjoy their company.* An idea began to take shape in his mind...

After dinner, once Stuart, Karen and the boys had left, Ken sat down with Peter and talked with him about laptops. 'I'd just like to be able to Skype Ben from my own home... and anyone else, come to that,' he said.

Peter screwed up his face. 'It would be expensive just for that,' he replied.

'Well, I'd also like a website to exhibit my paintings, and maybe sell some via the site,' he added.

Peter shrugged. 'In that case, you *would* need a laptop, but you'd also need internet access.' He raised his eyebrows. 'We can look into it all this afternoon if you'd like,' he said.

'Are you sure you have time?' Ken asked. 'I have arranged to have basic computer lessons at the Age UK office in town sometime. A laptop would mean I could practise.'

'Okay, let's order you one,' Peter said, much to Ken's surprise. 'Do you want your internet access with BT?' he asked. Peter then had to explain to Ken how it all worked, and eventually Ken decided that he would use BT because they already provided his phone line.

'I'll tell you what to say and you give them a call tomorrow to arrange it,' Peter said.

***

Peter had offered to drop his dad back at home, and as Ken was about to get out of the car Peter promised to let him know about the internet access.

'It's been lovely to be with you all,' Ken said. Thank you, and thank you for helping me with the internet.'

‘I enjoyed today too,’ Peter said with a surprisingly cheerful wave.

Ken was excited, and as soon as he had his coat off he picked up the phone to ring Eric.

Eric shared his excitement. ‘We can talk more about it on Thursday,’ he said. ‘As soon as you’ve set up Skype, we’ll give it a go.’

As he sat beside his fire that evening, Ken reflected on the day. It had been good to be with Peter and the family. It felt good, too, to be supporting one another, and a computer would be another exciting addition to his already blossoming life.

CHAPTER 20

Despite the good cheer of the day before, on Monday Ken found that he woke with a weary heart. It was barely light; the heating was on, but it had hardly taken the chill off the bungalow.

He threw his dressing gown on over his fleecy pyjamas and sat on the edge of the bed to get his balance.

First, he would turn on the gas fire to warm the lounge, and hopefully his heart. The cold weather did nothing to alleviate the arthritis in his knees. Then he would get a cup of tea and maybe get back in bed until the bungalow had warmed up a bit.

He didn't want to waste too much time, though – he wanted to paint today, and he had also decided he would ring his newfound friends and see if any of them would like to join him for a pre-Christmas 'Christmas tea'.

He took a sketch pad with him when he went back to bed with his cup of tea, and began to outline another painting. This one was a secret. He wanted to surprise everyone and he wanted it to be at the centre of his works in the art exhibition; that reminded him that he needed to ring John to make sure that there was still space for his work at the exhibition.

He used pen and ink to outline the new painting. This project excited him, but he must remember that he needed to finish the others as well.

By eight o'clock he was up and having breakfast and by nine o'clock he was painting. He had begun a painting that he had entitled *Connection*. It was a picture of a spider's web, which he hoped to finish in time for the Christmas tea with his friends that he had begun to plan.

He lost himself in his work, and when he realised the time it was half past eleven. He stopped to make coffee and decided to ring John.

John was delighted with Ken's decision about the exhibition, and when Ken told him about Helen and asked him whether he knew anyone who exhibited sculpture, he was over the moon.

'It's quite a large room I'm renting for the exhibition. I rented that one because it's cheap, but it will be so much better if I can fill it,' he said. 'Sounds like Helen could help with that!'

'My granddaughter helped me to look up some of Helen's work on her website,' Ken said. 'It looks pretty good to me, though I'm no expert.'

After giving John the website address, he remembered that he'd wanted to discuss Christmas too. 'John, I was thinking – how would you like to come to a Christmas tea party I'm thinking of putting on for some friends. So many people have been key to my recovery since Edith died, and after the accident, that I thought it would be good to have a little party.'

John was delighted, especially when Ken suggested that he might like to bring someone.

'I'd like everyone who is invited to bring someone who has helped them recently,' Ken explained.

'What a nice idea,' John said.

'I haven't set any date yet, or thought it through completely. I'm just sounding people out to start with,' he said.

When he came off the phone, Ken was excited. He hadn't had a party of any sort for a few years. For almost as long as he could remember, Christmas had been at Peter's house. Edith had always done the decorating and catering when they were younger, but once the children were grown and they'd got into the habit of visiting Peter every Christmas, their own celebrations had dwindled. They somehow didn't think of having their own party.

It doesn't have to be too elaborate, he told himself. *I'm sure Meg would help me to decorate the bungalow.*

Ken couldn't contain his excitement as he began to plan the decorations and how he would lay out the food. *I definitely want a tree,* he told himself.

He decided to ring Dora while he was still in party mode. 'How do you fancy a bit of an afternoon Christmas party, here at my bungalow just before Christmas?' he asked her.

The response was more than he could have wished for. 'I'm in if I can make the cake and some of the food!' she exclaimed.

And so the party was born.

Later, once he'd finished painting for the day and made his calls about an internet connection, Ken rang Meg. She was delighted. 'I'll help you, Granddad. Any way you want me to.'

'I need a tree,' he said.

'Artificial?' she asked.

'Yes, that would be less trouble and I'd still have it next

year.’

‘I’ll come round and we’ll order one online,’ she said.

***

A week later, with all the guests invited, the tree ordered and the date set for the Saturday before Christmas, Meg picked up her granddad and they went shopping.

First they went to Marchers Store and bought cheap decorations, all colour co-ordinated by Meg. ‘We’ll decorate the tree in the same purple, black and white,’ she said.

Next they went to the pound shop and looked for a tablecloth and serviettes in the same colours. Her granddad looked disappointed when they didn’t find any.

Meg gave him a nudge. ‘Hey, don’t get downhearted – there are three different pound shops in town.’

They found a purple-and-white Christmas tablecloth and serviettes in the second shop. ‘Told you!’ she said with a smile. ‘Now, is there anything else you want to get today?’

‘I’d like a little gift for each of the guests. Not something expensive, just a little token. But I haven’t thought what yet.’

‘Okay,’ she replied. ‘Let’s go home now then, and we’ll think about it.’

Ken was happy with that suggestion; he was tired now.

Before they had even reached the car, Meg had conceived an idea. ‘So, for the gifts – what about a Christmas tree ornament that means something for each person?’

Ken’s face lit up. ‘From the person that they helped!’ he shouted. ‘That’s brilliant – inexpensive but effective… and it can be presented at the party.'

Meg nodded. 'Sorted,' she said. 'Now you just have to buy a few, and also tell those who are bringing their inspirational helper with them.'

'I'll tell the others this evening,' Ken said.

The traffic was heavy and it took quite a while to get back to the bungalow. 'I won't come in,' Meg said, 'because I'm off to view a couple of houses near here.'

'Oh, good luck,' Ken said.

She dropped him off outside and he waved as she drove off. He loved how they were helping each other.

CHAPTER 21

When the day of the party arrived, Ken set up his pièce de résistance in the corner of the room. He had painted it with all these friends in mind, and his plan was to cover it with a cloth and then unveil it this afternoon at the party.

With Eric's help, Ken had arranged to have postcards printed of the picture on the easel, and he had put these in envelopes, with one to be placed at each table setting.

It was mid-morning before he got the call from Helen. She was in tears, and at first he could barely make out what she was saying. She had fallen from her crutches when she got out of bed that morning and was now in too much pain to move. It wasn't serious, but she wouldn't be able to get to the party this afternoon.

When Ken put down the phone, he was tearful himself. Helen had been such a delight and was an encouragement every time he and Eric met her at the gym. She worked her way through the pain in order to keep mobile, and he had learnt to do the same with his arthritis, which was now far more under control.

He rang Eric first.

'Her sheltered accommodation is warden controlled,' Eric told him, 'and they have an events room as well as the residents' lounge.'

Ken interrupted him. 'I get your thinking!' he exclaimed. 'Take the party to her.'

Eric laughed. 'Don't get too excited. We'll have to ring the warden and check it's not being used.'

'And Meg isn't going to be very pleased with me when I tell her we've moved the party,' Ken laughed.

'I'll give the warden a ring and call you back,' Eric said.

Five minutes later, Eric had confirmed that they could use the events room, and the party was reborn.

Ken rang Meg first, who sighed with frustration but agreed it was a good idea.

Next, he rang Helen. When she heard that they had changed all the arrangements and were bringing the party to her, she cried again. 'Even my family don't put themselves out for me that much,' she sobbed.

'We couldn't have the party without you,' Ken said. 'Just rest there until we come and collect you from your flat.'

The next person he rang was Dora, as she was due to arrive early with the food, and then he rang everyone else to let them know of the change of venue.

About half an hour later, Meg arrived to move the party. This meant she was the first one to see the spider painting.

'That's stunning!' she said. Ken explained its meaning to her and she shook her head gently from side to side. 'Granddad, you're amazing,' she said.

'No,' he said, 'it's everybody else that's amazing.'

'Are we taking the Christmas tree?' Meg asked.

'Too right we are,' he replied. 'Eric says they haven't got one in the events room so we'll take mine.'

Fortunately for Meg, she had convinced him that his bungalow would only accommodate a small Christmas tree. Even so, taking off all the decorations and laying it on the back seat of the car was quite an operation; she didn't want to bother taking it apart and putting it back together again.

While she put the tree in the car, Ken put all the tree decorations in a small box. That was all they needed; Eric had assured him that the events room itself at the warden-controlled flats was already decorated for Christmas.

'You realise,' Meg said, 'that the decorations probably won't match your serviettes and tablecloth now, don't you?'

He nodded. 'Yes, and it's a shame after we hunted them down, but it's more important that Helen is there.'

'I agree,' she said, lifting up the box of decorations to take it to the car. Then she put the easel on the floor in the back of the car and the food, drinks and paper plates in plastic crates in the boot. 'You'll have to carry the painting,' she said.

'Did you put the bag with my gifts for people in the car?' he asked, anxiety creeping into his voice now.

'Yep,' Meg replied, cheerfully. 'I think it's just you and the painting to squash in now.'

Ken began pacing the room, running through his mental checklist, hoping everything was going to work out – and wondering why he had thought having a party was a good idea in the first place.

Then he took a deep breath and stopped; he knew the reason, really. Each of these people had helped him move forward when his life had felt so stuck, and some of them were bringing people who had helped them at significant times too.

It's easy, he thought, *to be cynical and ungrateful, but the world is full of joyful, helpful people.*

***

Meg pulled up right outside the main door so they could unload the car, and Ken got out and rang the bell.

The warden answered the door. 'You must be Ken,' she said, offering him a hand, which he shook. 'I'm Beth.'

She was younger than he expected, probably about fifty, with kind eyes.

'I've put up a couple of tables at the side of the room and made sure that you have enough chairs,' she said.

Then she proceeded to help them empty the car. Ken kept hold of his painting and Meg brought him the easel. He set the easel up in the corner of the room and covered the picture with a black velvet cloth.

Meg and Beth had already brought the tree in by the time Ken had finished with the easel – Beth worked fast. Ken brought in the tree decorations next and left Meg to arrange them. She was infinitely better at it than he was.

Meanwhile, he put the tablecloth on the long table, carried in the food and set it out on plates. Paper plates and serviettes were laid to one side and Beth brought in cutlery.

He wanted it all to be beautiful, to express the love and gratitude that he had for each one of them. He placed white candles in purple candleholders at the centre of each table. Then he added purple-and-black crackers that Meg had spotted one day – she'd rung Ken to see if he wanted them.

On a table at the side of the room, Ken also laid out a bowl of mulled wine, which Beth had heated for him, and there were soft drinks. Down the centre of the drinks table was a purple-and-black table runner. Sleek black vases decorated this table, each with a single purple gerbera.

The small individual gifts were placed beneath the Christmas tree.

Ken and Meg, with Beth's help, had finally got every detail in place when Beth said she would go and call for Helen.

'She really did take a tumble,' she said. 'I'll bring her down in the wheelchair.'

It took a few minutes for Beth to get Helen ready and push her to the events room, but when Helen arrived she was delighted. 'It looks beautiful,' she said. 'I don't normally get invited to parties. I can't believe you brought the party to me.'

'Well, you are one of my favourite guests,' Ken said. 'Bringing the party to you was Eric's idea. He'll be here in a minute. He's organising a few games.'

About ten minutes later, Eric arrived with a laptop and a folder with quizzes and competitions in it. Another man was close behind him as he entered the room.

'I've got the competitions here,' Eric said, patting the folder to his chest. 'Ah, sorry –this is Martin, he's my next-door neighbour and he's been brilliant to me since my wife died. He's also wonderful at checking if I need anything when he's going into town.'

'That's fantastic! It's lovely to meet you, Martin,' Ken said. 'Do help yourselves to drinks... Oh, actually it looks as if Meg is bringing mulled wine round.'

Dora arrived next with two friends, each carrying food prepared by Dora.

‘This is Vi,’ Dora began, with her arm outstretched towards a very tall, elegant lady, ‘and this is Amira,’ she continued, indicating the woman on her left, who wore a beautiful pale brown sari trimmed with dark green.

Ken greeted them both and Meg came over with a tray of drinks.

Eric had bought a small present for his neighbour, and Ken watched as Dora also put down two tiny presents under the small Christmas tree. Everyone had remembered to bring presents for their guests.

Ken watched Helen from a distance. She was engaging with everyone but she hadn’t mentioned a guest.

Dora went out to the car and brought in the Christmas cake. It was iced to look like a beautifully wrapped Christmas present.

‘That’s amazing,’ Ken said.

She nodded. ‘Thank you! I haven’t made one for years because I always go to family for Christmas – I think they get theirs from M&S.’ Dora laughed.

Ken looked elated. ‘Well, yours looks far better than anything I’ve ever seen in M&S.’

‘Probably got a lot more brandy too,’ she said with a wink.

John turned up with Peggy Day, the lady who ran the art club, and looked a little embarrassed. ‘I didn’t really have anyone to invite,’ he said apologetically to Ken while Peggy was talking to Eric.

‘Don’t apologise,’ Ken said. ‘People who give up their time to run clubs like that are amazing. Sometimes they’re the only person that others see, and in your case she has encouraged your brilliant talent. I’m just so glad you’re here because you've played such a big part in my recovery.'

John looked a little uncomfortable, and Ken called Eric across to introduce him.

'Eric,' he said as John wandered towards Meg, who was still handing out drinks, 'could you keep an eye on John for me? He's a bit shy, but he's the one who's offering to exhibit my paintings and who got me motivated. He's brought our art club leader, Peggy, but she's very sociable and probably won't stay with him.'

Beth suddenly appeared with a CD player. 'Helen sent me to her flat to get this,' she said, 'and... this!' She produced a CD of Christmas songs.

'What a brilliant idea!' Ken exclaimed. 'I hadn't thought about music.'

He left Beth to set it up and mingled with the guests. His carer, Angie, arrived; she had brought her sister, Emma, with her.

'Emma came round every day after my husband left. I was left with two young children and went into depression,' Angie explained.

There was joy on Ken's face. *Every story is precious,* he thought. *These stories don't make the news but they change the world little by little.*

As he was still mulling these thoughts over, his Age UK 'home from hospital' volunteer arrived. Kate was alone. 'The person who has been the most help to me is here already,' she said. 'I am so delighted to be invited.'

Ken looked puzzled. 'Who is the person who helped you the most?'

'You are,' she replied. 'I started volunteering because my children had grown up and I wanted to do something with my time. I missed the children so much when they left home, and I'm a single mum so I was all alone. You taught me a lot about recovery by sharing all the things others were sharing with you.'

Ken smiled to hear this. 'Kindness really does go round and round, doesn't it?' he said. He beamed with delight as she went to the table and put a small gift under the Christmas tree.

After a little while, Ken called the party to order. 'We'll start with a game to break the ice,' he said, 'although it doesn't look as if it needs breaking. Over to Eric.'

Eric organised everyone into groups of two or three and then handed out Christmas anagrams. 'All the words spell out something to do with Christmas when you rearrange them,' he explained.

Dora and her friends won that game, and he gave them each a pencil with a fluffy Santa Claus head on it.

The next game was a musical one. He had recorded some Christmas songs and they all had to guess who sang them.

Eventually, everyone sat round in a circle and played a game of pass the parcel in which every layer contained a ridiculous Christmassy item that the recipient had to wear. There were silly hats and gloves and scarves, but the final prize was won by Helen – it was a Christmas jumper that made her look like a Christmas pudding. She loved it and laughed and laughed.

'Next,' Ken said, 'we'll have some food – help yourselves from the table. After the food I want to show you my latest painting, which is dedicated to you all.'

The food was excellent and disappeared fast as everyone

helped themselves. When they had all sat back down with their plates, Meg helped by taking drinks round again. After about forty minutes, Ken got Dora to cut her cake, and everyone had a little of it.

While they were eating the cake and making appreciative noises to Dora, Beth's son, Tim, arrived.

'They told me you'd be here,' he said from the doorway, holding her gaze to avoid anyone else's. 'I went to your flat and got no reply.'

Beth apologised and was about to leave with him when Ken called them back. 'Join the party,' he said. 'Get some food and catch up!'

Tim crept into the room, Meg watching him with interest. He sat next to John and engaged him in conversation.

Meanwhile, Ken shouted over the hum of conversation to get everyone's attention.

'There is something else for you all – there's a personal gift for each one of you, bought by the person who has been changed because of your kindness. What we're going to do soon is hand out those presents one at a time, and the person who bought the present will come and explain what it means, and what the person means to them, as the gift is opened.'

Then Ken had another thought.

'Before we start, though, please help yourselves to all the chocolates that everyone has brought – because if I have to take all of those home I'll get very fat. They're over on the table.'

Nobody got up so Ken made a move for the chocolates himself; after a few moments, people followed his lead and mingled around the table.

Ken was delighted to notice that Helen was sitting next to John and holding forth in an animated conversation. Hopefully John was offering Helen a space at his exhibition.

Once most people were seated again, Ken headed for the tree, passing Meg on his way.

'I'll bring round trays of tea and coffee as the presentations are made,' she said.

Ken started to sort out the small parcels under the tree, squinting to read each person's handwriting. He began setting aside all those that belonged to people standing nearby.

He was intrigued to find one in particular – he had seen his Age UK supporter put a present under the miniature tree for him, and he wanted to know what it was.

Ken eventually found his present halfway down the pile, but he decided he'd better be patient and go through all the other presents before he opened his own.

While he was still engrossed in his task, Meg came up to him in concern. 'There won't be a present for Tim,' she said.

Ken had noticed how much attention his granddaughter had been paying to Tim and Beth, and a little smirk crossed his face.

CHAPTER 22

The presentation of the gifts became the major event. Ken hadn't planned it that way, but that was how it turned out.

Once he'd been through all the wrapped items and ensured they all had labels that he could read, he picked them up one by one at random and called out the name of each person who was to collect the ornament. Then the person who bought the present was to give a brief explanation of what that person had meant to them, and why they'd chosen that gift.

The first gift Ken took from under the tree was for Eric's neighbour, Martin. Ken called Eric up to present it to him.

'Martin is the most wonderful neighbour that anyone could wish for. If the weather is really cold he calls round to make sure I'm alright. If he's going to the shops he calls in to see if I need anything... After my wife died he and his family were a real gift to me,' Eric finished.

Martin opened the present. It was a glass reindeer.

'I thought your children would like this,' said Eric, 'but I hope you hold on to it as a keepsake, because you have brought gifts to me that nobody could measure, just like Santa's reindeer.'

The second present selected was for John. 'This one is from me,' Ken said. 'John has encouraged me with my art, even offering me space at his next art exhibition. I would never have thought that I'd get back to my painting, much less be made such a fantastic offer.'

John opened the gift. It was a glass ornament of an acorn.

'John,' said Ken, facing him, 'you have planted a seed in me, a seed that I'm sure will grow. Thank you.'

Next up was Emma, the sister of Angie, who had been Ken's carer in the weeks after he came out of hospital.

'I bought this ornament for Emma because she stood by me, came in every day to see me, helped me with the children and never let me go when I sank into depression after my husband left me,' Angie said.

Emma opened her gift – a glass teardrop.

'The teardrop represents the way that you were there for me when all I had was tears,' Angie said. Emma hugged her sister and they sat down again together, with Emma clutching the teardrop.

Ken bent down towards the tree and picked up a beautifully wrapped present. He would have guessed that it was one of Dora's and it was. It was for Amira.

Dora came to the table with Amira. 'Amira is quiet and delicate and everything that she has ever done for me has been done without fuss,' Dora said, 'but whenever there is no one else that I can turn to, she is there, whether that is by listening when I feel low, or helping practically.'

Amira opened up her present to find a delicate snowflake.

When Ken picked up the next present he could hardly wait to present it. It was for Meg.

'You have been there for me from the time I came out of hospital,' he said. 'You have sacrificed your time and energy, you helped me with the party, and although this ornament may seem sentimental to some, to me it's just right for you.'

Meg unwrapped the glass bauble with an angel inside.

'It's as if you were sent from heaven for me,' Ken said.

She hugged him tight. 'You deserve it, Granddad,' she said, before sitting back down by Beth and her son.

Dora's gift was next. Ken had bought it, and he handed it to her with a light kiss on the cheek. 'You've become a good friend and been brilliant company over these last few weeks since we met on the way to outpatients,' he said.

She opened the tiny package and found a colourful glass bell.

'You are always bright and cheerful and full of good news and happy stories,' he said, 'so I bought you the bell.'

Meg went around with more drinks on a tray as Ken picked up the next gift. Eric's was the next to be presented.

'This one is for one of the people who transformed my life after I was admitted to hospital,' Ken said. 'From the time we met, Eric encouraged me enormously. I thought my life was over when Edith died...' – he slowed down as he thought of his wife once again – 'but Eric showed me how to begin again.'

Eric opened the gift and revealed an old-fashioned lantern. 'You showed me the way forward, lit the path for me, as I attempted to get back up and live life again.'

Beth was next, and she was utterly surprised that she had a gift at all.

'Ah well,' Ken said, 'it's from Helen.'

Beth opened the gift before Helen could speak, and found a heart.

'You are all heart to all the people in this accommodation,' Helen explained. 'I'm sure there are people who do this job routinely, but there is nothing routine in the way that you treat each of us. You share your love and kindness with us all. Nothing is ever too much.'

Peggy Day's gift was the next to be brought out from under the miniature tree. John fumbled his words a little trying to explain her importance to him, although Ken was staggered that he had managed to speak in public at all.

'I never had very much confidence in anything that I did, and you helped me to believe that my art was worthy of exhibiting and even selling to others. I have now had three successful exhibitions and it is all thanks to you and the art club.'

Peggy's ornament was a butterfly. 'Because that is what I feel like,' said John. 'You found the curled-up, closed-up chrysalis and patiently waited for the butterfly.'

He was shaking when he sat down, but by the broad smile on her face Peggy was delighted with her gift, and John sported a proud expression. He had done it.

Ken picked up the next small parcel. 'This one is for me,' he said. 'Who bought this?'

'I did,' Angie, his carer, replied. 'Because although you thought I was helping you when you came out of hospital, you were actually helping me too. I'm a single mum and the last of my children have now left home. I didn't know how to get out of the empty nest syndrome, but in helping you I helped me,' she said.

'I think that's quite an emerging pattern,' Ken said thoughtfully. 'Kindness and helpfulness can be interlinked, and they come back around to us.'

He opened the gift and found a glass cat.

'You brought me comfort,' Angie said.

As it turned out, his present for Angie was the next item he picked up.

'You were more than a carer to me,' he explained. 'You talked to me like a human being, you spoke to me with dignity and you would do anything to help.'

She opened the box and revealed a golden angel playing a violin. 'It was as if you brought music back into my life.'

Helen's present was next to be taken from under the tree. She was pushed forward in her wheelchair by Beth.

'I bought this,' Ken said, 'but it's really from Eric and from me, because we are both so grateful for your friendship.'

He looked up and Eric was nodding enthusiastically.

'I think both of us were a little reluctant with the exercise when we first went to the gym, because it was a bit painful at first, but your encouragement to work through that to develop greater mobility was invaluable, and I think that both of us would confess that we have less pain and are more mobile because we stuck with it.'

Helen opened her gift – it was a sleigh.

'Now we can all get about more!' Ken laughed, then hugged her. 'I won't hug you too tightly because I'm sure some parts of you still hurt from the fall, but if I could, I would hug you tight.'

Helen smiled, and wiped away a tear. 'Thank you,' she said, 'and thank you so much for moving this party here today so that I could attend.'

A present for Dora's friend Vi was taken from under the miniature tree next.

'I had given up on Christmas forever when I first met Vi about five years ago,' Dora explained. 'I'd just lost my husband and I couldn't face a busy family Christmas, although any of my children would have had me over. Vi invited me to her house and let me be myself, exactly as I was, and we had a lovely time in the end, just the two of us. Thanks to Vi, I can enjoy Christmas again now, whoever I spend it with.'

Vi opened her box to find a green glass Christmas tree.

There was one present left now.

'Last but not least,' Ken said, 'is Kate's present. Kate volunteers with Age UK and came to visit me when I came out of hospital just to make sure that I was reconnecting with my life and didn't need any other help. She contacted my old art group and found out about other support for me.'

Kate opened her gift. It was a soldier – the little drummer boy.

'She is a stalwart,' Ken continued. 'One of those people who just soldier on unseen, doing their work helping others.'

Meg got up next. 'I've just been hearing about another kind person,' she said, 'and so I'm taking this robin off my granddad's tree to give to Tim. He also helped his mother at Christmas two years ago at a difficult time. It wasn't so much what he did, but him being there for her brought cheer into her life. When everything is dark and cold, the robin still turns up and cheers up the garden.'

With the present-giving successfully completed, Ken sat down for a while to chat with John, but then he got up to speak again, waving to attract the whole group's attention first.

'Carry on eating and drinking if you like,' he said, 'but

now I want to reveal my painting, which is dedicated to you all.'

With that, he pulled the black velvet cloth off the easel to reveal his finished oil painting of a spider's web.

The web was incredibly realistic, with fine, dark grey lines. It was beautifully intricate and had beads of rain on it. Some of the beads of rain were painted drops of water, but others were tiny jewels he had crafted into the painting.

'Oh Ken, that's amazing,' Beth said. Dora's mouth fell open. John nodded his approval. Admiring smiles surrounded him.

'Every one of us is one of those jewels,' he explained, 'and every one of us is joined to another by an almost invisible line. That is what kindness, help and support have done. There is a postcard copy of this painting for each of you in the envelopes on the table, so that you will always remember that you are the jewel that changed someone else's life.'

***

When Meg dropped her granddad home after the party, she helped him carry everything inside.

'You are amazing, Granddad,' she said. 'I have just one question – however did you think you'd fit all those people into your bungalow? The lounge might be a good size, but it's just as well in a way that things turned out as they did. The events room was a much better place for a party.'

Ken laughed. 'You're right. One or two people turned up with extra guests that I wasn't expecting. I'd use that room again.'

Meg looked at him, astonished. 'Do you mean you're going to make a habit of it?'

Her granddad merely shrugged. 'I don't know yet... But it's a really good room if we ever need one.'

CHAPTER 23

Ken had arranged with Peter that they would pick him up for Christmas dinner at around midday.

Peter had protested to begin with. 'You don't want to wake up on your own on Christmas Day,' he insisted.

'It's a funny thing,' Ken had replied, 'but as you get older it feels good to have time to reflect – just not all night and day, as it was when your mother died.'

Peter nodded and gave up trying to persuade him.

What Ken hadn't told his son was that he had also arranged for Helen to pick up John, Eric and Dora so they could all have a Christmas breakfast at nine-thirty at his house before they all went off to families for the day. They had agreed to stay until eleven-thirty, and then Helen would drop them home ready for relatives to pick them up for Christmas dinner. That would give Ken half an hour to clear up before Peter was due to arrive.

When the big day arrived, Ken sang to himself as he covered the dining table with a green tablecloth, which was embroidered with gold Christmas trees. He had found it in the airing cupboard and ironed it. He laid out a light breakfast of croissants and fresh fruit salad, aware that they were all likely to be fed inordinate amounts of Christmas dinner later on.

In the living room he put out five champagne glasses on the coffee table, along with a bottle of pink champagne in a chiller of ice.

Then he stood back to admire his work and clapped his hands together. 'This is the most exciting Christmas I've had in a long while,' he said aloud to himself.

He picked up Edith's photo. 'I wish you could be here to share this,' he said. 'You'd be singing in the kitchen today.' He brushed away tears and with them the rising sadness. His friends would be arriving soon.

Oh – music!' he said suddenly. He put the photo back on the shelf. He considered carols but settled for an album of Christmas songs by Elvis. 'This one is for you,' he said as he picked up the photo again, kissed it and put it down.

It had seemed a challenge to get up and ready by nine-thirty, but by quarter past everything was prepared. Ken sat down by the patio door looking out into the garden, reflecting on the past and thinking about the joy he was feeling right now. Just a few weeks ago he wouldn't have thought it would be possible to enjoy Christmas at all, but here he was, waiting for his new friends on Christmas morning.

He heard the car pull up outside and got up to open the door. 'Come in, come in,' he said, standing back from the doorway.

'Wow! Look at you all dressed up!' Dora said to Ken. 'That green really suits you.'

'I thought I'd make an effort,' Ken replied.

They made a lot of noise as they tumbled inside. He took their coats and they sat themselves down in the lounge around the fire.

'Pink champagne, anyone?' he asked.

'Ooh, yes please,' Dora replied, and then added, 'Ah,

that was a bit keen, wasn't it?'

Ken poured the champagne as he spoke. 'Not at all. It's Christmas.'

'I wasn't going to drink alcohol until lunchtime... and I'm driving,' Helen said. 'But I could just have a very small one – as you say, it is Christmas.'

'We'll just have one, anyway,' Ken replied. 'We don't want to turn up drunk at our family dinners, do we?'

'It might make mine more tolerable,' John retorted.

'Well, you can have more if you like then,' Ken replied.

After enjoying the champagne, they moved into the dining area, where Ken served warmed croissants and they ate as they chatted.

Dora and Eric discussed gardening, while John, Helen and Ken talked about the exhibition for a while. They all moved easily from one subject to another and time passed quickly. Ken couldn't help noticing that at one point John and Dora chatted for a long time about cooking.

At ten-thirty Ken moved across to the kitchen to make coffee, and John followed him.

'Thank you, this is the best Christmas I've ever had,' he said.

'Well, I didn't think I'd ever enjoy Christmas again after Edith died, but you've all proved me wrong,' Ken replied. 'I think you're the kindest friends I've ever had.'

'Don't go getting all sentimental on me,' John said. 'Here, give me that tray. You shouldn't be carrying it.'

Once they had finished the coffee, Helen tried to get them out of the house, but every time she tried someone had started another conversation.

'Come on,' she said eventually. 'Ken's son will be here to

pick him up in a few minutes.'

They finally all made it to the door at the same time and were still saying goodbye on the doorstep when a car pulled up, but it was Meg at the wheel, not Peter.

Ken looked surprised as she approached, but then so did Meg when she saw his friends leaving. She said both hello and goodbye at the same time and went inside with her granddad.

Once they were alone, Meg looked him up and down, mildly amused.

'Well, I must say you are looking exceptionally dapper this morning,' she said.

'Are you laughing at your old granddad?' he asked.

'Not at all... well, yes,' she said, and then she couldn't contain her laughter any longer.

'I'm dressed for Christmas,' he said.

Secretly, he could tell, she was proud of him. 'Those brown trousers really go with that fern-green shirt,' she said. She appreciated good colour sense.

'Anyway,' Meg continued, 'it's a good thing I came instead of Dad. I don't know what he'd have made of your little breakfast party.'

'I agree,' Ken replied with a wicked grin. Then they both burst out laughing.

Meg picked up cups and glasses and plates and carried them into the kitchen. 'We'd better wash these up and tidy round just in case Dad drops you back here and comes in,' she said.

Having cleared everything up, Ken picked up the bags of presents that he had packed up for the family and headed for the door.

‘It’s cold out, Granddad,’ she said. ‘You’ll need a coat.’

‘Oh yes. Silly me.’ He picked up his jumper from the back of a chair and went to the hall to put on his overcoat.

As they left the house, he put the bags down on the doorstep while he locked the door. Meg picked them up and carried them to the car boot.

‘Let’s go,’ she said.

***

‘You took a long time,’ Peter remarked as they stepped inside the house.

‘Yeah, Granddad wasn’t quite ready,’ Meg replied, with a subtle wink at her granddad. He in turn was trying to suppress a smirk.

Ken felt surprisingly energised. He wasn’t offended at Peter’s overprotection of him; by giving time to himself he’d left himself more content and he felt better able to be kind to the rest of the family. *Now that’s a lesson I wish I’d learnt earlier,* he thought.

‘Glass of sherry or a beer?’ Meg asked him. ‘Mum says dinner will be about half an hour.’

‘Then I’ll have a sherry,’ Ken said.

When dinnertime arrived, Meg made sure that she was sitting next to her granddad. ‘So,’ she said, ‘when are the famous five meeting again?’

‘I don’t know,’ he said, ‘but we all have each other’s numbers.’

Meg laughed. ‘You sound like a group of students. Are you all on Facebook?’

‘No,’ he said. ‘Should we be?’

She shrugged. 'It's just that you could arrange private events and invite each other.'

'You'll have to show me how that's done,' he said, and then he changed the subject. He knew that Meg had seen Tim a few times since the Christmas party.

'What about you? Are you still seeing Tim?' he asked her.

She blushed a little. 'Yes. We talked about dancing when we were at your party, and last time I saw him he told me he'd go if I would.'

'So are you going to?'

'We've booked lessons for the New Year,' she replied. 'He's with his family today but we're meeting up tomorrow evening for a while.'

By the time they reached the Christmas pudding stage, Ken was full up. 'I couldn't eat another thing,' he said.

'I'm not surprised,' Meg whispered.

'Shh. Don't give me away,' Ken said under his breath.

The afternoon passed much the same as every previous Christmas afternoon. They went for a short walk in the park behind Peter's house, and this was followed by the present-opening ceremony, which took the rest of the afternoon.

Meg's present to her granddad was tickets for the flight to Cyprus.

'Oh Meg, this is amazing. Thank you! I can't believe you just booked it. A week in Cyprus,' Ken marvelled, hugging the tickets to his chest in delight.

'It's actually eight nights, because that worked out cheaper and the flight times were better,' Meg said.

'That's brilliant – thank you, Meg.'

There was an even bigger surprise for Ken from Peter, who gave him a lightweight suitcase. 'Oh, bless you both,' Ken said, looking from Peter to Sarah. 'That means so much to me.' He couldn't stop smiling.

Nobody ate much for tea but Sarah put out a light buffet and forced everyone to have a slice of Christmas cake.

After tea, they played charades, and when Meg offered to take her granddad home Peter suggested that he stay the night instead.

'Thanks, but I'm happy going home,' Ken replied. 'As long as Meg doesn't mind taking me?'

She shook her head and went to fetch her car keys from the dish by the front door.

As she got her coat on, Ken hung back to speak to Peter. 'Thank you so much for the case,' he said. 'It means a lot to me to have your support.'

'Are you sure that you're alright about going home?' Peter asked, frowning.

'Absolutely,' Ken replied. 'I'd like a little time to be alone.'

'Okay,' Peter said. 'I'll pick you up at teatime tomorrow then.' They'd arranged to meet Stuart, Karen and the boys for Boxing Day.

'Sure, I'll be ready.'

After Meg had dropped him home, Ken sat for a while, thinking about his day.

I only wish I'd learnt how to do things my own way when you were still here, he whispered to a photo of Edith. *But*

I'm grateful for the time we had together, and I can't go back, I can only go forward from here.

He smiled, with tears streaming down his face.

CHAPTER 24

It was two nights before the exhibition launch, and sleep eluded Ken. He had lived and breathed painting for weeks and had managed to produce twelve paintings, which had been his target for the exhibition. That included the four he had done before Christmas, which John insisted he wanted on display.

As he lay thinking about it, Ken marvelled at all they had achieved since Christmas. If he was honest, it had provided a welcome distraction from the low feelings he had experienced in the aftermath of the celebrations. Meeting with John and Helen for coffee to discuss the content and layout of the exhibition had kept him buoyant; it had rescued him from the heaviness and loneliness.

He was pleased with the postcards. He'd been surprised to learn that Dora was good at photography; she had taken the pictures for him, and he was delighted with the job the printers had done.

With no one else to talk to, he whispered to Edith in the dark. *What would you say to all this, Edith? Are you proud of me?*

He had put a lot of thought into the workshop he was going to run, 'Sea-painting with Acrylics', but now he was getting nervous. Would it be successful? Had his acrylics practice in recent weeks really prepared him to run a workshop? He ran through it in his head, making sure he knew what he was trying to achieve.

Then, as he lay there, unable to sleep, he began to think of everything that he still had to do. 'I should have made a list,' he said to himself under his breath.

He sat up and switched on the old-fashioned bedside lamp. There was no point trying to sleep while his head was tossing ideas backwards and forwards like a tumble dryer, so he got out of bed and made a cup of tea. He took it back to the bedroom with a notebook and pen.

Why, oh why, do I leave it so late? he asked himself, but he got no reply. When he'd finished making the list, he looked at it, shook his head, drank his tea and lay back down again. This time, instead of worrying that he would forget something, he worried that he wouldn't have time to complete everything on his list. But eventually he fell asleep.

By morning, he was tired but determined. When the alarm went off at eight o'clock he yawned and heaved himself out of bed.

It wasn't long afterwards that Meg called. 'Tim says he'll bring the van round this evening at about half past five to collect your paintings,' she said.

'That's fantastic,' Ken said. 'I wasn't sure how we'd get them all in your car safely... along with everything else. Has he got time?'

'Yes. He has to go out to a couple of properties early afternoon to talk through options for landscaping jobs, but after that he'll be free.'

'That's very kind of him,' Ken said.

'I didn't have to persuade him. He just appeared very eager to help.'

'I'm sure he did,' Ken replied with a hint of a wink in his

tone.

'He's helping John and Helen too, so that's only a rough time,' she added.

'I'll be ready,' Ken said, relieved.

After a quick breakfast he sat down to write a little about each painting. It took him much longer than he had anticipated, but by half past nine it was finished. He sighed and made a coffee. Now all he had to do was work out how to print them off using his new laptop and printer! In frustration, he rang Eric, who managed to instruct him over the phone.

'Thank you, Eric,' he said. 'That's one less thing to worry about.'

'Good luck,' Eric said at the end of the call.

Ken looked at his list. 'Collect postcards,' he said out loud to himself. He had checked on Monday that they were ready and agreed with John that he would go in on the bus and collect them from the printers. He stood by the front window willing the rain to stop. *I'll leave it until a bit later and hope that the weather improves,* he thought.

Next he had to cut out the information he had printed off about each painting, so that the pieces fitted the wooden blocks that John had given him.

By eleven o'clock they were cut to size and stuck to the blocks of wood. He placed them carefully in a plastic box and put it in the corner of the lounge with the paintings, which were encased in bubble-wrap ready for the exhibition.

When he sat and thought about collecting the postcards, he decided to call a taxi. Not only would it be quicker, because he wouldn't have to wait around, but the rain had settled in now – and anyway, he hadn't given any serious thought to how he would manage with the box on the bus. He ordered the taxi for half past one.

While he was thinking about an early lunch, the phone rang. It was Dora.

'I've cooked dinner for you, John and Helen for this evening. Come round to mine when you've set up the exhibition,' she said.

'Oh Dora, you are a star. Thank you,' Ken replied.

The taxi arrived on time and Ken went to collect the postcards. The box was much larger than he had expected and he was glad he had taken a taxi.

When he got home, the kind driver carried the box inside for him and Ken put it in the corner with everything else.

'Right,' he said, taking a quick glance at his list on the edge of the coffee table.

He went to the bedroom and returned with his suit trousers and a blue sleeveless shirt. The shirt looked a bit creased so he quickly ironed it. *I mustn't forget that I need to polish my shoes,* he thought. So he added it to the list, but then decided that if he did it straight away then his outfit for tomorrow would be complete, and that would be another thing he wouldn't have to think about anymore.

It was twenty to six by the time Tim and Meg arrived – Tim in his van and Meg in her car. Ken laughed when he opened the door. 'However did you manage to get here at precisely the same time?'

'I followed Meg,' Tim said, with a bright smile on his face.

Ken nodded. 'Ah, right,' he said as he stepped back to let

them in. 'I've got everything ready in the corner of the lounge.'

It only took Tim and Meg a few minutes to load everything into the van. They put the large painting that Ken had done for the party at Christmas into the back of Meg's car, and Ken sat in the passenger seat.

'It's only ten minutes from here by car,' Meg said.

***

When Ken stepped through the door of the exhibition room, he stopped in his tracks for a few moments. The plain walls had come alive. He stood gazing with his mouth gaping. Now he believed it – it was really happening.

Last time he had seen the room it had been empty; now there was a reception desk by the door, John's paintings were already on the wall, and Helen was just finishing putting her sculptures on plinths in various places around the room. At each end there was a padded bench where viewers and prospective customers could sit and look at their leisure, and there were spaces on the wall for Ken's artwork.

Ken handed the box of postcards to John, who arranged some of each in separate little piles on one end of the table opposite the reception desk, next to the small wooden carvings that Helen had brought to sell. He left the rest of the postcards behind the table.

It was a modern gallery, with a lot of light coming in from the far end and from the skylight in the centre.

'This,' said Ken, holding up the harbour painting against a wall the colour of caffè latte, 'would go nicely here.'

John agreed, then added, 'I think we should put the Christmas painting at the end of the gallery on an easel.'

'Great idea,' Ken said. 'We'll try that and see what it looks like.' He turned around with a watercolour painting of his favourite bluebell woods in his hands. Meg looked at it from a distance.

'I think that would go well on the pale moss-coloured wall,' she said, taking it from him and hanging it on the other side of the gallery.

'Oh yes!' he exclaimed. 'Bluebell woods fit better on the darker side of the gallery.'

She nodded, and from then on she helped him to find the optimum place for each painting in terms of background and light.

He picked up the final three small paintings. 'The best place for the triptych is here,' he said, holding them up against the caffè-latte-coloured wall.

'I agree. Hang them up and you're done!' she said.

Meanwhile, John was arranging champagne glasses on one end of the reception desk.

'Is the champagne at your house?' Ken asked him.

'No, no,' John replied. 'It was delivered earlier. It's out in the kitchen. I'll put the first few bottles in the fridge overnight.'

'Good idea,' Ken said.

By half past seven, it was all set up and Meg agreed to drop Ken and John at Dora's house for dinner. Helen had left earlier and was arriving on her own, and by eight o'clock they were eating.

'Thank you for doing this,' Ken said.

Helen agreed. 'Yes, thank you. I'm glad I didn't have to start cooking now!'

When Ken arrived home, he was weary but exhausted. Despite the excitement, he was too tired tonight to stay awake, and after a quick hot chocolate he fell asleep.

CHAPTER 25

Ken couldn't decide whether he was excited or terrified. He had set the clock for half past seven to make sure he was awake to hear Helen on the radio at eight o'clock.

He turned the radio on and tuned it in to the local station. At eight o'clock he was elated to hear Helen's voice, clear and confident, talking about their exhibition. He'd already heard her speaking about it to others and she interviewed well. This interview was a short one letting local people know the details of the event. He was delighted with how it went and was sure that John would be too.

The launch was scheduled for two o'clock but they'd all agreed to be there by midday to ensure everything was set up and ready to go. Would anyone bother to turn up? Would people buy the artworks? Would his workshop tomorrow go well, Ken wondered? He already had eight people booked in and that was all the little room would accommodate.

Never having done anything like this before, Ken was nervous. John had confided last night that despite having done exhibitions before he was still nervous, which had settled Ken a little, but he was still pacing the room by the time Helen picked him up at quarter to twelve, as she had promised, giving them plenty of time to get to the gallery.

Today the gallery looked even more amazing to him. It wasn't any different from last night, but somehow despite his earlier reservations he was ready now. John was already there and had set up a cash box for small purchases, complete with change. Larger items would be reserved and paid for at the end of the exhibition.

'I've brought everything in ready for my workshop tomorrow,' Ken said.

John nodded. 'That's fine. It can stay here until tomorrow. There's plenty of room in the cupboard.' John helped Ken to stack everything in the cupboard before returning to the exhibition room.

While they were talking, Dora arrived with the petit fours on beautiful vintage platters and Eric set out the glasses on the silver tray that Ken had provided.

'That looks great on that little table,' John said. 'I'm so glad you two could come and help serve the food and drinks. It leaves the three of us to engage the invited guests in conversation.'

'That's what I thought,' Dora said. 'I must have a quick look at everything before people start arriving.'

Eric joined her. 'I love the sculptures. I think they make the exhibition more interesting.'

'This is my favourite,' Ken declared as he stood in front of a sculpture of a mother and child.

'I love the owl,' Eric said. 'It looks as if it could fly away.'

Helen laughed. 'Well, I hope it doesn't. Not before the exhibition, anyway.'

To their surprise, at two o'clock, the entire Christmas party group turned up. And shortly afterwards, even the mayor surprised them with a visit. He couldn't stay long because he had a meeting to get to, but he did seem interested in the inspiration for Ken's spider's web painting, and chatted to him for quite a while about collaboration.

Dora managed to get a photo of the mayor alongside Ken's painting on the easel, and John proclaimed that it would be a good photo to send to the local press.

Dora laughed. 'I'll see how it looks when I put it up on the computer. I won't send it if it's out of focus!'

***

By the end of the day, they had sold twelve postcards and five little wood carvings.

Two of John's paintings had been reserved, but most surprising of all was that a local business owner had commissioned a sculpture from Helen for the entrance to his company office. He had told her that the entrance was large and intimidating and that it needed something less formal.

He had then approached Ken and asked him if he was able to paint something like the bold sea picture but much bigger, also for the office entrance. Ken had been stunned and knew it must have shown in his face; the shock silenced him briefly.

'There's no rush,' the businessman had said. 'I just think it would really improve the first impression we make on our visitors. We have very plain walls and an enormous entrance area, so it looks quite clinical.'

Ken agreed to take on the commission, and the man took his number and promised to ring him to discuss the details. Ken couldn't help thinking that if this sale came off it would pay for him to hire a cleaner, as he'd promised himself.

There were lulls in the visitor numbers once their Christmas party group had left, but the gallery was never empty. John particularly enjoyed speaking to one couple who had heard Helen on the radio and had been intrigued.

'We live just down the road and we both paint,' the wife said. 'I'd really like to meet with other artists.'

John told them about Peggy's group and gave them her number.

And Ken had a fascinating conversation with a man who played the harp and had always wanted to play in an art gallery. They exchanged numbers and Ken agreed to ring him.

At the end of the day, the group declared the exhibition a success so far.

'Forty-five people passed through the doors,' said John with quiet pride.

'And we've met some very interesting people,' Ken added.

***

Ken slept a little better that night but still woke once in a cold sweat about the workshop. He was worried that it might not be what people wanted or expected.

John had assured him that workshops were all different; that was the joy of them. 'People don't always have preconceived ideas about what they will achieve,' he said.

Ken needn't have worried – the workshop the next day was a complete success and he enjoyed it tremendously. All eight people who booked turned up. One had only ever painted in watercolours before and was delighted with her initial efforts in acrylics.

'I find it easier to create depth with acrylics or oils than with watercolours,' Ken had said, while admitting to her that the watercolour painting of the harbour in the exhibition was the first time he had tried painting the sea in watercolours.

Afterwards Ken declared that, on reflection, there were a few things he would have done differently.

'Well, it's always good to reflect on events and think what you'd change next time,' John said. 'So what would you do next time that you didn't do today?'

Ken thought for a moment. 'I wouldn't try to achieve quite so much. Simple ideas would be best, I reckon. Also, I gave them notepads to take notes, but I think it would be more time-efficient to have handouts.'

The gallery was only open from ten until four but the first full day still felt long to Ken, who wasn't used to going out to work anymore. That night he fell asleep from happy exhaustion before he had time to be anxious.

The same thing happened for the next two days. When the final day was over, Ken, John and Helen, together with Dora and Eric, went for a meal at the local Chinese restaurant.

'Well, I think that was a great success,' John said. 'We made quite a few sales, and hopefully people will come again when we have our next exhibition.'

Ken laughed. 'Not so fast! We've got commissions to do, I need time to paint more pictures, and I'm off to Cyprus with Meg next month.'

John nodded. 'That will be a good opportunity to sketch even more interesting pictures.'

CHAPTER 26

Ken picked up the phone casually.

'Hi, Granddad. It's me.'

'I know, Meg. I can read it on the handset,' he quipped.

'Yeah, I don't know why I say that every time,' she laughed. 'Granddad,' she continued, in a serious tone, 'I've got good news and bad news.'

'Give me the good news first then,' he said. He heard her take a deep breath.

'I've been promoted. I'm now... a senior housing officer!'

'That's fantastic!' he said. 'Congratulations. You deserve it. That will help with the mortgage when you get your own place.'

'Yes,' she replied, and then hesitated.

He helped her out. 'Let me guess. You can't come to Cyprus in March?'

She sighed. 'Well, I might be able to...'

He interrupted her. 'It's hard with a new role, especially a promotion. Another time would be better for you. Don't worry.' He was disappointed, but he knew how important Meg's job was to her, and he was genuinely pleased for her.

'What I did wonder,' she continued, cautiously, 'was whether one of your friends, maybe Eric or John, would like to go with you? I've already got the ticket and it would just mean transferring it. I wouldn't need paying – not now

I'm going to be earning so much more!' She didn't wait for a response before she added, 'I'd just be glad that you could go.'

Ken thought for a moment. 'Well, Eric likes travel but he's still not as mobile as he'd like to be... John's never been much of a traveller, but we could make it a kind of art trip, so maybe I could talk him into it.'

'Just see what they say,' Meg said. 'I do want to go and see Uncle Ben one day, though.'

'Yes, and I'm sure he'd love to see you too. But don't worry about March. I'll see what I can do. If neither of them wants to come I might go alone – but don't tell your dad I said that.'

Meg laughed. 'I wouldn't dream of it. Not until it's too late for him to do anything about it, anyway.'

'Ha ha, you're as bad as me!' Ken exclaimed.

When he came off the phone, Ken began to think. The more he thought about it, the more going with John seemed like a good idea. With John it would become a painting holiday. He would try John first.

It was with enthusiasm that Ken got out his paints that evening. Somehow life had worked in his favour ever since he had taken a step towards rebuilding his life. In a way, Edith's death had felt like his death too in the early days, but he hadn't felt so alive for a long while as he felt right now.

I'll call in and see John tomorrow, he thought.

***

'I'm not sure,' John said when Ken mooted the idea with him. 'I've never flown before.' He stood up and stared out of the window. 'The first time I went abroad was a couple of years ago,' he volunteered. 'I went by ferry to France.'

'Well, now might be a good time to start!' Ken said, not put off by John's reluctance. 'Since Edith died I've realised that when you take a brave step forward life seems to come and meet you.'

John sat down and smiled. 'You do make me wonder if I'm just being a coward.'

Ken let out a protracted, 'We-e-ell,' which made John smile again. 'I think we all have fears and anxieties, but mostly we can begin to overcome them by taking one little step.'

John sighed deeply. 'I really want to say yes, but I don't want to wake up tomorrow and regret it.'

'You don't have to say yes right away,' Ken said.

'Okay,' John said. 'I'll think about it.'

They talked for a while about their current painting projects and drank coffee.

'Try one of these,' John instructed his guest, bringing out a plate of home-made biscuits.

'I do envy you your baking skills,' Ken said, taking a chocolate shortbread. 'I must admit I've always been lazy about cooking. Edith was so good.'

'Well, I've always found that when you take a brave step forward...' John began, and Ken burst out laughing.

'Seriously, though,' John said, 'I went to cookery classes when I was younger because I got tired of eating the same old things.'

Ken sighed. 'I don't think I've got time for any more

classes, although I reckon Eric would tell me that I could follow instructions on YouTube.'

'I quite like watching cookery programmes on the television,' John said. 'I pick up lots of ideas from those, and then you can always get the recipe on the website.'

'That's a good idea. Mind you, there are lots of cookery books in my kitchen. I guess they're fine if you follow the instructions carefully.'

'I challenge you to try and bake a cake in time for this week's art group,' John said with his hands on his hips.

'I accept!' Ken said, 'although I might regret it... and so might everyone else.'

'You'll be fine,' John replied, waving a hand dismissively as he sank into the cream leather sofa.

Everything about John's house was tidy. Ken smiled to himself. *John must feel uncomfortable in my muddle,* he thought, although John had never mentioned it if he did.

'Can I see your art studio?' Ken asked. He had heard about this art studio from other members of the art group.

'Of course,' John said. 'When we've finished our coffee I'll take you out there.'

He told Ken the history of the art studio. When his mother died, he had inherited her large house, but he had no use for it so he sold it to buy his smaller house and pay for a purpose-built studio in the garden.

'I've always wanted my own exhibition room too,' he added, 'but that would need to be central and would be very expensive to buy.'

Ken was intrigued. He had always seen John as a bit retiring and dull, but John had a quiet strength and confidence that Ken envied. *He might not be adventurous in some ways,* Ken thought, *but there are some risks he isn't afraid of.*

Ken offered to help wash up the cups and plates but John wouldn't hear of it. 'It won't take me long. I'll take you out to the studio now,' he offered.

So Ken heaved himself out of the chair, stretched his legs a bit and followed John out of the kitchen door and under the covered walkway to the studio.

The studio was much larger than Ken had imagined, stretching across most of one side of the garden. Inside, it was light and airy, yet warm. He was surprised just how many projects John had in progress.

'Do you work on them all at once?' he asked.

'I like to have three or four on the go at any one time because I feel inspired in different ways on different days,' John replied.

Ken was intrigued. He had sometimes done a couple at a time, but never three or four.

'How is it heated?' he asked, looking around for clues.

'It has under-floor heating.'

Ken nodded. 'Do you ever do workshops in here?'

'I did one, a long time ago,' John replied. 'I'm a bit of a loner, really. I feel inspired on my own.' He looked up at Ken. 'You like company, don't you?'

'I do. I miss Edith terribly but you've all helped me to recover.' Ken changed the subject back to his host. 'It's a lovely studio. You're so fortunate.'

When they had finished looking around the studio, he followed John back into the house. He didn't sit down again though.

'I'd better go,' he said. 'I still have a cake to make!'

John laughed as he fetched Ken's scarf and coat from the old-fashioned coat stand in the hall. 'I'm looking forward to it,' he said as he handed Ken his things.

Ken had enjoyed his afternoon with John and felt sure that he would enjoy his company in Cyprus too, if only he could talk John into going.

CHAPTER 27

Ken didn't have to wait long for the answer. John rang him the next day. 'Okay, I accept your challenge but I won't have a clue what I'm doing because I've only ever been to France.'

Ken was jubilant. 'No worries,' he replied. 'I'll help you with anything you need.'

When he came off the phone he was still excited. He rang Meg to let her know. She would need more of John's details to transfer the plane ticket into his name, but she was glad to hear that the trip was going ahead.

'I'd have felt awful if you hadn't been able to go,' she said.

'Well, you don't need to feel bad because we're going,' he replied. 'I must let Ben know next... I hope to see as much as I can of him while I'm there but I suspect it will be much more of a painting holiday now.'

Meg was delighted. She knew how much her granddad loved his painting, and visiting Cyprus with a fellow painter had to be a good thing to spark his creativity. 'If you need any help with anything, let me know,' she said.

Ken guessed that they would be less likely to hire a car than if he had been going with Meg, and more likely to get around by taxi. He didn't mind that; he'd become quite accustomed to using taxis. When Edith was around, he would have been too aware of the cost because she was much more money-conscious.

'I'll miss you,' Eric said when Ken told him at coffee on Thursday.

'We're only going for just over a week!' Ken replied.

Eric protested that he would miss out on the gym. 'Don't be daft,' Ken had said, laughing. 'Helen will be there, so there's no excuse.'

***

The preparations were a little hectic because Ken had been preoccupied with the exhibition for so long, but eventually he found the time to shop for some new clothes. He'd only ever bought clothes on his own once before, and he struggled with matching colours.

But it's okay, he had told himself. *I managed with the Christmas shirt, so I can do it again.*

He had chosen a fern-green T-shirt, remembering that Dora had told him the colour suited him, and a new pair of tailored shorts because Ben had said that, in some years, Cyprus could be quite warm in March. Now all he needed was a hat and a new beach towel. *Just in case it turns really hot,* he thought. *And a couple of small sketch pads.*

In the end, Ken was proud that he'd managed to get everything together. It was a few years since he and Edith had been away together and she'd always done the preparations.

It had been arranged that Meg would drop him and John off at the airport at ten o'clock on the Friday morning. She was to collect John first and pick her granddad up at about half past eight.

'Make sure you're ready,' she'd instructed him, wagging her finger playfully.

When the time came, he was indeed packed and ready. Meg arrived surprisingly punctually and even dropped them off early at the airport.

'I hope you have a lovely time,' she said, lifting the cases out of the boot of her car and then giving her granddad a hug. 'I can't wait with you 'cause I took the whole day off and Tim and I are meeting up this afternoon. Give my love to the family.'

'We'll have a great time,' Ken replied. 'And one day soon you'll be going to see them all yourself.'

'I hope so,' she said with a smile.

They successfully checked their cases in, with John helping to lift Ken's onto the conveyor belt, and got their boarding passes, then settled down in a café for a cappuccino.

'We're booked for lunch on board so we don't need a lot to eat,' Ken told John.

John was fiddling with his boarding pass and still had his passport in his hand.

'You can put those away for a while, if you like,' Ken said. 'You don't want to go leaving them in a café.'

John took a deep breath and put the passport and boarding pass in his inside jacket pocket.

After finishing their coffees, they decided to go through security so that they could get it over with and relax. Security was busy but they had plenty of time, and they each bought a bottle of water once they had got through to departures.

John's face brightened once the security process was out

of the way, and he offered to buy them another coffee while they waited. Then they browsed the duty-free shops until it was time to board.

They were seated together on the plane, and Ken let John take the window seat. The sky was cloudless and they had a clear view of the city below as they took off over the river.

John may have been nervous when they started out but he was enjoying himself now, and he chatted away for a little while before retreating into his book. Ken got out his sketch pad.

'I'm impressed,' John said. 'You've started already.'

They passed the flight reading, sketching and chatting.

When they had landed in Larnaca, got through security and, finally, collected their cases, they were surprised to find Ben was there to meet them – they had expected to take a taxi.

Apart from a few streaks of grey in his otherwise dark hair, Ben didn't look very much older than the last time Ken had visited his son's adopted home; but then, Ben had always kept fit.

'I was hoping to get here all along,' Ben said, 'but I didn't know if I could get the time off work so I thought it best not to promise.'

Ben hugged his father tight. It was their first physical contact since the funeral, and Ken held the embrace for several moments.

Next, Ben shook John's hand. 'It's so lovely to see you both,' he said with a smile. He took both cases and led them to his white Mercedes.

'Beautiful car,' John said.

‘Yes, they withstand the dusty climate better than other makes... Was the flight okay? At least it was near enough on time,’ he said.

‘The flight was fine, thanks,’ John replied.

As they headed towards Limassol, Ken and Ben shared all the family’s news. After a while, Ben asked John about his own family.

‘I don’t actually have a lot of family,’ John answered. ‘I see them at Christmas but not much otherwise. You’re all very lucky to have each other. I’m fortunate to have made good friends with Ken and the others in our circle.’

Ken was pleased to hear John opening up so much – perhaps the location was working its magic on him already.

‘We all get on so well,’ John continued. ‘The art exhibition we held recently was a wonderful success because they all helped out.’

Ken smiled to himself. In his case, it had taken Edith’s death, and the accident, to show him the difference it made to have help and support from so many people.

‘I’ll drop you off at the apartment first because then you can sort everything out,’ Ben said. ‘We have dinner quite late out here, so I’ll give you a while to unpack and then come back to collect you... By the way, Jane has stocked the apartment with all the essentials and plenty of food, so you’ll be alright for a day or two after that. But you must have dinner with us tonight – Jane is desperate to see you.’

‘I can’t wait to see her either. It was so sad that she couldn’t come to your mum’s funeral.’

‘Yes.’ Ben sighed. ‘She was so disappointed.’

***

As they entered the apartment, Ken looked around. It was a typical holiday apartment with tiled floors and minimal furnishings. *Well,* he thought, *at least it won't take a lot of cleaning.*

John put the bags in the bedrooms and started to explore the rest of the apartment. Ken headed for the kitchen and opened the fridge, which was packed full, and then the pantry cupboard, which had also been well stocked.

'Wow! Look at this, John,' he said. 'We won't have to buy anything all week unless we want to. Jane is so kind.'

'And look at the stunning view,' John called from the balcony. 'I can't believe it's so close to the sea...! And I love all the pottery,' he added. 'The colours are so bright. I think we're going to enjoy it here.'

Ken joined him. 'I'm sure we are. I can just imagine us sitting on this balcony in the sun with a cold beer in one hand and a paintbrush in the other.'

'Just as long as you don't end up drinking your paintbrush water, you'll be fine,' John quipped. 'Ah well, we'd better unpack before Ben comes back.'

It didn't take long. Neither of them had brought a lot of clothes, and what they had they quickly put away in the bedrooms.

Ben returned to pick them up at about eight o'clock.

'I'll sit in the back,' Ken offered.

'No,' John insisted, 'you sit in the front with Ben.' He opened the back door and got in.

John said little on the journey, adjusting his jacket and fiddling with the buttons. He appeared rather overwhelmed, his old nervousness returning at the prospect of meeting someone else's family.

Ben navigated the narrow streets with ease and pointed out landmarks along the way. Ken was amazed at how many churches they passed en-route – even on the main roads.

Little else was visible in the fading light, apart from the advertising billboards along the way, and when they turned off the main road, darkness engulfed them.

Once they'd arrived, John couldn't seem to get himself in through the front door – he stood for many moments looking over his shoulder at the view.

'Wow! That is just amazing. It would make a fabulous painting.'

Ben smiled and seemed happy to linger. 'The view was what sold the house to us. We didn't want to be right in Limassol, and although we love the sea, we wanted a community. The village centre is wonderful in the evenings – it's quite quiet at the moment but very sociable in summer.'

Ken nodded in appreciation, and Ben continued.

'Sometimes we just sit out on the balcony with a glass of wine or a beer and watch whatever's going on down below... I love the wildness of the sea in winter, but we're not far away and we walk along the front quite often.'

'I love the white walls and brown roof tiles,' Ken said, looking up.

'The roof tiles are quite typical. It had an attractive front door and shutters when we bought it but the whole house needed renovation and the door was rotten. We considered replacing the door with a similar one but decided against it in the end.'

Jane came out to meet them. 'Come in, come in,' she

said, hugging and kissing both her guests enthusiastically. 'Dad!' – she had called Ken 'Dad' ever since her marriage to Ben twenty-seven years earlier – 'You look so well!'

Ben stood by, looking a little embarrassed at her uninhibited show of affection, but she ignored him and continued her excitement inside the house.

'Don't look at me like that,' she said to Ben. 'I'm entitled to get excited. I didn't make it to the funeral with you and I was so disappointed. I'm so pleased they've come to see us.'

She turned back to John and Ken. 'I'm sad not to see Meg, but I'm thrilled she got the promotion. I know how much her job means to her... Her cousins were a bit disappointed, too.'

Jane went back to preparing the evening meal in the open-plan kitchen.

'I love the view from this room,' Ken said. 'I could sit and watch the activity in that square for ages.'

'We had to choose,' Jane replied. 'The old house in Limassol was closer to the sea, as I'm sure you remember, but as Ben said, this is more of a community.'

'And it centres on the square, I imagine,' Ken replied.

'Yes, that's right,' she nodded.

'And the church, presumably?' John added.

'That's correct. It's all very much part of the way of life... Anyway, I'm glad *you* could come, John. I gather from Ken that you haven't been to Cyprus before. It will be a wonderful place for painting... Although,' she continued, addressing John over her shoulder as she worked, 'I was a bit worried about Ken. From what Peter said, he wasn't managing all that well a while ago? Mind you' – she turned back to Ken now – 'it did occur to me that he hadn't really given you much time to come to terms with Mum's death...'

Ken had forgotten how much he loved Jane's zest for life, and her insightfulness. He hoped he would see more of her while they were here.

'You're right. Peter's better now but he was trying to carry on as if nothing had happened, and he was expecting me to do the same, I think. Things are much better now that I've had a bit of help – and found my amazing new friends,' he said, looking over at John.

As Jane served the starter, she steered the conversation around to art.

'I hear you have a keen interest in art, just like Dad,' she said to John.

'Yes... our styles are quite different but we appreciate each other's work,' he said, 'and we get on well together. Our exhibition last month was a great success and we plan to do it again.'

'This is halloumi, by the way,' Jane said, serving the grilled cheese on a small bed of salad.

Then she sat down with them. 'I've always been an art enthusiast, but never painted anything myself. There are quite a few small galleries and art shops here – you should take a look. I have Tuesday off so I could take you round a few if you're interested?'

'That would be wonderful!' John said, a surge of enthusiasm breaking down his typical reserve. 'I'm hoping to get a chance to see some of the icons in the churches while we're here too–'

'–oh, and I'd love to go to the Agia Napa Orthodox Cathedral,' Ken said. 'It's in the old part of Limassol. I'd love to sketch it and have a go at painting it.'

Jane laughed. 'So much to do, so little time. The week will go fast.'

'He painted a lovely one of a Cypriot church, with a stunning blue background,' John said.

'The Church of Lazarus in Larnaca,' Ken said.

Jane's eyes lit up again. 'That church is amazing, especially on a sunny day. I'd love to see your painting.'

'Taxis are an easy way to get around and are relatively cheap,' Ben said. 'That way you can get dropped off close to wherever you want to go.'

Jane got up and filled the table with dishes for the main course. She motioned to the food and urged them to help themselves. Ken handed John the pork afelia and then the Greek salad.

'This food looks lovely, thank you,' John said as Ben filled their glasses with red wine.

Jane engaged them in conversation throughout the meal, asking questions and sharing local information.

'So how are the family doing?' Ken asked, eventually. 'You've asked us so many questions that I almost forgot!'

'Well, hopefully you'll get to meet them all at some point,' Ben said. 'They're all looking forward to seeing you. Simon is excited to get an opportunity to talk to you both about art.' He added, as an aside to John, 'He's the oldest – he teaches art and English at the local secondary school.'

'How is Lucy doing? She's almost finished her estate agent training, hasn't she?' Ken asked.

Ben raised his eyes heavenward and sighed. 'She is such a scatterbrain – too easily distracted. She lives with her partner, Georgios, who is a pharmacist, but her life outside of work is far more important to her than work.' He shook his head. 'I despair of her ever finishing her training.'

'Oh, you worry too much,' Jane interjected. 'She's enjoying life.'

'And Michael?' Ken asked.

'You'll definitely get a chance to talk to him because he still lives at home, so he'll come out with us for a meal at the end of the week, if that suits you both alright. He's playing his cello in a recital over in Larnaca tonight.'

'That would be lovely,' Ken said, turning briefly to check that it was okay with John.

Ben looked at his watch. 'Do you want to stay longer or would you like a lift back? We don't want to keep you up if you're tired.'

'I *am* beginning to get a bit tired,' Ken said.

'Yes, me too,' added John. 'I got a bit anxious about travelling and that's exhausting.'

'Jane will be in touch before Tuesday so that she can take you out,' said Ben. 'She's got your mobile number, hasn't she?'

Jane checked her phone. 'No, I'd better put it in now, while I remember.'

***

Back at the apartment, Ken and John made themselves comfortable in the lounge and talked over the events of the day.

'Ben is quite quiet, isn't he?' John said. 'Well, compared to Jane.'

'Mmm, always has been. We were all surprised when he

first met Jane but I think she's good for him. He's confident at work, and gives presentations all around the world, but he isn't as sociable as Jane.'

John leant back in the chair. 'I'm looking forward to seeing some of the galleries with Jane.'

'Me too. What shall we do tomorrow?'

'We could wander into the town and just look around to get the feel of the place,' John suggested.

'Okay, let's do that. We'll have a leisurely breakfast and wander a bit. Stop for a coffee and take a look at the seafront, maybe.'

'Sounds good,' John said. 'I think I'll go to bed now. All that worrying did drain me.'

Ken laughed. 'I think it always does.'

CHAPTER 28

Bright sunlight peeped round the curtains the next morning, smearing itself in narrow streaks across the wall of Ken's bedroom. There was total silence in the apartment.

He crept into the lounge, opened the blind and let the full force of the sun in. It was gently warm rather than hot, which was pleasant. The brightness cheered his soul and he felt the desire to share it with Edith. For a brief moment he felt sorrow; there was a strange sense of emptiness in a holiday apartment, in the echo of wood and tiles, the bareness of the walls and the sparseness of the furniture. It wasn't homely.

Ken was used to cheering himself up these days, reframing the way he saw things. Creating a blank canvas. He smiled to himself. This was an opportunity; one he couldn't afford to squander. He told himself it was okay to be in a reflective mood, okay to miss Edith, but not okay to let it overwhelm him. Edith would be delighted to see him painting again; she had always loved his artwork. He needed to be in this moment, now, to take in the beautiful view, the wonder of a new and interesting place.

By the time John woke up, Ken felt better. He would enjoy today, here, with John.

'It's a beautiful morning. Quite springlike,' Ken said.

'I feel dozy,' John replied.

'Would you like a coffee to help wake you up?' Ken

asked.

'That would be wonderful.'

The kettle had already boiled and Ken poured water on the instant coffee that Jane had supplied. 'Is it best if we each make our own breakfast?'

'I think that's a good idea,' John replied.

They sat beside the balcony door for breakfast – the door was slightly ajar and a warm breeze lapped their legs.

The view over the bay was even more stunning this morning. John stood up to admire it. 'I would love to live here.'

'So far from family and friends?' Ken asked.

'Well, I would miss the art group... and our friendship group too, now, I guess. I imagine it's just the warmth and the colour and the sea that make me feel that way. Actually doing it would be another thing entirely.'

John sat back down and poured himself some orange juice. 'We can take our time getting ready this morning, and then wander down to the beach and maybe find a café?'

Ken nodded as he started to clear a few things from the table. 'I agree. No need to rush.'

Opening cupboards in the little kitchen, he discovered a coffee machine. 'I hadn't noticed this before. I think I'm going to have a decent cup of coffee. Do you want one?'

They sat a while longer before getting dressed and ready for the day, and by quarter to eleven they were ready to head out. Ken smiled to himself when John appeared; he had hardly ever seen him in short sleeves but today he had braved a polo shirt – brand new, judging by the folds in the fabric.

Ben had given them a key each so that they could come

and go independently if they chose. They chatted as they wandered down to the beach. John wrote down the way they had come, determined not to get lost.

This weather reminded Ken of an English summer's day. The light breeze that licked at his skin tempered the heat of the March sun. Ben was right – this was a good time of year to visit. Not too hot, and less crowded too.

'It's packed in the summer,' Ken said. 'It's lovely that there's not too many people now – it gives me a sense of freedom. That sea looks amazing... I'm thinking of painting more pictures of the sea. It's so energising.'

'I love the sea best when it's stormy,' John replied. 'I've never painted it, though. It's very calm today. I was just thinking that I should have a go.'

'I've painted a few pictures of the sea,' Ken said, 'but always back home where the hues are affected by the clouds, making it all darker. The colours in this sea are vivid and clear. Would you do it in oils or watercolour?'

'I have acrylics with me, but I'd want to sketch it first. We could bring our sketch pads and paints down this afternoon and see how it goes,' John said.

'I'm in awe of your ability to remember what you've seen. I always have to take photographs first.'

'I remember images quite clearly,' John replied. 'I was a bit of a dunce in school because I didn't easily learn what I'd read, but if they showed me a picture I could always recall the details.'

'Which is how you became so good at art, I guess,' Ken said.

They strolled along the beach until they came to a section in sight of a line of shops. John spied an ice cream kiosk. He didn't say a word, just looked from the kiosk to Ken. Ken laughed.

'Well, since there's nobody here to stop us I think it would be a grand idea,' Ken said.

They took a long time deciding which flavours to have. Ken kept changing his mind but eventually settled on chocolate and pistachio. John chose rum and raisin – 'Two scoops,' he said.

They continued their walk at a leisurely pace, eventually stopping at a café for coffee. They found two seats outside, facing the beach, and Ken went inside to order the drinks.

Every time he opened his wallet, Edith was looking at him. He had decided to bring her photo with him even at the risk of upsetting himself. Today he didn't feel upset; he felt proud of himself for his adventurous spirit and was sure that Edith would be too. In that moment he wished that he and Edith had been more courageous when it came to holidays, but he couldn't change the past – that was then, not now.

He shut his mind up and returned to their table with a tray.

'I wish I'd gone on holidays more often,' John said as he arrived.

Ken smiled. 'I was just thinking the same. Edith and I went on holiday each year but almost always to Wales or the Isle of Wight. Just seeing a different culture is enriching somehow.' Ken put the tray down on the rustic metal table. 'Of course, it's much easier here than some places because they all speak English.'

They sat in comfortable silence for a while, people-watching. After they'd had their fill of that, they meandered through side streets with interesting little shops, stopping to browse every now and again.

Finally, they decided to head back to the apartment for lunch as Jane had got a lot of food in and they didn't want it to go to waste.

'It would be good to make a list of all the things we want to do while we're here or we'll run out of time,' John said as they set off.

'You're absolutely right,' Ken agreed. 'We can grab a piece of paper when we get back to the apartment and write it all down. Next Saturday will be here in no time. A week isn't long, is it?'

The apartment was close to both the beach and the seafront shops. It only took them ten minutes to wander back to the apartment and John immediately got out paper and a pen.

'Okay,' he said, pulling up a chair at the dining table, 'what do we want to fit in?'

John started a list. 'The Agia Napa Cathedral,' he said. 'That way, you see the cathedral and I see some icons.'

'Agreed,' Ken said. 'And I know Jane has got a fair amount of food in for us but I'd like to go out for meals a few times. It just seems part of the culture, somehow.'

John nodded. 'I agree. Are you interested in any of the archaeological sites?'

'Not particularly, but I'm happy to go if they interest you,' Ken said. 'I quite like the look of the tiny castle outside Limassol – Knossos, I think it's called – but it would mean taking a taxi. We don't have a lot of time, though, so I'm happy to give it a miss if it doesn't interest you.'

John laughed. 'We should probably do *something* historical while we're here – we don't want to look like complete philistines, do we?' John looked pensive for a brief moment. 'I know you couldn't walk too far when we got there, but I'd love to see one of the villages.'

'Yes, me too,' Ken said. 'Some of them still do lace-making, and many of them have little cafés at the centre where everyone congregates, a bit like Ben's village... I'm not sure if it's a bit early in the year, though?'

'We could ask Jane on Tuesday,' John suggested. 'Do you think they would let us take the family out for a meal on Tuesday evening? That way, we get to find a decent restaurant and see the family all in one go.'

Ken agreed to give Ben a ring and arrange it. 'That's a brilliant idea. I'd pay because it's my family. I do think it would be nice to have lunch out sometimes, too.'

John nodded. 'Yes, let's do that. I also heard about a cocktail that we must try while we're here. It's called brandy sour and was developed in the thirties for the King of Egypt. It contains brandy and lemon plus Angostura bitters and soda.'

'That sounds too good to miss – we'll try that one evening!' Ken said.

***

The afternoon was spent on the beach painting. John sketched out his first project, but Ken had put paint to paper immediately and was a little further on. Both did more work on their paintings when they returned to the apartment in the late afternoon.

They ate out that evening at a restaurant they had seen just down the road from the apartment. It turned out to be a friendly little place where nothing was too much bother. The waitress chatted to Ken and John about their visit and told them about her own attempts at painting, which she had abandoned – John encouraged her to join a course and try again.

The food was simple but tasty and both of them ended up having brandy sours with their coffee at the end of the meal, much to their delight. The waitress even wrote out the recipe for them.

'I love this place,' John announced as they sat chatting on the balcony back at the apartment, enjoying the warmth of the evening. 'People are so friendly.'

'Yes, I'm so pleased we came. What shall we do tomorrow?'

'Well,' John said, 'the first thing on our list is the cathedral, so maybe that's a good place to start.

'Okay, great,' Ken replied. 'I think I'll go to bed, then. I'm looking forward to seeing that cathedral.'

'Me too. Whoever wakes first puts the coffee machine on!' John said, laughing.

'It's a deal,' Ken replied.

CHAPTER 29

When Ken woke the next morning, he discovered that John was already awake and busy.

'I guessed you weren't awake and didn't want to disturb you,' John explained, 'so I opened the balcony doors quietly. It was beautiful when I first woke. Dawn had broken through and there were a few wispy clouds. So I did a bit of sketching.'

Ken picked up John's sketch pad and admired the pencil drawing.

'I want to paint it and capture those vivid colours on the doors and shutters,' John told him, pointing.

Ken looked across. *The colours are happy,* he thought.

'Do you note down the colours?' he asked.

'I'll remember them,' John replied. 'Well, near enough anyway.'

'I wish I could,' Ken said. 'I take photos.'

John put a cup of coffee in front of him. 'We don't need to rush, do we?'

'Not at all,' Ken replied.

When they were both ready, they rang for a taxi and were dropped within sight of the cathedral. They had checked the service times online and were pleased to see that the cathedral was quiet now.

Ken pushed the gate open and then stood back momentarily. He marvelled at the brightness of the sun reflected on the marble-effect courtyard at the cathedral entrance and pointed it out to John. The cathedral's exterior was grand and imposing; its two towers rose up like monuments pointing to heaven and its pillars and arched windows added to the majesty.

As he passed through the door, Ken breathed in the silence, and the incense that lingered from the early-morning service. He lifted his head up, gazing towards the dazzling opulence of the altar, which glistened with white and matt gold, punctuated with the vivid colours of Greek iconography.

He had heard much criticism over the years of the Catholic and Orthodox churches for their wealth, but he felt that they reflected majesty and glory that he didn't feel anywhere else. *Better that,* he thought, *than the drabness of some of the churches back home.*

John approached an icon of Jesus, seated on a throne and holding an open book. He crossed himself and stood in front of it for a while with his head bent forward in a reverent pose. He looked up briefly and Ken caught his eye.

Ken stood beneath the dome, looking up into the eyes of Jesus. The gaze was penetrating. Angels were depicted around the base of the dome and he felt that it drew him closer to heaven, which sent a slight tingle through his skin. He lit a candle for Edith.

The sheer size of the building was awe-inspiring to Ken. He looked across and saw John kiss an idol. He sat for a while to give him time for reflection but found himself unconsciously thinking of Edith. His eyes welled up and a tear settled on his cheek. He wiped it away but he didn't mind any more.

'One day,' he said under his breath, 'I will see you again.'

As he raised his head, he saw the dazzling tear-shaped crystals of the chandeliers. God understands my sorrow, he thought.

At that moment, John turned and walked towards him. It was good to have friends again after feeling so lonely. *Life goes so fast,* Ken thought. *I need to make the most of every moment I spend with people.*

'What do you think of it?' Ken whispered to John as they reached the door.

'It's beautiful,' John replied. 'I wonder how much time it takes to paint an icon. How does an artist even begin to feel the emotions in a painting like that?'

Ken didn't have the answer. 'I have no idea.'

'If I ever came across a workshop that dealt with painting icons I'd sign up,' John said.

Ken raised his eyebrows. 'Really? That surprises me because it's unlike anything else you paint.'

Once in the courtyard, John stopped and looked back at the cathedral. 'There's something about icons. The faces have an expression that I don't see in any other painting. They combine artistic ability with the spiritual.'

Ken stood beside him, nodding gently. 'Mmm,' was all he said.

John continued. 'I feel that it would access a part of me that I've only dabbled with.'

'Well,' Ken mused, 'there must be workshops for icon painting. There are workshops available for almost anything these days.'

'True,' John replied, taking out a tiny spiral-bound notebook and pen from his camera case. 'I'll write it down and look it up when we get home.'

'I might buy a notebook this afternoon,' Ken said. 'I've nearly filled the one I brought with me, already.'

Ken stood back from the cathedral and took a few photos. 'I just want to go over the road and take a couple from further away.'

'That's fine. I'll stay here and sketch a few things,'

Ken wandered across the road and took more photos until he got distracted by a quaint street. The houses were close together and the street was narrow, but every house was whitewashed and had shutters and doors in vivid colours in the classic Mediterranean style. Ken eyed up jars of home-made jam outside one house and eventually succumbed.

When he arrived back at the cathedral, he held the jar out to John as if bearing a precious gift.

John smiled. 'Lovely. We'll have it with lunch back at the apartment. Where did you get it?'

Ken pointed across the road. 'There was a little street with Mediterranean-style houses. One of the ladies was selling it from her house.'

'Ooh, I'd love to sketch that!'

Ken turned around instantly. 'Let's go. The great thing about a holiday like this is that we can do exactly what we want and change our plans at any time.'

John's face lit up the instant he set eyes on the street. 'Of all the pictures I've seen of Cyprus, this is what I really wanted to see – and eventually to paint.'

John spent nearly half an hour making small sketches in his notebook, mostly of angles of buildings and close-ups of flowers and home-made wares.

'They'll work well with your photos – if you're happy to share them with me,' John said.

Ken nodded enthusiastically. 'Of course! I'll email them to you, if I can remember how. Did you manage to sketch everything you wanted at the cathedral?'

'Yes. There was a stunning statue of an eagle.' John took out his notebook again and showed the sketch to Ken.

'That will make an awesome painting.'

They ambled to the seafront and settled on a little café with seating outside in a walled garden.

After lunch, they wandered on to a small harbour and sat on the wall watching the seagulls. It reminded Ken of the last time he had sat on the harbour wall in the Isle of Wight with Edith, and he was quiet for a while. John didn't seem to mind. He was accustomed to his own company.

As the temperature began to drop, they wandered across to a taxi company and got a taxi back to the apartment.

John went for a rest on his bed with a book while Ken got out paints and began to outline the houses they had seen in the beautiful little street.

John appeared about an hour and half later. 'Since you're outlining your painting and I've got sketches I'd like to do, why don't we walk to the shop down the road and get a pizza rather than eating out. We can have some of the salad that Jane has got in the fridge and carry on with what we're doing after dinner.'

'Great idea!' Ken replied. '

Ken put on a jumper and they strolled to the shop. John picked up a pizza and Ken spotted a notebook. 'Ooh, I'll take this too,' he said, throwing it into the basket.

They stopped for a while and chatted to the young

woman who served them, who said her name was Sophia. Her English was excellent, like that of most of the people they had come across.

It was getting dark by the time they left, and as they approached the apartment only the lights of the houses lit the way.

'I'm quite looking forward to pizza,' John said. 'I don't often have it at home.'

'Me neither,' Ken said. 'Edith always called it junk food and wouldn't buy it.'

They both settled down to sketching and outlining. John took out his notebook and transferred his sketches to a larger pad before fleshing each one out a little. After that, he sketched out the statue of the eagle. They worked in silence for a long while.

Eventually John got up and went to the fridge. 'Would you like a drink of anything while I'm up?'

'I was just wondering about opening one of those bottles of wine we bought. We won't need it all with the pizza, will we?'

'Good thinking!' John replied, closing the fridge and taking a bottle from the wine rack on the kitchen counter. He found glasses in a cupboard and poured the wine, then handed one to Ken.

Ken took a sip. 'Ooh, I'm glad Sophia talked us into swapping the wine. This red wine is smooth and rich. I love it.'

The evening passed quietly. Ken took time out of painting to cook the pizza and make a salad. He even found some oven chips, which delighted John.

Most of the evening had already passed when John

began telling Ken something of his life story. Ken had often wondered about John's past but had never liked to press his friend on events that clearly troubled him. Maybe it was the wine that had loosened John's tongue; he had said very little about his life before, but now he seemed keen to share everything that had happened to him.

As a child, John had had everything that money could buy, but his dad died when he was nineteen, and two years later his mum also died. He inherited the house, he had money, but he was utterly bereft.

'I had no support, just when I was embarking on life... I meet a lot of people who live to make money, but it has no value for me. The house was too big for me so I sold it in the end, and bought the smaller one I have now. The difference in price paid for the studio in the garden.'

John paused. 'I would like to have married, but I don't think I could have coped with it when I was younger.' There was no self-pity in his voice, just honesty.

John had an uncle who had kept an eye on him when he was younger, but he didn't live nearby. 'Now my cousin invites me every Christmas, but it feels as if they see it as a duty.'

To Ken, it explained a lot about John. He was honoured that John felt able to share all this with him. 'You've done remarkably well for someone who was effectively orphaned. How many young people, left alone in the world at twenty-one, would have survived? Many would have taken a much more self-destructive approach to life.'

Ken could see the parallels with his own grief. 'It is hard to bear it when your loved ones die,' he said. 'I thought my life was over. I was about to put myself into a care home because I was so lonely. Life in the West is geared up to couples. Breaking my arm was the best thing that happened to me! It made me realise that it was okay to need help.'

John took another swig of his wine. 'I was too afraid of losing anyone else. It was only when I fell into depression that I sought help and had counselling. I wish I'd done it sooner.'

They both sat quietly for a while. Then John added simply, 'I use art to express my feelings.'

Ken smiled. 'That explains why your art is so rich in expression.'

John nodded in agreement. They sat in easy silence for a while.

The conversation left Ken feeling certain that their friendship group would remain close and support each other for as long as they all lived nearby.

John's thoughts appeared to have been running on similar lines. 'Sometimes I feel as if our friendship group is like the family that I don't really have,' John said. 'They're always there for each other.'

Ken nodded. 'It is a very special group.'

They went to bed soon after that. Ken didn't sleep straight away. He couldn't help imagining what his life would be like now if he had booked himself into a care home and given up on living.

He loved this life, even if he did miss Edith. He was grateful for the new friends in his life, but he also took pleasure in knowing that he had helped others too. And he'd learnt a lot about John today. It felt good to have friends.

He fell asleep content.

CHAPTER 30

John woke first on Monday morning and took a cup of coffee in to Ken.

'What time is it?' Ken said, sitting up and running his hand through his dishevelled hair.

'Nine o'clock.'

'Gosh, I hardly ever sleep in that late!' Ken said. 'Have you been awake long?'

'No, only as long as it takes the machine to produce the coffee.'

Over breakfast they discussed how they would spend the day.

'I was wondering if we could do something that didn't take too much energy, as we're clearly a bit tired today,' John suggested.

Ken went to the fridge and got out the pot of jam he'd bought the previous day, then put it on the table next to the rack of toast.

'Ooh, I'd forgotten about that,' John said.

'Had you got anywhere specific in mind?' Ken asked.

'Not really. We could get on a bus to one of the villages and sit sketching in a café.'

'Sounds good to me. Tomorrow will be a full day, with Jane taking us to art galleries and then us meeting up with the family in the evening.'

John reached across the table and handed Ken a leaflet.

‘Omodos is the village that they take tourists to,’ Ken said. ‘Looks as if it’s popular in the summer. I guess not everything will be open but that doesn’t matter.’

They found the bus stop and waited about twenty minutes before the bus arrived. The journey itself didn’t take as long as they had imagined.

They spent the day in cafés and wandering through the village and the surrounding countryside. John took the cobblestone path up to the stone-built monastery but Ken decided to stay in the village and rest. John returned having sampled a few of the local wines in the nearby wineries and having bought two bottles of his favourite.

It was beginning to get dark when they arrived back at the apartment. Ken found crisps and popcorn to keep them going until dinner was ready. Jane rang at quarter past ten and agreed to pick them up at ten in the morning – not too early, but giving them plenty of time to look around galleries.

‘We should go to bed at a reasonable time tonight,’ Ken said, setting the alarm on his phone for nine o’clock. ‘Tomorrow will be busy.’

***

Tuesday was a sunny day so they sat out on the balcony for breakfast. When Jane arrived, on the dot of ten o’clock, they were both ready. John tucked a larger notebook and pen into a day bag for this trip. Ken took his SLR camera and a small sketch pad.

‘I’ll start by showing you the public gallery,’ Jane said. ‘And then I’ll take you around some of the other galleries.’

Everywhere they went, Ken and John found plenty that took their interest. John was delighted to find iconic art. The variety intrigued them both; there were some old buildings, some new.

'On balance,' John said, 'the newer galleries appear to be purpose-built and are therefore more useful spaces.'

'I think I'd agree with that, although I love the architecture of the old ones,' Jane said.

They spent a wonderful day visiting the galleries and really appreciated Jane's knowledge of the art of the island.

On their way from the last gallery to the car, they stopped off at Jane's favourite café and sampled Greek coffee. 'It's a bit bitter, but I always take it with a little sugar –then it's called metrios – not sweet, not bitter.'

Ken shrugged. 'Ah well, we're here so we might as well give it a go.'

'Do you want to try it?' Jane asked John.

'Oh, go on then,' John said.

As she dropped them back at the apartment, Jane promised to pick them up for the evening meal at eight-thirty. 'We tend to eat later in Cyprus. In the summer it's too hot to eat early.'

'Have you decided where we're going?' Ken asked as they got out of the car.

'Yes. It's a seafront restaurant that's good value. I'll see you later,' she called.

John plonked himself down on the settee. 'I think I'll rest on the bed and read a book for a while.'

'Thank you for coming to meet everyone tonight. It means a lot,' Ken said.

'Well, it is a little nerve-wracking but it's just one

evening.'

'I think we're also meeting with Ben and Jane, and probably Michael, later in the week,' Ken said.

'That's not quite so scary as an entire family,' John laughed.

He took a cold beer from the fridge and went to his bedroom. Ken made a coffee and sat in the lounge. He was looking forward to seeing the family.

***

It was Ben who turned up to collect them at half past eight. 'Jane was hoping to get you but she wasn't quite ready,' he said.

It was only a short ride to the restaurant and all the family except Jane had arrived before them.

The family gathering in the busy seafront restaurant was an informal affair. It wasn't a posh or expensive place, but it was clearly popular with large local family groups.

The meal began relatively late and lasted almost until the restaurant shut, giving each family member plenty of time to talk to 'their Ken'.

After catching up with Ken a little, Simon took the opportunity to sit next to John and discuss art. Lucy commandeered her granddad next and chatted loudly, helping herself to far more than her share of wine, Ken noted with a smile. He liked Lucy – she didn't seem to be afraid to be herself – and from what he could see of her partner, Georgios, he fitted well into the family.

Michael held back to begin with, barely lifting his eyes from the table, but he soon relaxed a little. Anyway, Ken knew he would get another chance to talk with Michael when he met with him, Ben and Jane later in the week.

Ben ordered the food and wine, and by the time the waiter served it, Jane had arrived.

It was a sumptuous feast – far too much food even for their large group. The atmosphere remained relaxed as they all ate and drank. Ken glanced up at John a few times, and even he looked comfortable, despite having been a little nervous earlier on.

Jane had seated herself opposite Ken. 'Ben found it difficult when Mum died,' she said, early in their conversation. 'There was nothing he could do, and he does like things to be under control.'

'He always did like to know where he stood with things,' Ken said. 'Peter is fairly similar. He found it difficult when Edith died too.'

'Ben picked up on Peter's excessive anxiety over you,' Jane said. 'He got to the point where he almost didn't want to call Peter because it was always so negative. I actually wondered whether Peter was depressed at the time.'

'I think he was. It wasn't until the accident that we managed to talk about our feelings at all. You know what we're like,' he said with a smile, looking up at Jane.

She laughed. 'I do.'

'Michael seems quiet,' Ken said.

'He's still finding his feet in life. He's a good musician. I hope he can get into music college in Manchester, but I'll worry about him being so far away from us.

'He can come and visit me anytime he likes, and I'm sure that Meg would love to see him... and Peter too.'

'That would be good. It puts my mind at rest to know

he could go to family,' Jane said.

At the end of the meal, when they'd finished the coffee, Ben called the waiter over to ask for the bill, and Ken tried to get them to bring it to him. But when the bill arrived, the waiter gave it to Ben, who sported an expression of victory.

'Then let me pay half,' Ken suggested.

'Stop arguing with him,' Lucy said in a half-drunken slur. 'You can't win.'

Ken raised his hands in surrender. 'Alright, thank you.'

Ben shook his head from side to side. 'If Lucy had to pay for her own wine she'd be broke by now.'

Lucy raised her almost empty glass to him. 'Thanks, Dad,' she said. 'I've never seen the point of paying for something that someone else would cover for me.'

Lucy's partner, Georgios nodded. 'I would say that's true,' he laughed.

Ken joined in the laughter.

It had been a lovely evening catching up with each other; as they gathered up their belongings before leaving, even John declared that he had enjoyed it.

In the car on the way back to the flat, Ken was quiet, reflecting on how proud he was of the way his family had turned out. They cared about each other. Edith would have been proud of them too. He had seen the joy and excitement that each of them had for their work and for each other, and the desire to find more of that in his life again was welling up in him. He knew he was fortunate already, though, in that he had a family who loved him, a group of good friends, and a hobby that he not only loved but from which he was also beginning to make money.

'I've been thinking,' Ken said to John once they were

back at the flat. 'My family don't need me as much as they used to. Of late I've been more dependent on them than they are on me. I don't really know how to explain it but I feel as if I need a new project, maybe even more than my painting – something to get my teeth into.'

John sat for quite a while without replying, staring into space. He sighed before he spoke.

'I've been a bit afraid to ask this,' he said, before taking a deep breath, 'but I've been wondering if you wanted to come in with me to run an art studio and exhibition centre. Maybe create something unique in our area?'

Ken swallowed hard. John was such an accomplished artist and so experienced at running exhibitions that he felt a bit out of his depth. 'I'm not sure what I could offer. You seem to know exactly what you're doing.'

John laughed. 'I may have more experience but you're much better with people. You enjoyed doing your workshop, whereas I hate it. People have asked me when you're doing one again.'

Ken raised his eyebrows in surprise. 'Really! I must admit that was the bit I enjoyed most.'

'I'd like Helen to be involved too because her sculptures add a new dimension, and her workshop was very popular,' John added.

Ken could hardly believe it. The timing was perfect.

'People enjoyed your workshop too,' Ken said.

'That's true, but I hated every minute of it. I love teaching painting one to one, but workshops overwhelm me. You ran yours as if you'd been doing them all your life.'

Ken looked at John with kindness. The smile reached the wrinkles around his eyes. 'I'd love to help – if you think

I can.'

'That's brilliant,' John said. 'I can't decide whether to use the studio at the back of my house or find a bigger building somewhere else.'

They discussed the possibility of a bigger place, but Ken wasn't convinced. 'I think we could be rattling around in a big place, and then it becomes cold and formal. We could start in your studio and see how it goes?'

John agreed, and Ken put on the kettle. 'I think I'll have a hot chocolate and go to bed. Do you think tomorrow should be a painting-on-the-beach kind of day?'

'Yes,' John said, 'as long as it's warm enough.'

Ken couldn't sleep straight away. He imagined himself leading workshops, taking flyers out to shops, writing articles for the local paper, exhibiting his own work. This was a life he would never have thought possible; even in his dreams life never got this interesting.

He fell asleep thinking about Edith, imagining her encouraging him. 'Yes, Ken,' she would say, 'of course you can do it.'

CHAPTER 31

They both woke up late on Wednesday. Ken crawled out of bed, stretched and staggered into the lounge. He heard John stir but his friend didn't appear right away.

When John did eventually surface, Ken laughed at the state of him. 'How much wine did you drink last night?' he asked.

John shook his head. 'I don't even know. Lucy did top up my glass at least once... but I feel okay.'

'You should take a look in the mirror,' Ken said.

'I think I'll have a coffee and a shower and *then* take a look,' John said as he slumped down in the corner of the settee.

By the time John was ready to set off it was half past eleven and they were ready for another coffee.

'I reckon we should go down the road to the little café that we liked so much,' Ken said.

John jumped at the chance. 'That sounds great. We could have an early light lunch back here and spend the afternoon painting or sketching on the beach.'

As they sat in the café, John was concentrating on something outside the window. 'I have to sketch that view,' he said. His face was animated and his voice a little excitable. 'I think it's the faded pastel colours of the curtains and the bright colours of the materials and ceramics on the market stalls – the contrast is stunning.'

While John sketched, Ken watched a young family. It didn't seem all that long ago that his own children had been like that... and then his grandchildren, and now his great-grandchildren. *Wherever has all the time gone?* he wondered.

They wandered back to the apartment for a leisurely lunch. It was warm enough today to sit on the balcony and watch the world go by as they ate and chatted.

Then they packed a bag each of painting equipment and set off for the beach.

'I can't wait to set up my easel and paint,' Ken said. 'I love to paint freehand, no sketching or planning, just painting what I see and feel.'

'I always sketch first,' John said. 'It must give a feeling of freedom to just sit down and paint.'

Ken shrugged. 'Well, give it a go. I think we've both found that trying new things is good for us.'

They found a low wall at the top of the beach by the road and set up in front of it. Each had a small beach chair and an easel.

'I'm glad we're close to that ice cream booth,' Ken said.

'Me too,' John replied. 'I fancy strawberry and banana. I hope they have them.'

'We sound like two children. I hope we have time for a paddle.'

John couldn't stop laughing. 'That's the sort of thing that I think I missed out on most by not having children. I never got a chance to build sandcastles or sand cars without looking ridiculous.'

John set about painting without sketching and was surprised at what he produced. 'I still think I'm better sketching it lightly first, but I have to admit that I rather enjoyed trying without.'

'I like it. It reflects the freedom you felt in doing it. The lines flow well,' Ken said.

Two hours later Ken had an idea. 'Why don't I go and buy two buckets and spades and we make a sandcastle? We can look daft together.'

John laughed. 'Yes, let's do it. Nobody here knows us anyway.'

Ken crossed the road, selected his buckets and two long-handled spades and then caught sight of some little paper flags. He smiled to himself. *I haven't seen these in years,* he thought. He picked up a pack and took them with the buckets and spades to the assistant.

'Are you on holiday with your family?' she asked him.

'Some of my family live here,' he replied.

'You'll probably get stuck with making the sandcastles,' the assistant said.

'I'm sure I will,' he said, with a sly smile.

They made a detailed sandcastle, stood back to admire it, and took a photo. Ken grinned. He could see the freedom it was creating in John – as if he had accessed his inner child.

***

They had planned Thursday as their cultural day. Neither of them was enthusiastic about it, but they decided that while they were here it would be good to appreciate some of the history of the place. They would visit the castle and the Cyprus Medieval Museum.

'We needn't stay long,' Ken laughed.

It turned out to be a relaxing day, and once they had exhausted their interest in the museum and the castle they took a short walk to the harbour.

'I love harbours,' Ken said. 'They always remind me of Edith. We often used to sit on the wall of the harbour at Ryde, on the Isle of Wight.'

'They are busy but peaceful. I love that,' John replied. 'I'm going to make a few sketches while we're there.'

It took them less than ten minutes to walk to the harbour. The many new apartments overshadowed the marina. Ken's disappointment was evident. 'This is more upmarket than I'd expected.' He sighed.

John sighed too, and sat down on a bench to take in the view. 'It's still beautiful. Imagine if you lived in an apartment that overlooked the water like that.' He stretched out his legs, crossed his feet and clasped his hands behind his neck. 'Perhaps I could live here.'

'Then I guess you'd need a yacht to keep up with the neighbours,' Ken laughed.

'Stop mocking and take a photo of that big yacht there for me,' John said as he took out his notebook and began sketching once more. 'Anyway, I don't think I'd like sailing.'

'I'm not sure you'd have to sail it,' Ken said, 'just keep it as a status symbol.'

'I bet some of these penthouses cost a fortune.' John moved closer to the yacht to take a closer look.

Ken drew closer too. 'Do you want me to take some close-ups?' He didn't wait for an answer before starting.

'These big yachts look majestic. I love drawing them. I've never tried painting one, though. I'm going to try to paint this one when we get home.' John looked at it all misty-eyed.

'I do believe you are falling in love,' Ken said with a laugh.

'Well, she is my type,' John said.

For the next little while they were quiet. While John continued with his sketch, Ken wandered along the marina. He stopped and stared out across the water, softly talking to Edith, remembering times they had spent together.

I wish you could be with me now, he whispered to the wind. *I hope you can see me and would be proud of me. I miss you, so badly at times that my heart aches, but I have dreams and I'm sure you would want me to fulfil them.*

He hoped in his heart that his words reached her. He wiped away tears with the back of his hand and returned to see how John was getting on.

'Your sketches are amazing!' he told his friend. 'You could sell them.'

John smiled and nodded gently. 'Thank you.' Then he put his book away. 'I fancy a beer.'

'Good idea, let's go and find one!'

They spent the rest of the day in an equally leisurely manner and returned to the apartment quite early. It was still warm, so they sat out on the balcony sipping wine, watching the shadows that toyed with the people in the street below as the sun began to set. The sun hugged the sea way out to the west in a fiery glow.

***

That evening Jane picked them up for a much smaller

family gathering, a kind of farewell dinner. 'This will be quieter,' she said. 'It gets quite noisy when everyone is together. And this is a different kind of restaurant. This is Ben's choice.'

Ken studied her. When she dressed up and put her hair up, as she had tonight, she was still as elegant as she'd ever been.

Ben and Michael were already there when they arrived. Ken looked around. The room had four pillars and warm red-and-gold brocade curtains. Each table was carefully laid with linen tablecloths and serviettes. There were flowers in an alcove that matched the decor. This was much more the style he would expect of Ben.

When Ken mentioned it, Ben laughed. 'You're right, but we wouldn't bring the whole family here. It's too expensive. They drink more when I'm paying.'

'Ah yes,' Ken said. 'That brings back memories of when meals were always on me.'

Ben laughed. 'I'm sure it does.'

Once the food arrived, Jane engaged John in conversation and Ken and Ben reminisced, while Michael focused on his meal.

'Mum was such a soft touch,' Ben said after a while. 'We were her life.'

Ken noticed his son was holding back tears. He could feel his pain; he reached out a hand and placed it on his arm. Physical distance had caused an emotional separation – he felt now the connection they had lost, and a new warmth coursed through him. *Yes, I need a new challenge, but I need my family too – and they still need me.*

'At times like this I miss you so,' Ben said. 'I felt so

useless here – then dashing over for the funeral and having to get back so quickly for work. I blocked out much of what I felt.'

'We all did,' Ken said. 'It was impossible to imagine life without your mum.'

'In my better moments I know that her influence is everywhere – we are who we are because she gave her life to all of us,' Ben said. 'I remember her telling me once that all she wanted was to give us better opportunities than she had.'

Ken nodded. 'And she did. She was very proud of you both.'

While Ben collected himself, Ken spoke quietly to Michael.

'I'm told you want to come to Manchester to study music,' Ken said.

'Yes, that's right,' Michael replied.

'Which is your first instrument?'

'Cello,' Michael said, 'and I play violin too. I like the cello best, because of its mellow tone.'

'Your cousin Meg used to play the violin, but I think she's given it up now. I never hear about it.'

Ken looked at Michael with fondness. 'When you come over to England you must come and stay with me for a few days. Meg would love to see you again. She was disappointed not to be able to come to Cyprus.'

'I'd like that,' Michael said. 'I wanted to ask you if you're okay now, Granddad?'

Ken looked pensive and ran his finger around the top of his liqueur glass, which made a high-pitched sound. He cocked his head on one side as he spoke. 'I still have days when something triggers a little sorrow, but it isn't as raw as it was. I was completely lost to start with, but reconnecting with my painting has helped a lot.'

Michael stared at the table. 'I find that my music takes me into another dimension where stress seems to fade. It soothes and calms me, like a massage for the mind.'

His granddad nodded; he understood.

At the end of the evening, Ken felt pride in his family once more as each of them hugged him and kissed him goodbye, and then did the same for John.

Michael lingered. 'I could come round with my cello tomorrow if you'd like to hear me play it. About five-thirty.'

'That's a deal. I'll see you tomorrow,' Ken said.

After she had dropped them off outside the apartment building, Jane called out of the car window. 'I'll be here on Saturday to collect you at about ten o'clock. It'll take a while to get to the airport and you need to be there quite early.'

'Thank you,' Ken called back, and Jane drove off.

'You're so lucky,' John said. 'You have such a lovely family.'

It gave Ken pause for thought as he lay in bed. He had taken them all for granted; now he was beginning to appreciate them.

CHAPTER 32

For their final full day in Cyprus, Ken and John had agreed to find a pottery where they could see the pots being painted. The colours had fascinated John. Ben had told them that there were a few potteries near the foot of the Troodos Mountains.

Ken woke early that morning and crept into the lounge so as not to wake John. His mind was working overtime. He poured orange juice and quietly opened the balcony door. A mist hovered over the sea, which gave the place a magical air. It felt like a dream. In fact, the whole trip had felt like a dream.

Ken smiled to himself. Not long ago he had thought he was in a nightmare. He had no idea how he had survived those early days after Edith died.

He shook off regret and pulled his dressing gown tightly around himself; it wasn't warm yet. He went back inside and shut the door.

He got out his camera and flicked through all the photos he'd taken. It had been wonderful to have time to devote entirely to his artwork. *The strange thing is,* he thought, *that I not only enjoy the time I spend on art, but I meet other people too, and I've been able to help them. Maybe when we live our dream it creates an environment that encourages others to find their dreams too.*

Ken had already set the table for breakfast when John

woke. The beaming smile on John's face made it worth the effort.

'Wow!' John said when he appeared.

Ken laughed. 'I woke early and realised that, apart from tomorrow, when everything will be a bit rushed, this will be our last breakfast of the holiday. I thought it would be nice for it to be a bit special.'

Ken had begun poaching eggs to go with the carefully arranged smoked salmon and fresh fruit in glass dishes, and since John had woken up he'd also put the coffee machine on.

John sat down at the table. 'This is lovely.'

It wasn't until Ken sat down that John spoke again. 'Until I met you, I had never been invited to a party. I didn't want to tell anyone because it made me look a bit of a sad case, but your Christmas party was the first time I had ever felt really included. It made me feel as if I belonged somewhere. Every single person accepted me.'

John didn't look up and Ken found it difficult to know what to say. He opened his mouth twice to answer but was lost for words.

Eventually he found what he wanted to say. 'Until I felt alone and excluded, it never occurred to me how painful that was.' He thought a moment. 'We all sit in our comfortable little families and forget that there is a world outside... especially at Christmas.'

'Well, you've made up for it now,' John said.

Ken sighed. 'Thank you.'

John picked up the knife and fork. 'Well, let's not allow this to get cold after all your work!'

When they'd finished, Ken glanced up at the wall clock.

'I don't think I've ever taken this long to have breakfast.'

John smiled. 'Nor me. No rush though, is there?'

Ken shook his head. 'Absolutely not.'

By the time they were ready to leave it was twenty to twelve. Ken shrugged. 'Ah well, we'll just wander down to the taxi rank and see how the timing works out.'

'Good idea,' John replied.

The taxi driver was chatty and recommended a specific pottery to them. 'You can watch the painting there, although I don't think you can see them make the pots.'

The pottery painting was stunning and John talked to the artist at great length while Ken wandered through the shop taking pictures.

'I absolutely love this,' John said, pointing out a large ceramic pot decorated in sunny colours. It would look amazing on my patio.'

'I'd like to see you get that on the plane!' Ken laughed.

After a late lunch in a nearby café, they waited a little while for a taxi and returned to the apartment in plenty of time for Michael's visit.

'I'll cook for tonight,' John said. 'I'll do a chicken curry and use up some of the fresh vegetables that Jane left for us.'

'Thank you,' Ken said. 'It's probably best if we do most of the packing and clearing up this evening and get a reasonably early night.'

He poured two beers and took one to John, who was now standing on the balcony looking longingly out to sea.

Michael arrived on time to the minute, so much so that Ken wondered whether he'd been standing outside waiting until it was exactly five-thirty. He looked nervous.

'Come in,' Ken said. 'Would you like a drink – hot or

cold, we have most things, thanks to your mum.'

'I'd love a coffee,' Michael said. 'Mum's thoughtful like that but does tend to go a bit overboard.'

'I'll put the pods in the coffee machine,' John offered. 'I've been looking forward to hearing you play, Michael. I've always loved the cello. It has such a mellow, melancholic sound.'

Michael's shoulders relaxed a little. He put the cello case down on the floor and sat on the settee with his granddad. 'I'm so pleased you came to visit. I would have been a bit nervous of coming to see you and Peter and his family all alone while I'm in England, but I'll be less anxious now.'

John served the coffee and offered Michael food. 'I'd better not,' Michael replied. 'Mum will have cooked for me.'

'Of course,' said John, and he sat opposite Michael in the reclining chair. 'I think it's brave of you to go from living at home to crossing the world in order to study music.'

'It's just something I have to do if I want to go to one of the best places to study. I'd like to go to the Royal Northern College of Music in Manchester.'

'Well, it wouldn't take you too long to get to us from there,' John said. 'It would be lovely if you had time to meet our little group of friends too. Maybe you could play for us.'

'Oh, Dora would love that!' Ken exclaimed.

John talked to Michael about how he became interested in music, what drew him to the cello, what other instruments he played, and why Manchester, and Ken sat back for the most part and watched, only intervening every now and again to ask a question of his own. For some reason John and Michael got on really well.

Once they'd finished the coffee Ken nodded towards the cello. 'So are you going to play it for us?'

Michael jumped up enthusiastically. He appeared encouraged, animated by his conversation with John.

Ken smiled. On a one-to-one basis John was brilliant with people; he just wasn't comfortable in larger groups.

Michael took out the cello and checked the tuning before running through a couple of scales. 'I'm going to play you two pieces by Adam Hurst. The first is called "Sparrow", and the second is called "Desolation". Then I'm going to play you "Hallelujah" by Leonard Cohen.'

The fingers of his left hand moved with ease and strength around the fret board as the bow glided smoothly across the strings in slow, measured movements. Michael appeared to be unaware of Ken and John as he focused on the music. He made it look easy.

Ken gave voice to his enthusiasm for the performance. 'You must play very well to be that fluent and at the same time so expressive,' he said.

Michael's response was modest. 'I've heard a lot better,' he said, smiling.

'Well, I go to quite a few classical concerts and it sounds excellent to me,' John insisted.

'Adam Hurst is my favourite cellist,' Michael said. 'I love his compositions. His music moves me to tears. It's so haunting and magical. "Desolation" makes me think of the faces on people in refugee camps. It's beautiful but also profoundly disturbing.'

Ken studied him. Michael's sensitivity connected with

something in himself.

'I listened to a Croatian cellist on YouTube a little while ago. I can't remember how I came across him but he was amazing,' John said.

'Luka Šulić?' Michael asked. 'I would love to hear him live. He does tours with another Croatian cellist.'

They chatted for a little while longer until Michael started glancing at his mobile phone.

'Oh, don't let us keep you from whatever you're doing,' John said. 'We're delighted you came to play for us and hope to see you when you come to England.'

Michael packed the cello into the bag, put on his black fleece and set off.

'I'm glad I've renewed my connection with him,' Ken said. 'Like he said, that will make it easier for him to come and visit the family if he comes to Manchester.'

'True,' John said. 'Now... if I can get out of this chair, I'll cook dinner.'

As Ken sat reading, John received a message on his phone. 'Oh wow! Wait till you hear this. Dora has just signed up for a catering course at the local college. She sounds extremely excited. What shall I say?'

'Er, what about congratulations?' Ken replied.

She replied instantly. *Wouldn't have done it without you all.*

John turned to Ken. 'Who would have thought that our group of oldies could have started to live new lives and do something useful?'

Ken could see tears in John's eyes.

'I was always confident enough to run exhibitions,' John said, 'but doing it with other people has brought more customers – you're better with groups of people, and Helen is good at advertising. Working with others is definitely more fun.'

A thought suddenly struck Ken. *Interesting that Dora and John keep in touch away from the group...* But he kept his musings to himself.

Ken got up and stared out to sea again. In some ways it felt like a long time now since Edith had died. So much had happened and he had achieved so much. But in other ways it felt as if it was only yesterday that he had last been with her. *Memories are strange, timeless things,* he thought.

He felt pleased that, out of his loss and pain and injury, a group of people had come together, helped each other and given each other confidence to move forward.

He gazed out at the night-time view for the last time. He would miss this, but he was happy to be going home too.

CHAPTER 33

After a hectic morning of washing-up, stripping beds and cleaning, Ken and John said their goodbyes and headed for the airport, this time with Jane at the wheel of the white Mercedes.

The airport didn't seem so strange to John second time around. Things were all a little disorganised, but they eventually got through security and into departures, and after wandering round the shops a few times and perusing the duty-free shop, they finally boarded their plane home.

Peter was there to meet them at Heathrow. As they left the airport, the grey gloom hit Ken. 'Gosh, I'm going to miss the sunshine,' he said.

'I take it you had wonderful weather then?' Peter replied.

'It was fantastic,' John said.

'You should take the opportunity to go out and utilise that flat sometime, Peter,' Ken said. 'It has the most amazing view over the sea.'

They enthused about the cathedral, the family dinner, Michael coming over, the pottery, and the delightful food. Ken smiled as Peter listened to their eager descriptions of all that they had done, asking appropriate questions from time to time.

When he eventually dropped Ken off at home, Peter made sure that he had everything he needed and left quickly. With his final words he had invited his dad to Sunday dinner the next day. Ken couldn't wait to tell the family all about the visit, especially Meg.

The quietness of the bungalow was stark after all the company and activity, it was a little cold but Ken put the gas fire on and the lounge soon warmed up.

***

The next day, Ken rang Eric to arrange to meet.

'I did miss our little get-together last week,' Eric said, 'but I went to the gym anyway, and Helen and I went to lunch together after the workout. I can't wait to meet and hear what you got up to, though, and to see what artwork you've done.'

Round at Peter's, it was almost like a dream to Ken, a bit surreal, as he told the family his tales of all that had happened in Cyprus and talked about Ben, Jane and the grandkids.

Meg expressed her disappointment at missing out on the visit. 'I do wish I could have seen them all,' she said.

Ken's face brightened. 'Well, if I can do it, so can you!' he said. 'Just book it and go. I wish I'd gone more before.'

He told the family about his conversation with Michael, too. 'He played the cello for us,' Ken said, exuding excitement. 'I hope he does come over to Manchester. It would be lovely for everyone to meet him again now he's so much more of his own person... I'm so proud of you all,' he added, braving a glance at Peter. The smile on Peter's face and his nod of acknowledgement warmed Ken's heart.

Back at his bungalow, Ken looked at the family photos

on the board that Meg had helped him put together. 'I *am* proud of them all,' he said to a photo of Edith, 'and I know you would be too.'

It's all about balance, he thought, smiling to himself. *I have room in my heart and my life for projects and art and for family and friends too.*

It had been good to go away. He felt as if he was beginning to make sense of things.

He brought the easel into the lounge ready to begin painting again. He couldn't wait to get going and build on some of the artwork he had begun while he was away. He was looking forward to collaborating again with John and Helen on exhibitions and workshops.

***

Ken and John were oblivious to the events of the previous week as they arrived at the community centre for the art group on Monday, excited to share their experiences of Cyprus.

A wall of despondency met them, bursting their enthusiasm. Ken's eyes flicked from one gloomy face to another. He glanced up briefly at John, who merely shrugged, sporting a puzzled expression.

'What's happened?' Ken asked.

A forlorn look crossed Peggy's face. 'I've run this art club for years but now it looks as if it has come to an end. They're closing the community centre down.'

Peggy barely looked up as Ken, briefly stunned, took a moment to reply.

Eventually he asked, 'Did they say why?'

'It needs too much work to get it into a fit state to be more widely used, and anyway they can't afford to pay any staff. Apart from Ellie, the part-time worker, everyone who works here is a volunteer, and two of them have just left. I was warned a few months back that they were considering it but I didn't think they would actually do it. There's nothing else on this estate.'

Ken plonked himself down in a chair and sighed. This was really coming back down to earth with a bump. 'How soon?' he asked.

'There's not enough funding now. It's running at a loss but they'll keep it open until June,' she replied.

John suddenly took notice. 'What! That's only a few months away. Where will we go? What do they expect us to do?'

Peggy said nothing initially, merely shrugged. Eventually she replied, a little shakily, Ken thought. 'Almost every one of us has been coming here for years and there's nowhere else nearby that we could meet.' She stared at the ground. 'I just don't know what to do.'

Ken was deep in thought. 'Who currently uses the centre?' he asked, looking at Peggy.

She shook her head. 'I'm told that, on a regular basis, it's only us and a group of young people with learning disabilities. It's occasionally used by other people for one-off events – children's parties and that sort of thing.'

John paced the room. 'Oh,' he said with heavy sarcasm, almost angry, 'nobody who matters, then.'

Ken still had a faraway look in his eye, his mind ticking over. 'Then I think we could do better,' he said suddenly.

The entire group looked at him, puzzled.

'We could run it better,' he repeated, full of enthusiasm now. 'Tomorrow I'm seeing my friend Eric, who used to be a project manager. He also knows a lot of people. I'm going to have a chat to him about it. With a bit of TLC this place has potential.'

Peggy looked doubtful. 'That would be a lot of work... and look at it.' She shrugged. 'It hasn't had much done to it for years. The last time it was even decorated the old youth club did it... and it looks like it. Even the youth club itself has gone now. Let's face it, it's finished. We'll have to find somewhere else to meet.'

'For the time being we can meet in my studio,' John said. 'It will take a long while to set up the community centre again, even if we *can* eventually run it ourselves.'

Peggy almost cried at this offer. 'Oh, thank you, John!'

Ken's eyes were suddenly wide open. 'Do you realise, John, that this is also the answer to our need for a place to exhibit and to run workshops?'

John's mouth fell open. 'You're right!'

***

The next day, Ken met up with Eric. Before they got to the pressing business of the fate of the community centre, Ken shared with his friend some of his experiences of Cyprus – Eric couldn't wait to hear about Ken's exploits. Ken described the quaint little cafés to him, adding, 'and the pastries are to die for.'

'Oh gosh,' Eric said, 'now I'm going to have to order cake with my coffee so I don't feel left out.'

Ken laughed.

‘I got your postcard on Friday,’ Eric said. ‘Thank you.’

Ken described his experience at the harbour that was pictured on the card he’d sent, explaining to Eric just what it meant to him, along with his memories of Edith.

‘I hope I get to see some of the painting you did while you were there.’

‘Oh yes,’ Ken replied. ‘Next week, if you get a taxi over to mine, I can show you everything I’ve done and all that I’m planning.’

‘I’d like that,’ Eric said, his smile reaching his eyes.

‘I’m glad you went to the gym anyway – and met up with Helen,’ Ken said.

‘Me too,’ Eric replied. ‘She says that the exhibition has given her a new lease of life with her sculptures. She can see a way to be able to sell them now. She’s already started on the piece that businessman commissioned.’

‘Wow, that’s keen. I’d love to see how that’s coming on.’

Eric took out his phone. ‘Well, I can show you how far she’d got with it when we met up ’cause she sent me a picture on WhatsApp.’ He scrolled through his messages. ‘Here,’ he said, handing the phone to Ken.

‘Wow... I’m going to have to get in touch with him again too, about the painting,’ Ken said. ‘I promised him I’d get started on it as soon as I returned from Cyprus.’

Once the coffee and cake arrived, Ken broached the subject of the community centre.

‘Well,’ Eric responded, ‘I haven’t been in that community centre for years, but it seems to me that it’s central to the life of the community, just as its name suggests, and for that reason alone it would be beneficial to try. There must be loads more groups out there who would like to use it.'

Ken couldn't contain his excitement. 'It has a little café. It would be great to see it used in the area. There are a lot of older people and the Dalton estate itself has a lot of poverty. I think the area needs the centre but I think we could do it better than the parish council, just because we haven't got the constraints that they have.'

He took out the last notebook he'd been using while he was in Cyprus, and jotted down ideas from the café in which they now sat. 'Simple, but with a touch of class,' he said eventually. 'Not too many cloths and things to clean.'

'I imagine if we could make it a success they'd be delighted,' Eric said. 'Let's meet up again with our whole social group and gather ideas.'

'That way we can see what support we've got from our group before we start looking further afield,' Ken said. 'I'm sure the local community would help us – especially if they think we're going to create something useful to everyone. It's structurally sound but the decor is ugly.'

Eric eyed the cakes again. Ken laughed at him.

'I need the calories in order to think!' Eric protested.

Eric was in his element, and soon he'd arranged a meeting with a group of their friends for the next week. There were seven of them in total – Ken, Eric, John and Peggy were joined by Dora, Vi and Helen.

The meeting was held in Ken's house, and Dora had brought cake to go with Ken's tea and coffee – yet more calories to help them think, Eric quipped.

Dora's friend Vi, who had come to the Christmas party with her, became excited when Ken began to talk about setting up a café.

'I used to run a café. I wouldn't want to work full-time but I'd love to work a couple of days, and I know how to set one up.'

Ken clapped his hands in delight. 'That would probably be enough to start with. It might be better to begin slowly.'

'And while I'm doing my catering course I can get practice by helping her,' Dora said, excited.

'I spoke on the phone to Harry Walsh from the parish council,' said Eric. 'He told me that if they did grant us permission, the parish council would probably want to see progress after six months.'

John laughed. 'Well, an improvement on nothing isn't hard to achieve, is it!'

His joke served to lighten the atmosphere, which up to that point had been a little intense.

Once the group had got some idea of what they wanted to achieve, Eric arranged for him and Ken to meet with Harry from the parish council.

***

At the meeting, they were informed that any agreement would need to be put to a committee but that the council was hopeful they could allow them to run the centre. The group would need to put together a business plan, which Eric thought would be easy enough. They would also need someone with the right experience if they wanted to open the café to the public.

Things moved fast at the start. Peggy committed the art group to paying for the room each week once the hall was reopened. The learning disabilities group were delighted, and their leader even suggested that some of the young people and their families might be able to help with sprucing up the hall.

It transpired that quite a few of the young people had worked in cafés, and Ken thought that it would be a great idea to give them further experience once the café was up and running. 'Maybe even unemployed local youth too,' Ken suggested.

His next idea was for him and John to run an art exhibition, with the proceeds going to the centre.

Eric, meanwhile, had begun a crowdfunding appeal and was advertising on social media as well as in the local paper. The adverts mentioned their need for skilled volunteers to help with refurbishing the centre.

'Also,' he said to Ken when they next met up, 'Martin, my next-door neighbour who was so good to me when my wife died, is a plumber. He says he'll check out all the plumbing and is happy to plumb in a new kitchen.'

Ken couldn't believe their good fortune. 'I guess that's what happens when we all work together.'

When Meg arrived at her granddad's house that evening, she caught him wiping away tears as he opened the door to her.

'Are you okay, Granddad?' she asked.

He looked into her eyes. 'I will be. I was just thinking how exciting all this would have been for your grandma.'

Ken went through to the lounge, with Meg following, and sat down on the settee.

Meg thought a moment. 'I imagine that you would never have done all this if Grandma was still around.' She sat down beside him.

‘I’d give it up in a flash to have her back,’ he said with a sigh. ‘I couldn’t have come this far without the support of the family.’

‘It’s another phase of your life – and I’m proud of the way you’ve turned it around.’

‘It’s okay. I won’t give up. I just still miss her sometimes.’

‘That’s understandable,’ she said. ‘That was a different age! So…’ She linked his arm and gave it a squeeze. ‘Tell me how far your plans have got.’

CHAPTER 34

The wheels of the parish council turned more slowly than those of the group, who were determined to make their plans work.

'Never underestimate the power of a group of friends with vision – however old,' Ken said to his granddaughter when she called in on him next.

'This time you may have just bitten off more than you can chew,' Meg said.

A broad grin crossed Ken's face. 'I'm not doing it alone.'

She pursed her lips and raised her eyebrows.

He reached out and laid his hand on her arm. 'I know we look like a lot of old folks, drinking our coffees and meals with wine, and whiling away our days, but every one of us has skills, and that community centre should belong to the people of the Dalton estate. You and I have money and can go to other places for entertainment, but many people can't.' He sat back.

She raised a hand in front of her defensively, eyes and mouth wide open. 'Wow! Granddad, I had no idea you had that in you – but that centre has never really served the community since they closed down the youth club.'

He looked her in the eye. 'You're right, and that is why we think we can do a better job. The parish council has too many financial constraints to run it well – and not enough staff. We have people who have run businesses, people with catering qualifications, and skilled tradesmen. It's possibly the most exciting project I've ever been involved in.'

She nodded gently to herself. 'Then I'm pleased for you, Granddad, and for the sake of the community I hope you succeed.'

***

When they eventually got the go-ahead from the parish council Ken almost went into meltdown. It was only a basic agreement in principle, but it was a good start.

'What have we done?' he exclaimed to Eric the next time they chatted in the café. It was just two days after he had been informed of the decision. 'This is so outside of my comfort zone. Can we really do this, do you think?'

Eric looked miles away; he was thinking something he wasn't sharing. When Ken repeated his concerns, Eric looked up.

'Don't go getting cold feet on me,' he said with a laugh. 'It will be a fairly long process and we'll have to take it one step at a time. We won't be reopening the centre any time soon.'

Ken looked anxious. 'We only started because we lost our meeting place for the art group,' he sighed.

'Exactly – think how few places there are for people to meet up in the area. That whole estate stretches almost from your place right over to mine, and yet there is nothing there except one small shop. It's exciting to be able to provide a community resource.'

'We have to succeed,' Ken said. 'The community needs this place.'

Eric shrugged. 'And it would be worse to have the idea and never try. Let's get as many of our group as possible together next Saturday, and invite the local community, and then arrange to meet with Harry Walsh again after that.'

Ken could see why Eric had been such an encouragement to him when they had been in hospital together; nothing appeared to daunt him. It was actually not very long that they had known each other, but their friendship, the first that he'd made since losing Edith, was as strong as ever, and when they chatted it felt as if they had known each other for a very long time.

Ken looked up at Eric with pleading eyes. 'Will you chair the meeting?'

Eric looked excited. 'Are you sure? Don't *you* want to?'

Ken shook his head. 'You'd be much better at it than me. Your belief in what we are doing is self-evident, and that matters.'

They agreed to share out the list of people to invite to the Saturday meeting and ring half each. They would need to let the people on the estate know too, and they had invitations for some of the business owners from the nearby business park and anyone else who might be able to help in any way.

'I'll ring Helen now to see if we can use the events room at her sheltered accommodation,' Ken said.

'Good idea,' Eric replied.

They had another cup of coffee while they waited for Helen to ring back.

'We're on!' Helen said. 'Wow, this is exciting. It's booked for one-thirty.' Her voice was so loud and excited that Eric could hear what she said from the other side of the table.

'That's great,' Ken said. 'The meeting will start at two o'clock.'

Ken and Eric met up the next day to discuss what recommendations they would put to the group and what resources they would need. Ken stared, agog, at Eric's notebook. It contained a vast list of resources and services they would need – everything from leaflets to a sink to someone to plumb it in, and kitchen equipment, to say nothing of volunteers for painting, cleaning and social media duties. They would also need some staff to run the centre, and board members with particular skills.

They knew that there was even more that they needed to consider, but they had to put together as much as they could for now, ready for the next meeting, in order to get things rolling.

'I'll put together a PowerPoint presentation. Give me a call if you think of anything else you want included,' said Eric.

Ken nodded slowly to himself. 'And that is why you're better to be doing this than me.'

***

Ken and Eric arrived early the following Saturday and were met by Beth, who had already laid out chairs, along with a table at the front of the room for the laptop. Eric and Ken were glad of the help; Eric still had difficulty walking far and Ken couldn't carry anything too heavy yet.

Beth had also set out cups and saucers and arranged for

one of the more able residents to serve tea as people arrived. Dora arrived soon afterwards with chocolate brownies.

The attendees arrived in dribs and drabs and quickly formed small groups, talking with great excitement about the community centre. For those who lived on the estate, this seemed like their only chance to save the centre – a place where they hoped they could continue to have children's parties at a rate they could afford, attend support groups and hobby groups, and generally strengthen their community in all sorts of ways.

For those in business, there was the potential to influence the refurbishment to contain a conference room that would complement the stretched facilities at the business park.

At two o'clock, Eric stood up to begin.

'We'll have time for discussion after each section. The more ideas we have at this stage the better, so don't be afraid to share any thoughts you have.'

He outlined their plans and asked everyone to share the Facebook page to recruit followers. 'Especially those who live on the estate,' he added. 'We'll be having leaflets printed, too, and they'll be delivered to the whole of the Dalton estate.'

'It would be great if we could get a youth club going again,' Helen said.

'I agree with you,' Ken said. 'There's nothing around here for them.'

Eric acknowledged their contributions and replied, 'I think we need to start by improving the facilities.'

Dora raised a hand. 'I reckon that opening up the café will generate interest, even if it can only be opened for a few hours a week. There's not a single coffee shop on the estate.'

Ideas were mooted throughout the meeting, with plenty of interaction from those present. One of the businessmen offered to donate to the project if a room was refurbished to a standard that meant they could use it as a conference room.

'Yes,' another agreed, 'I could hold small events here if the building was improved.'

A young mum from the estate asked if they could have a room for a playgroup, and the café idea was popular with everyone.

'If any of you know any plumbers, carpenters, painters and decorators or electricians who could help, please take my number and give it to them – encourage them to get in touch with me,' Eric said. 'That also goes for anyone who knows accountants or lawyers or anyone who might be willing to serve on a board to manage the centre.'

Ken was relieved. He knew that the meeting with the councillor would be much easier now that they had so many more ideas and so much support from local people and businesses; there were so many more groups looking for a venue than they had realised.

'Once we've improved the facilities we can put the word out to business networking groups and advertise the rooms more widely, but we don't want to jump ahead of ourselves,' Eric said, sounding more cautious than Ken had ever heard him.

'Help yourselves to another cup of coffee or tea, everyone,' he continued, 'and if you have any more questions or suggestions let us know. Once we have further information we'll be in contact again. And thank you all for coming.'

***

Two weeks later, they had the keys.

Meg had offered to contact larger businesses in the local area and attempt to get sponsorship. In that respect she was a great asset to the group. She quickly acquired three new toilets and washbasins, and a double sink from a plumbing supplies shop on a nearby trading estate, on the condition that the group advertised the fact on social media.

She also found a shop that would donate a commercial microwave and dishwasher to the centre.

Eric laughed as he and Meg arrived at the centre to take delivery of the donation. 'We never even asked for a commercial dishwasher!'

Meg shrugged. 'Well, once you're on a winning streak you might as well milk it.'

'Martin will plumb everything in,' Eric said.

Eric had done much of the social media work himself. 'The crowdfunding page is doing well,' he told Meg as they waited, perched on two lonely chairs in the centre's main space. 'Money is coming in little by little. I'm going to try and put together a bid for Lottery funding to help cover wages. It's quite a task, but the rewards will be great if we succeed.'

'That would be brilliant. It takes such a lot of money to get it up and running, doesn't it? There are local charities that might help too.'

Eric nodded. 'Yes, I've thought about that but haven't got around to contacting them yet. I'll do that tomorrow. I have a bit of spare time.'

Slowly but surely, their community centre was beginning to take shape.

CHAPTER 35

Originally, most of the group had anticipated opening the centre fairly quickly, but it soon became evident that Eric was right and it would take longer than they'd reckoned on. Altogether, it was over ten months before everything was finally in place.

Eric and Ken discussed at great length who should open the community centre. Ken was adamant that Eric must be in overall charge because he had done the lion's share of the work.

'But it would be good if we could get someone like the local MP to do the official opening,' Eric said. 'I'll contact his office and see if he's available.'

Eric rang Ken two days later, announcing with great excitement that the MP had agreed to open the centre. The same day, Eric contacted the local paper to make sure the event got coverage; they needed the free advertising to ensure that local people utilised the facilities.

'One more month and the centre will be open,' Eric said to the group when they got together in the skittle alley at the local pub that Saturday.

The group broke into applause.

'You've all worked hard to make this happen,' Eric responded. 'Thank you.'

***

Early on the day of the opening, in mid-February, Ken wandered around the building alone. He couldn't stop smiling.

His moment of peace soon ended, however, when the rest of the group arrived and the hard work of preparing for the opening began. It was a frantic morning, but everyone worked together to make sure the event would go smoothly.

'I bet you were a tyrant project manager,' Ken said to Eric.

'I had to be!' Eric replied. 'Although,' he laughed, 'you're all far better than a lot of the paid workers I've managed.'

'I'll take that as a compliment,' Ken replied as he continued hanging the paintings.

Dora's cakes were on the kitchen work surface, covered in cling film, alongside the cups and saucers that Meg and Tim had put out. Leaflets about the work of the centre were laid out on a table in the entrance, along with information about how to book the rooms, and, finally, Ken tied the ribbon across the front door.

'It's ready!' he declared.

They all went for a swift lunch, and returned via the back door at half past one, ready for the official opening at two o'clock.

Eric paced the room, looking out of the window every now and again, waiting for the arrival of the MP.

Dora brought him a cup of tea. 'Sit down and relax,' she said. 'He'll be here.'

He didn't even have time to drink the tea – as Dora spoke, their MP came in through the back door, and Eric walked across to meet him.

'Thank you so much for doing this, sir. It means a lot to all those who have worked so hard to bring us this far.'

'Thank you,' the MP replied. 'Call me David.'

'Would you like a brief look around before we join the people outside for the opening?' Eric asked.

They went from room to room, with the MP nodding appreciatively at the transformed centre. 'I haven't been here for a few years, but the whole centre looks like a completely different place. You've done amazing things with it.'

Eric beamed, and pointed Ken out. 'Ken had the original idea, and it just grew as we all worked together. It was a joint effort.'

'Which proves what can be achieved when a group of people collaborate on a project,' the MP said.

Even the weather was accommodating. It wasn't a warm day, but it was good enough for people to congregate outside while the MP spoke.

He took his place in front of the microphone, which a local band had set up for them, and smiled as he began his brief speech. He thanked all those involved, and encouraged the local people to support the centre and use the facilities in any way that they could.

He finished with a quote from an American elder statesman, which made Ken smile.

'Colin Powell once said, "A dream doesn't become reality through magic; it takes sweat, determination and hard work". And that is what has made this a reality here.'

The MP cut the ribbon and the centre was opened.

'Who would have thought, even a couple of years ago, that this would be where your journey would take you?'

Meg said as she stood beside her granddad and watched people mingle.

He smiled. 'That was then, not now. I was a different person.'

Meg returned the smile. 'We all were.'

Printed in Great Britain
by Amazon

73799669R00169